"What do you think you're doing?" Emma demanded.

"I thought I would ⬚⬚⬚⬚⬚⬚⬚⬚⬚⬚⬚⬚⬚⬚ itch up the oxen and get re⬚⬚⬚⬚⬚⬚

Emma's expression ⬚⬚⬚⬚⬚⬚⬚⬚⬚⬚⬚⬚⬚⬚⬚⬚⬚⬚
Nathan's gaze slid t⬚⬚⬚⬚⬚⬚⬚⬚⬚⬚⬚⬚⬚⬚⬚⬚g?

"I figured I'd get ou⬚⬚⬚⬚⬚⬚⬚⬚⬚⬚⬚⬚⬚⬚ better.

Her frown only intensified. "Lie back down." She blocked him from moving anywhere but deeper into the wagon.

"Get some rest," Hewitt said. The man walked off and Nathan wanted nothing more than to be able to do the same, to find somewhere private to lick his wounds. But he was still near face-to-face with Emma.

He gave in, lying back and staring up at the white underside of the bonnet.

When she spoke again, her voice sounded cheery. "The good news is you won't have to bear my company all day."

It was a relief. He didn't know how to converse with her.

But he also felt a small twinge of disappointment.

"What am I supposed to do confined to the wagon?" he asked.

"Rachel and I would be cheered if you were to serenade us as we walk."

He stared dumbly at her until she dissolved into giggles. How long had it been since he'd made anyone smile?

* * *

Journey West: Romance and adventure await three siblings on the Oregon Trail

Wagon Train Reunion—
Linda Ford, April 2015

Wagon Train Sweetheart—
Lacy Williams, May 2015

Wagon Train Proposal—
Renee Ryan, June 2015

Lacy Williams is a wife and mom from Oklahoma.
She has loved romance from childhood and promises
readers happy endings in all her stories. Her books
have been finalists for the RT Reviewers' Choice
Award (three years running), the Golden Quill and
the Booksellers' Best Award. Lacy loves to hear from
readers at lacyjwilliams@gmail.com. She can be found
at lacywilliams.net, facebook.com/lacywilliamsbooks or
twitter.com/lacy_williams.

LACY WILLIAMS

Wagon Train Sweetheart

H HARLEQUIN® LOVE INSPIRED® HISTORICAL

Special thanks and acknowledgment to Lacy Williams
for her contribution to the Journey West series.

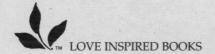

Recycling programs
for this product may
not exist in your area.

LOVE INSPIRED BOOKS

ISBN-13: 978-0-373-28310-1

Wagon Train Sweetheart

Copyright © 2015 by Harlequin Books S.A.

www.Harlequin.com

Printed in U.S.A.

Be strong and courageous. Do not be afraid;
do not be discouraged, for the Lord your God
will be with you wherever you go.
—*Joshua* 1:9

With gratefulness to my friends from the
OKC Christian Fiction Writers chapter of ACFW,
who helped brainstorm and always encourage me.

Chapter One

"He's a stinkin' thief!" The belligerent voice hurled the accusation like a stone. "We don't need his kind on this wagon train!"

Nathan Reed stood against the words, hands bound in front of him with rope, the way they had been since last night. Like a common criminal.

Like he deserved.

But not for stolen hair combs. He was innocent—this time.

He kept his eyes squinted where the rising sun was lighting the top two jutting buttes that formed a narrow canyon—he'd overheard someone call it Devil's Gate. The landmark was outside the circle of their wagons, where they'd stopped the night before.

"You're sure you saw this man—Mr. Reed—climbing out of our wagon with my sister's hair combs?" Ben Hewitt asked of the preacher.

The small committee had gathered in the predawn light, wanting privacy from the rest of the travelers in their westbound wagon train. This was Nathan's judge and jury—the men who would decide his fate.

Hewitt was a broad-shouldered, sandy-haired and

seemingly good-natured man, from the few interactions Nathan had had with him. But Ben Hewitt didn't know Nathan. Didn't count him as a friend. Nobody did, that's why Nathan was the only suspect.

Out of the corner of his vision, Nathan saw that Hewitt's sister Emma stood next to him and the group of men, the breeze blowing her deep green skirt a little. Probably sending wisps of her honey-brown hair dancing against her cheeks.

He didn't look at her. Didn't want to see accusation or recrimination in the vivid blue eyes he'd had only glimpses of when driving the Binghams' wagon.

He saw enough of the emotion when he had a chance to spy his reflection in a stream or pond.

He knew, probably better than anyone, that defending himself would get him nowhere. He was friendless on this Oregon-bound wagon train. No one to stand up for him.

The wind blew his long, unruly black hair across his cheek, but he didn't raise his bound hands to push it away.

"Erm…well, it was getting dark. It looked like him." It wasn't solid proof. It sounded as if the preacher didn't fully believe it himself. But that didn't seem to matter to the other men.

"Everyone else was accounted for," Ernie Jones blustered. Jones wasn't a committeeman, but had claimed to have witnessed the theft, along with the preacher.

"You got anything to say for yourself, Reed?" James Stillwell asked. The man had been watching Nathan with suspicion since Stillwell had joined up with the wagon train.

Nathan didn't know why. Maybe he just looked suspicious, or maybe the man could see his past in his face.

Again, Nathan said nothing. What was the use?

The breeze felt good against his overheated cheeks. The rising sun played tricks with his eyes as he kept them locked on the gradual rise of the red rock slope in the distance.

He felt dizzy and a little nauseated. He hadn't had much of an appetite the past few days, and maybe not eating enough was catching up to him. Being on the trail day in, day out wore on a body. With no wagon of his own, he depended on the kindness of others for his meals.

And Nathan didn't like depending on anyone. Joining up with the wagon train was his last chance to find a new start for himself. A chance to finally outrun the past that dogged his every step.

"Did anyone find the combs on Mr. Reed's person?" Emma Hewitt's soft voice was almost lost among the men's murmuring.

No one except Nathan seemed to hear her.

Without his consent, his gaze slid to her. Luckily, she was looking at her brother, not at him.

He'd been right. Her skirt fluttered. The brisk wind had set wisps of her honey-gold hair dancing at her temple and against her cheeks, like a vision out here in the wilds of the Wyoming Territory. Something beautiful that didn't belong.

He forced his eyes back to the craggy rocks in the distance.

Then her brother spoke up. "Did anybody find Emma's hair combs among Reed's things?"

"He ain't got much." Miles Cavanaugh, a committeeman, tossed Nathan's satchel on the ground at his feet.

Nathan ground his back teeth against the protest that

wanted to escape. Those were *his* belongings. Meager though they might be.

What right did they have to go through his things? Just because someone *thought* they'd seen him committing theft? In the dark?

But he doubted anyone would be on his side if he demanded fairness.

"He could've hid the combs somewhere. Along with the other stolen goods," Stillwell argued. What did the other man have against Nathan, anyway? A lot of suspicions, that's what.

"Can anyone verify your whereabouts last night before the party?" Hewitt asked Nathan, not unkindly.

Nathan kept his eyes on the brightening horizon. He'd been minding the oxen last night, separate from everyone as they'd washed up and chattered and prepared for the party.

Most of the time he didn't care that he was excluded from the gatherings. But last night it would have been nice to be one of the group. Then he wouldn't have been in this predicament.

Not that it mattered much in the scheme of things. He hadn't stolen those hair combs, but he'd done enough thieving and snitching that he deserved whatever punishment they would mete out.

Would they exile him from the caravan? He could live off the land, trapping and hunting the way he'd done for years. But he'd hoped for more. The small amount Mr. Bingham was to pay him for pushing the oxen to their destination was to be socked away so Nathan could purchase land.

Or would they deem that his misdeeds were enough to hang him? He'd heard of it happening in other situations. The thought sent a shudder through him.

Someone else was talking but a peculiar buzzing sound blocked the words and his light-headedness got worse. His stomach pitched from the dizziness.

Everything around him began to darken—but that wasn't right, was it? It was morning, it should be getting lighter as the daylight brightened.

Then he blacked out.

The men had fallen into low-voiced squabbling and, at first, Emma Hewitt was the only one who witnessed Nathan Reed slump to the ground.

And when the men noticed, they went silent.

No one rushed to help him.

"Really," she huffed quietly. Emma did not like being the center of attention, but did the men have a shred of decency in them?

They couldn't seem to come to agreement on anything. After she'd discovered the missing hair combs yesterday, her brother had filled her in on the ongoing investigation. She'd heard talk among the other travelers; whispers of a thief among them, but the bite of violation remained this morning.

Someone had rifled through *her* things.

But that didn't matter right at this moment.

She picked up her skirt, intending to go to the fallen man, when her brother Ben touched her arm to stop her.

"Wait. He might be faking. Pretending to swoon so if someone gets close he attacks or takes them hostage."

The alarming white pallor of Nathan Reed's face indicated otherwise.

"He's not playacting," Emma insisted, tearing her arm away from her brother's grasp.

She went to the prone man, meeting Mr. Stillwell,

her brother's friend, at his shoulder. Ben followed a few paces behind.

Mr. Stillwell squatted as she knelt at Mr. Reed's side. Stillwell touched his forehead. "He's burning up."

But he didn't look as if he intended to do anything about it.

She shook Mr. Reed's shoulder. "Wake up," she whispered.

She moved to touch his face, then faltered. If the great, burly, bear of a man was one of the children, she wouldn't have hesitated to examine him as necessary, even if it seemed far too intimate with a grown man.

She would think of him as a little child. She must. Even though he was the furthest thing from it.

Holding her breath, she peeled back one of his shapely lips. His thick beard abraded her knuckles.

He might've fainted from the fever or lack of sleep or food, but the marks inside his mouth confirmed what she'd already guessed. The contagious disease that had plagued their caravan had claimed another victim.

"It's measles," she murmured.

Her brother crouched at her side, Ben's presence reassuring. "You sure?"

She was. "Some of the children had the same white spots on their gums. See there?"

Ben's nose wrinkled and he only glanced cursorily into Mr. Reed's mouth.

"What do we do now?" Stillwell demanded.

Before she could think to prevent it, he raised his hand and slapped Mr. Reed's cheek. His dark head knocked to one side.

Emma gasped.

She could not abide injustice. In any form.

"Don't touch him like that again," she commanded.

But maybe Stillwell hadn't heard her. His eyes passed over her almost as if she wasn't there at all.

Stillwell stood, directing his words to the other men. "He's a thief—"

It was easier for Emma to direct her words to the unconscious man on the ground. "Whether or not he's a criminal, he's still a human being and deserves basic kindness. And care."

She looked up and met Ben's gaze. The men stood behind him, none paying attention. She'd spoken so softly that likely many of them hadn't heard her.

That was normal. Her opinions were rarely heard. And for a long time, it hadn't mattered to her. It did now.

But when Ben spoke, people listened. And he spoke now. "Emma's right. We can't punish a man in this condition. We'll stay the verdict until he's on his feet again."

The group of men grumbled. "What're we going to do with him?"

"We should just leave him behind," Mr. Stillwell said.

"You can't," she cried. "How would he survive?"

But perhaps her distressed cry had only been loud in her own mind. Because again Mr. Stillwell did not pay her any heed, only turned his back to talk to the other men.

Nathan Reed moaned, a low, pained sound that seemed as if it came from the depths of his soul, instead of from suffering a simple fever. He did not return to consciousness, and that worried Emma the most.

"He needs care," Emma insisted.

Ben nodded to her. He'd heard, at least. He argued with the men and left her with the prone Mr. Reed.

Emma was not a nurse. She'd had no formal training, only the difficult duty of being constantly at her father's bedside those final years.

Yet she was an expert at completing tasks that no one else wanted to do. At being available when there was no one else.

And since she'd nursed many of the children in the wagon train when they'd been afflicted with measles, it did not surprise her when the men agreed to leave Mr. Reed under Ben's care and delay his sentence until the time that he awoke. Ben would be busy driving the family wagon and carrying out his duties as a committeeman, so caring for Mr. Reed would fall to her. Ben did not ask for her agreement. He assumed she would consent.

It was unsurprising, but a bit disappointing. Of course she would have agreed to help Mr. Reed. But the fact that she hadn't been consulted rankled, just the tiniest bit.

Maybe it was because, as one of the committeemen, Ben needed to make a quick decision so the wagon train could move out for the day, under the guide Sam Weston's direction.

Or maybe it was because her siblings had come to rely on her without having to ask. That was a family blessing. And also a pain.

Her brother and sister were the only people with whom Emma's natural timidity didn't manifest itself. Most of the time. Sometimes, she still felt she couldn't speak up, even to them.

In the safety of her journal, Emma wished she could find her backbone. Had she gotten in the habit of being so very quiet at her father's bedside that now no one listened?

Sometimes she feared her voice would fade away completely. That no one would hear her or see her at all.

Ben returned and reached out a hand to draw her up from where she knelt next to Mr. Reed. "They've agreed to stay the verdict until he recovers. I've sent Cavanaugh to bring a stretcher."

She stood, her eyes lingering on Nathan, his dark head lolled to the side. "Where will he stay?"

"With Abby's family."

She opened her mouth to argue, but Miles Cavanaugh and two other men arrived and Ben was distracted with helping roll Mr. Reed onto the canvas draped over two long poles.

Ben's fiancée was Abigail Bingham Black. They had been sweethearts years before, until circumstances— and Abby's mother—had driven them apart. Widowed and back in her parents' household, Abby had been on the wagon train and she and Ben had reconnected. And fallen in love all over again.

Mr. Bingham had had trouble driving the oxen and Nathan Reed had arrived in the wagon train as a hired driver. With no wagon of his own, she knew he'd slept in the open air most of the time. But that wasn't an option now.

If the disease followed the same course it had with the children, he would be incapacitated with fever and weakness for a day or more. And remembering the glimpse Emma had had of the interior of the Binghams' wagon revealed the difficulty Ben hadn't thought of; their wagon had been overstuffed with all the things Abby's now-deceased mother hadn't wanted to leave behind.

She trailed the men carrying the still-unconscious Mr. Reed through the bustling camp. Women doused their cookfires, men harnessed oxen, children ran among the lot, all in anticipation of the call to ride out. They all worked with intent.

Was it only Emma who felt as lacking in direction as a puff of dandelion blowing in the wind? She needed to find her purpose again. For so long, her purpose had been caring for her father. Praying, hoping, believing that one day he would recover.

After his death, she'd been lost, drifting. Until she'd found the orphanage in the town nearest to their ranch, a small affair that had been run by one very motivated woman. And Emma had believed she'd found a new purpose.

Until the day her brother had come into the house, waving Grayson's letter. Ben and Rachel had been so excited about the trip, about leaving behind the difficult memories. About starting a new life.

But Emma hadn't been sure.

And she'd hesitated too long to mention that she didn't want to go West. Once plans were made, she hadn't felt she could broach the subject, not without sounding selfish and petty.

Her own fault. Now where was she to find a purpose? Was it possible that she could find it with a family of her own?

Her eldest brother, Grayson, had written of the widowed local sheriff, Tristan McCullough, who had become his close friend in the Oregon Territory. Tristan had three young daughters who needed a mother. Both Grayson and Ben seemed in agreement that the man was a match for Emma.

She wasn't entirely convinced that this was her purpose, even if her brothers seemed to be certain. She would wait until she met the man before she decided what to do.

Unanswered questions swirled in Emma's head as she trailed the men carting Mr. Reed to their wagon, but the biggest remained: Where would Mr. Reed stay? Obviously, he couldn't walk to guide the Binghams' oxen.

And from what she knew of Abby's wagon, there wasn't room for a mouse, much less a man as tall as Mr. Reed.

Ben had made himself Mr. Reed's caretaker when he'd stood up for the ill man. Would Ben—and Emma by association—be forced to keep Mr. Reed in the Hewitts' wagon? If he must stay in their wagon, the precious little privacy she fought for on this dusty wilderness trail would be gone.

When they arrived at the family campsite, Rachel and Abby were there, packing up the breakfast dishes.

"What happened?" Abby asked, moving toward Ben, almost as if by instinct.

"We need to clear a space in your family's wagon," Ben told his fiancée. "Reed fell sick—measles."

"Will there be room…?" Abby's question trailed off as she moved with the men toward the Binghams' wagon. Emma remained near the fire with Rachel.

"Did the committee reach a verdict?"

Emma shook her head slightly. "He collapsed. Ben demanded they hold the verdict until he is recovered."

Rachel watched Emma carefully. "You don't think he is guilty?"

Her sister saw too much. They had always been close. But Emma did have one secret—that she hadn't wanted to come West at all.

She shrugged, moving to pick up the breakfast skillet to take it to the family wagon. "Even if he is guilty, he deserves to be treated fairly. No man deserves to be left in the wilderness to die."

A shiver raced through her, just thinking about it.

"That's his punishment? How utterly unfair!" Rachel was a passionate person—and much more outspoken than Emma.

She went on, spouting her thoughts as if she was defending Mr. Reed in front of the committeemen herself. "I'm just glad Ben was there to stand up for him."

Emma was, too. Part of her wished that *she* had been able to stand up against the injustice. Perhaps that should become her new purpose.

Finding her voice. Or risk losing it forever.

Chapter Two

"Your presence here is quite inconvenient."

Emma bathed Mr. Reed's face with a rag dipped in tepid water from the small basin she'd tucked between two crates in the cramped Conestoga wagon. She was down to the dregs of what she'd started with—most of it had splashed onto her as the wagon jostled over the rough terrain.

She dared speak to him so rudely only because he hadn't regained consciousness after his collapse early this morning. If he was awake, she never would've had the courage.

And he probably wouldn't have heard her, anyway.

His continuous unconscious state worried her. Where her knuckle inadvertently brushed against his cheek, his skin burned her. His fever was high. Dangerously so.

"Crossing the creek again," Ben called out from outside the wagon, where he walked beside the oxen.

Again?

Emma braced one hand against the sideboard. The wagon lurched and she slid forward, then another unexpected drop sent her sprawling, her arm resting across Mr. Reed's massive chest and her chin on his shoulder.

"Sorry," she muttered, even though he couldn't hear her. She quickly pushed herself upright and away from the man.

After endless days of walking—sometimes as much as twenty miles—Emma had never thought she'd want to hike again. Until this very moment. *When* would they stop for luncheon?

There was no *space*. The Hewitts' wagon hadn't been overfilled as Abby's family wagon had, but their provisions were many and there wasn't room for two grown people back here.

She was alternately worried for Mr. Reed's health, and embarrassed about their shared close confines.

More so because she knew Mr. Reed didn't like her. She had no idea why, or what she'd done to offend him. But it had been very clear from their few interactions at the evening meal that he had no wish to be friends. The Hewitts shared a campfire with the Binghams and Littletons to conserve fuel. As Mr. Reed drove the Binghams' wagon, he ate supper with their group. Several times when Emma had offered Mr. Reed a supper plate and attempted polite conversation, he'd avoided her gaze completely and nearly ripped the tin plate from her hands before disappearing into the shadows. As if being in her presence irritated him.

After the third time, she'd quit trying to be kind and merely served his plate in silence. Unlike the times when papa's illness had made him difficult, she didn't have to accept the rudeness from a stranger.

He moaned, a low sound of pain that tugged something in the vicinity of Emma's gut. He was alone, with no one to care for him.

Her innate compassion dictated that she do for him

what no one else would. She hoped someone would do the same for her should she need it.

"I know you don't like me very much," she whispered, dabbing the cloth over his forehead again. "But it would be lovely if you would *wake up*."

But Mr. Reed made no response.

The caravan slowed and stopped for the noon meal and Emma was relieved to escape the wagon for a few moments.

Ben allowed the oxen out of their traces and led them off to graze for a bit. Rachel and Abby had their heads together, probably planning supper or trading news from elsewhere in the wagon train.

And Emma was left standing in the shade of the wagon. She arched her back, hands at her hips, attempting to shake the aches that being hunched over and jostled all morning had given her.

The landscape had changed subtly in the past days to bare, sandy plains. There was little vegetation, only the occasional wild sage. Ben had told her earlier they should come upon the Wind River Mountains by the end of the day.

"How does your patient fare?"

Emma looked over her shoulder at the familiar, friendly voice calling out. Clara Pressman. Disguised as a man. "Clarence" Pressman was only a ruse to hide the truth.

Emma had discovered the masquerade after they'd left Independence, Kansas. Clarence had gotten a nasty cut on his back and Emma had been called to aid him. While cleaning the wound, Emma had discovered his secret. Clarence was Clara.

And Clara was pregnant. Very much alone, after her husband had died, with no family in the East and no home to return to—her husband had sold everything to make the journey West—she'd decided to go on alone and meet up with her sister who already lived in Oregon. She'd felt it necessary to hide her true identity, fearing the organizers wouldn't allow her to make the trip if they knew she was a pregnant woman on her own.

She'd probably been right. Emma didn't necessarily agree with the ruse, but Clara had held up remarkably well on the journey so far.

Nearby, Clara was unhitching a yoke of oxen along with Mr. Morrison. Emma waved at her friend and called out a greeting to both.

Clara nodded, but the second man turned red and then turned his face away, not acknowledging Emma at all.

Emma's stomach pinched. Had her shout been too forward? She didn't know how to relate to men properly. When other girls her age had been attending socials and picnics and learning to flirt, Emma had been at her father's bedside.

Maybe her naivety and inexperience with the opposite sex was also the reason she didn't understand why Mr. Reed had snubbed her those several times.

What would Tristan McCullough think of her?

She hadn't allowed herself to hope that the sheriff Grayson spoke so highly of in his letters would like her once they'd met.

What if Mr. McCullough found her natural shyness irritating?

Perhaps he wouldn't even be interested in her once they met. Her cautious nature caused her to hesitate more than hope. She would wait and see how things turned out.

A soft whine drew Emma's attention to the long grass beneath the wagon, where a small brown dog crouched, panting. Watching her, almost asking a question with its eyes.

"Hello, you," she said, squatting. This was Mr. Reed's dog. She'd seen the brown-and-black mottled mutt from a distance, witnessed the man sharing snatches of his supper with it, but had forgotten about the animal in the rushed moments of finding a place for Mr. Reed before the bugle had urged the travelers to move out.

"Have you been following us all day?" She reached out and was astonished when the creature let her scratch beneath its chin. "Yes, your master is inside that wagon."

Pitiful begging eyes reminded her of the family cat, Buttons, that had been her childhood friend. "Hungry, are you?"

She knew the animal couldn't really understand what she was saying, but the dog's tail *whupped* against the grasses as if it did.

"I'll share some beans with you, but only if you promise not to tell your master."

She was so tired of the trail fare. Cold beans and bacon for dinner. Every single day. Unless one counted the times they had fresh buffalo meat to break up the monotony.

She wanted a real stove, not a camp stove and a fire. Real walls.

"Unfortunately, we've got a ways to go," she told the dog.

"What're you doing?"

Emma jumped at the sound of the unexpected voice and thumped her head on a bucket hanging from the side of the wagon. She backed out from where she'd been crouching, rubbing the top of her head and grimacing at Clara.

"If you must know, I was making a new friend," she groused.

Clara glanced behind her to where the dog still sat beneath the wagon's bed.

"I need one today," Emma finished.

Now Clara turned a raised eyebrow on her. "It's going that well with your patient, then?"

"Oh, Mr. Reed has been perfectly amiable, entertaining me with his lovely conversation and sweet nature."

"Ah." Clara's lips twitched. "So he hasn't woken up?"

Emma's friend kept the straight face for several moments before a smile broke through. Emma couldn't help sharing a chuckle with her. Between her father and two brothers, she well knew that men could be irritable when they were ill.

"And how are you this morning, friend?"

Just then, Amos and Grant Sinclair, brothers traveling the trail together, passed by.

Clara stiffened and waited until the men had passed out of hearing distance. "Fine."

Up close, Clarence's secret was no secret at all—although her womanly figure was covered with men's clothing, Emma could see straight through the ruse. She didn't understand how everyone else saw only a man.

Clara unobtrusively put her hand at her lower back. She nodded at the horizon, and Emma followed with her gaze. "Storm's coming."

Clouds built on the western horizon, directly in their path. Even as Emma watched, the slate-gray mass twisted on itself, forming a thunderhead.

And Emma had hated storms since she'd been caught out in one as a small child.

The ominous clouds had delivered on their promise. The caravan had been forced to end its day early because of driving rain.

Now in the twilight dimness, Emma was secluded with the still-unconscious Mr. Reed, with no end in sight of the intense storm.

Ben and Rachel were hunkered down in the family's tent, probably soaking wet instead of the mere damp that Emma suffered.

Rain pelted the wagon bonnet, rattling the canvas until Emma felt as if her teeth rattled with it.

"I don't suppose you'd like to wake up now," she said to the comatose man. She worked in the dark, still attempting to cool his fever. She'd lit a candle twice but wind had gusted in through the flaps and blown out the light—and once knocked over the candle. She was too afraid of catching their wagon afire and losing all their goods to try again.

Late in the afternoon, when they'd still had light, she'd watched the measles rash climb Mr. Reed's chest and neck. She imagined it had crept into his cheeks by now, but his heavy, dark beard obscured her view.

His continued unconsciousness worried her. None of the children had experienced a prolonged period like this. She guessed that measles could affect adults differently than children and that his body was likely attempting to fight off the burning fever.

"Not that I object to nursing you in particular," she went on. "It's just…I had hoped to leave behind the need to use my nursing skills."

She'd been so beaten down by her time at her father's bedside. The hours spent caring for him, praying for his recovery—only to be bitterly disappointed when he had died.

She'd hoped to, planned to, help the children at the orphanage with her other skills. Sewing clothing. Cooking. Loving on the children. But it was not to be, not when her family had decided to pull up their roots and travel West. And now she was here with Mr. Reed.

Static electricity crawled along her skin, making the

fine hairs on her arms stand upright and raising goose-flesh in its wake.

Bright lightning flashed, momentarily filling the interior of the wagon with brilliant white illumination. Thunder crashed so loudly that Emma instinctively raised her hands to press against her ears. The earth trembled, the entire wagon shaking with it.

When the thunder receded, Emma's eyesight retained large glowing spots, an aftereffect of the bright light that rendered her momentarily blind.

She reached out and clutched the first thing she found, attempting to ground herself in her state of disorientation.

The nearest thing turned out to be Mr. Reed's shoulder.

A muscle twitched beneath her palm, but he remained still and silence reigned inside the wagon, only the cadence of rain drumming all around them.

Emma squeezed her eyes tightly closed, bent over and breathed through the fear, inhaling the scent of stale sweat and man. Not for the first time was she made aware that she was nursing a man and not one of the children. The firm muscle beneath her fingers also made it impossible to ignore that this was not her father in his frail condition those last months.

Mr. Reed was a fine specimen of a man. Fit, tall, broad-shouldered. A bit unkempt for her tastes but everything else that usually made her tongue-tied.

Except he was unconscious.

"That was a close one," she breathed.

An echo of thunder rumbled from far away. Just how large was this storm? How long could it last?

Her nervousness and fear made her ramble on, though she attempted to keep her thoughts on the past and not the storm. "My father lost everything in the Panic. His spirit was broken and he was never the same after that. He got sick."

Emma allowed her hand to move until her fingertips brushed Mr. Reed's temple. Still hot.

In the dark, she fumbled for the rag and bowl of cool water. She dabbed at his forehead, feeling that her efforts were in vain. What if Mr. Reed died? The man wasn't even her acquaintance, yet she felt responsible for him.

"It wasn't that I resented being the one to care for Papa," she murmured. "But it was…difficult. Being closest to him when his spirits suffered. He battled despondency and often there was no comfort I could bring him…"

She was surprised when a sniffle overtook her. She'd thought she had mourned her father completely, but perhaps this trip was calling for more from her.

"Dealing with his bodily functions…"

She paused. "Perhaps I did resent my siblings a bit," she admitted. "For not asking if I needed their assistance."

It felt good to say the words, admit to her unkind feelings, knowing that no one would ever hear her.

"Of course," she went on to excuse them, "it wasn't as if Ben and Rachel ignored their responsibilities. Ben was constantly busy running the ranch. And Rachel took over the entire household. The situation was difficult on all of us."

And that was why her siblings had wanted a new start.

But the truth was, she'd hoped to find her new start right at home.

Nathan lay in the dark, knowing he should tell Emma Hewitt he was awake.

The booming thunder had shaken him out of the place of darkness that had claimed him…all day apparently.

Or maybe it had been the clutch of her small hand against his shoulder that woke him.

He should tell her.

But some small part of him that hadn't died with Beth had savored the soft brush of her fingers against his blazing forehead, the thought that someone wanted to converse with him.

Oh, he wasn't kidding himself. He knew she was caring for him out of basic human kindness—even that was as foreign to him as a store-bought candy. As out of it as he'd been, he had still heard her soft-spoken words and had felt her each time she'd smoothed back his hair, had bathed his face and neck with water, had helped him sip water from a tin cup.

No one treated him this kindly. Not since Beth.

Most people acted as if he didn't exist, or if they had no other choice but to talk to him, treated him like dirt.

It was what he deserved.

But that one small part of him held his limbs captive and numbed his tongue so that he just lay silent and still.

He didn't particularly like the dark, confining space. He was used to sleeping outdoors, even in the rain.

He couldn't see her, but he could make out a darker shadow that must be her form sitting close at his side. Beneath the damp smell of rain floated the scent of their foodstuffs. Flour, sugar, coffee. And a hint of wax, perhaps a candle that had guttered out.

And something he couldn't identify. Flowers or freshness...it must be *her* scent.

She was still speaking in a low voice.

"Once Ben received Grayson's letter, there was no talking him out of his plans. And Rachel on board, as well...how could I hold them back from their dreams?"

What about her dreams? It didn't sound as if Emma

had wanted to take the trip West. Why not? Curiosity stung him. He might not ever get answers, not if she stopped talking. Because he would never ask.

Light flashed again, not so brightly this time, perhaps farther away. Thunder rolled. Water from the cloth she was using trickled down his jaw and behind his ear.

It tickled, and he used all the willpower he possessed not to move.

"I hope your little dog found a safe place to curl up for the night."

Mutt. The animal didn't really belong to Nathan. It had attached itself to him the second night he'd been in camp. He'd waited for someone to claim the dog—it was friendly enough to belong to a family. But no one ever had. And maybe the little dog's protruding ribs meant no one would.

Just like no one claimed Nathan.

He hadn't been able to avoid the slight feeling of camaraderie with the animal, so he'd taken to feeding it scraps from his meals. It had started following him around, but Nathan didn't regard it as a pet. It would wander off at some point.

"Storms like this are just one of the dangers on the trail," Emma whispered. "Illness, poor nutrition, early winter, stampeding buffalo, snakes…"

She recited the list as if she'd read it in a book somewhere. Nathan had spent so much time trapping and living off the land that he didn't even notice the critters she'd mentioned. If you were listening, you could hear stampeding buffalo from a mile off and get out of their way. Snakes didn't bother you unless you got in their space.

It was the humans in the caravan that were the real danger. And didn't he know it? His past had taught him that men couldn't be trusted. He might have acquaintances back at Fort Laramie that he did business with, but there was always a part of him that held back. And look what had happened after he'd joined the wagon train. He'd been falsely accused.

There was a sudden muting of the rain outside. Prickles crawled along his skin and light flared. He caught a glance of Emma's chestnut hair and bright eyes before he had to close his eyes against the painful brightness.

There was a loud crack, then a boom, shaking everything until he was sure his teeth rattled.

And this time was different from the last. Voices cried out. Screamed.

Emma's hand gripped his wrist painfully.

A loud thump against the side of the wagon startled her and she jerked, releasing him.

"The Ericksons' wagon got struck by lightning and caught fire!" That was Ben Hewitt's voice. "Stay put for now, I'll come for you if I need you."

What a disaster. The torrential rain should help, but the lightning could've hurt the family inside the wagon or caused significant damage. He should get up to help, but he still couldn't figure out how to get his legs to work. Maybe he was sicker than he'd thought. Or had they tied him up so this suspected thief couldn't get away?

Emma shifted beside him. Another lightning flash and he saw that she'd curled up into herself, drawn her knees up to her chest and wrapped her arms around them. Her head was tucked down and she was rocking very slightly back and forth. She was muttering something, but he couldn't make out the words over the continuing rain.

She could be praying.

Or upset.

How many times had his sister curled up just like that during one of their father's angry spells?

Unexpected emotion ran hot through his chest and he did something he hadn't done in years. He reached out for her.

Fever still coursing through him, his arm shook, but he cupped her elbow in his hand.

Somewhere in the haze of the day, he remembered her saying something about him not liking her. The statement was something of an untruth. He didn't like *anyone*. No one liked him.

But when she stilled beneath his touch, he scrambled for something to say and what came out was, "I don't dislike you." His voice was raspy from disuse.

There was a beat of silence. As full and tense as that moment before the lightning had struck.

"You're awake," she said, surprise in her tone.

"I'm feeling a mite better." It wasn't entirely true but he figured she was probably tired of nursing him. Likely she'd want him out of her wagon any minute. "You all right?" he asked.

He sensed more than saw that she went still again.

"*How long* have you been awake?" she asked quietly. Caught.

He hesitated. "Long enough." He cleared his throat. His whole body felt as though it were on fire, and he figured half of it must be from the fever and half from the hot embarrassment that spiraled through him.

But instead of giving him a well-deserved shove out of the wagon, she shifted beside him. "You need to drink some water. Do you think you could keep down any food?"

She wanted to *feed* him?

"I don't know," he said slowly. His head felt stuffed with cotton.

She pressed a cool tin cup into his right hand. He tried to rise up on his elbows. Tried and struggled.

And she put a hand beneath his shoulder and helped him. She must be the kindest person on the face of the earth.

He frowned as he sipped from the cup, the tin metallic against his tongue.

She was too nice. He didn't know why she was being kind to him. Experience had taught him that everyone wanted something. But with his head hot with fever, he couldn't figure what her motive might be. Had her brother forced her in here to make sure he didn't abscond with the goods he hadn't actually stolen?

The water was a relief to the parched desert of his throat. He drank until the cup was empty, then wiped his chin with the back of his wrist.

Lightning flashed again, illuminating the interior of the wagon and giving him the visibility to see her flinch.

Thunder boomed again, rattling two pots hung above and behind his head.

And he had some strange impulse to comfort her. Maybe if he started a conversation with her, she would be distracted from the storm's fury. Not that he knew how. He'd been on his own for too long to know how to talk to a proper woman. Which was why the most impertinent question popped out of his mouth.

"Have you always been scared of storms?"

He heard the small catch in her breath, felt the stillness between them. Even though rain pattered on the wagon's bonnet, he thought she must be holding her breath.

"I was four years old when I got caught out in one."

Her words came slowly at first, and then he was surprised when she went on. "My family was at a town picnic and I was playing with a friend. The storm came on quickly and as everyone rushed to get out of the open, I was separated from my friend and couldn't find my family. It might've only been minutes, but I was alone in the wind and rain and thunder. And I've never liked storms since."

He couldn't say that he blamed her. Lightning flashed, burning into his brain an image of her as a small girl lost in the storm. His gut tightened. His cheeks got hot.

He didn't want to feel the stirring of compassion or the small surge of protectiveness for a lost little girl.

His discomfort made his next words sharp.

"If you didn't want to come West, why did you?"

Her grip tightened on his elbow. She didn't answer outright. "Will you tell my brother I was complaining about the journey?"

"Why should I?" He'd spoken to Ben Hewitt when necessary in the weeks since he'd joined the wagon train, but it wasn't as if they were friends. They didn't share confidences. As far as he was concerned, if she hadn't told her brother she didn't want to be here, it was her business.

"There are many difficulties on the trail," she said. "As you know. I was…finding my way back to being happy where we were, after Papa died."

So she'd given up her own desires to go West with her family. It reminded him of Beth, his sister, who had often given in to his whims.

Thunder rolled again and he sensed her shiver.

The bitter taste of fear remained from his past. And he didn't want that for her.

He tried a different tack.

"So you're going to Oregon to get married?"

She inhaled sharply. "Have you been eavesdropping on me? What a childish thing to do—"

In the dark, he couldn't tell if she was angry or teasing. "I just hear stuff is all."

It was true. Always on the fringes, half-hidden in the shadows, he heard a lot. Whispered complaints against the committeemen. Young couples sneaking kisses and making plans.

He just wished he'd had some clue as to who had stolen her hair combs. Then he would've been able to prove his own innocence.

"I might marry Tristan McCullough. If I decide to." Did he detect a note of petulance in her voice?

It was too dark to see her expression, so he was left guessing. Not that it was his business, anyway.

His head was pounding now and he shifted his elbows. She seemed to realize he needed to lie down again and pressed one hand against his shoulder as she guided him back down.

"My brother Grayson is already settled there," she said briskly. "He knows Tristan. His friend is looking for a mother for his three daughters."

"A ready-made family." There was something poking his back, beneath the blanket they'd spread. He tried to reach beneath himself to adjust it, but it wouldn't budge.

"I suppose. It isn't as if I'm unused to taking care of…"

"Your pa. Yes, you said."

He still couldn't get comfortable. He shifted, moving his weight. And she was there, helping him, reaching under his back to move the box or crate that had poked him.

He still couldn't see her face; he imagined her frowning. But at least if she was miffed at him she wasn't thinking about the storm.

"Do you want to marry a man you've never met before?"

"I don't know."

"I don't know."

Emma helped Mr. Reed settle again in the crowded wagon. He was warm, even through the barrier of his shirt. Though he had awakened, his fever had not abated.

Perhaps she should feel guilty about her indecision over Tristan McCullough. Her brother Grayson thought they would make a fine match, but how could she be ready to marry a man she'd never met before?

She'd spent the past several years caring for her father. Given up so many things—social events, time spent with friends, even time to herself.

Joining a new family with the demands of three young girls…she'd be jumping right back into the same type of situation. Housework, caring for the girls and the demands of a husband. She'd just begun finding her feet again, had found a worthy cause in the orphanage back home before their move had uprooted her. Did she really want to take on an entire family?

Or was this the purpose she'd been petitioning God for? Had He provided this family, these girls who needed a mother, just when Emma needed direction in her life?

She didn't know.

She should be uncomfortable speaking so candidly with Mr. Reed, but somehow the darkness and the intimacy of their situation had erased her usual awkwardness with the opposite sex.

And then he said, "It sounds like it's moving off."

It took her a moment to realize he meant the storm.

And he was right. Thunder rolled in the distance, but the patter of rain had slowed on the wagon bonnet.

Had he engineered the whole conversation to distract her from the danger the storm represented?

She loosened the ties and opened the back flap in time to see several flashes of light at the horizon. The storm would be completely gone before much longer.

"Fire's out," someone called out. There was much more activity than the camp usually saw after dark.

"Do you think you can hold down some food?" she asked again, turning back to her patient.

There was no response.

When she knelt at his side, his breathing had gone shallow and he didn't respond when her fingertips brushed his forehead.

He'd fallen unconscious again.

Chapter Three

Nathan—Emma found she thought of him by his Christian name after their late night conversation—did not rouse at all the next day as they came within sight of the Wind River Mountains, majestic snowcapped peaks miles to the north. She knew they would grow bigger as the caravan approached.

By the time they'd made camp that evening, she was exhausted from her efforts attempting to cool his fever and forcing water down his throat.

And he'd begun coughing, a deep racking cough that worried her.

Rachel came for Emma after supper. The rest of the camp was settling for the night, the sounds of conversations and music and laughter quieting as dusk deepened.

"Get out of that wagon," Rachel ordered. "It's time you had a break. That man isn't going to die if you leave his side for a half hour."

But Emma was half-afraid he might.

"He's still burning up. His fever should have broken by now." She was worried, her fear taking on an urgency that made her movements jerky.

After sharing a few moments of conversation with the man last night, she felt…responsible for him.

He moaned, a low, pained sound, then coughed again. She tried to support his shoulders as the hacking shook his entire body. She bit her lip, not knowing what to do…

"If bathing his face in water was going to cool him off, he'd be frozen by now. You've soaked his shirt through at least twice," Rachel said.

It was true. Wetness stained the collar of his worn shirt.

When Emma still refused to disembark from the wagon, Rachel disappeared. Emma couldn't hope it would last very long.

"Wake up, Nathan," she whispered. If she'd hoped using his name would rouse him, it was in vain. He remained still in the wagon bed, his cheeks flushed with fever.

She brushed the damp waves of his hair away from his temple. If he'd been awake, she never would have dared so familiar a touch. But he wasn't awake, and that was the problem, wasn't it?

"Emma."

Ben's stern voice from behind startled her and she hid her hand in her skirts as if she'd been doing something improper. Which she really hadn't been.

Her brother stood with hands on his hips. Emma could see Abby and Rachel standing shoulder to shoulder several yards behind him, both wearing matching expressions of concern.

"Come down for a while," Ben said. Except it sounded more like an order than a request. And she was tired of others dictating her actions.

"I'll stay for a bit—"

But her voice faded as he spoke over her. "You've

been cooped up in the wagon for two days. It's time to come down. Abby can sit with Mr. Reed for a few minutes."

He hadn't even heard her protest.

"But—" Emma swallowed back the entirety of her argument as her brother reached up and clasped her wrist.

She allowed herself to be assisted—hauled—from the wagon, but when Rachel offered to accompany her to the nearby creek, Emma insisted she stay in camp.

Perhaps Rachel sensed Emma's upset because she didn't follow.

The muscles in Emma's back and legs burned as she walked briskly through the small space of prairie and then down through the brush to the meandering creek.

The tension in her shoulders remained.

There were other women nearby, some bathing protesting children in the cool, clean water, some scrubbing clothes. Emma would never have been brave enough to come alone, not with the threat of Indians. Not to mention the troublemakers among them—whoever was committing the thefts in the wagon train.

But she knelt on the bank somewhat apart from the other women. She knew many of them, had helped some of them when their children had been sick.

But she couldn't stomach making casual conversation with anyone tonight.

She splashed water on her face, shivering at the coldness against her overwarm skin.

Ben and Rachel didn't understand. Nathan Reed couldn't die.

Ben hadn't sat at their father's side as the man who'd once been so full of life had faded away. Oh, her brother had been there at the end—those painful moments had been burned into Emma's brain so that they were unforgettable—but he hadn't been constantly on call at Papa's bedside.

Rachel couldn't know how many hours Emma had spent praying for Papa to recover. To come back to them. And he hadn't.

Watching Nathan Reed struggle was bringing all of those memories back. It was like living through Papa's decline all over again. But this time, it was happening much faster.

Just yesterday, Nathan had been a virile, powerful man. And now he was laid weak with fever, the disease killing his body.

And she couldn't do anything to stop it.

"God, please..." she whispered, her face nearly pressed into her knees on the creek bank. She didn't even know what she was praying for. That Nathan would be healed, or that she would be relieved of the guilty burden she still bore from Papa's passing?

When she couldn't stand the heaviness in her chest any longer, she stood up on shaky legs. How long had she stayed by the water, prostrate and crying out silently? She didn't know.

Most of the women had left, only a few remained far down the creek, speaking quietly. The dusk had deepened around her and urgency gripped Emma as her feet turned back toward the wagon. Whether it was the fear of the unknown wilderness, or fear for the man, she didn't know.

Ben had pitched the family tent near the wagon and stood nearby, for once away from Abby.

"You should send someone for a doctor."

Ben frowned and she rushed on, "Some of the other travelers we've passed said there are doctors traveling with other trains. If someone took a horse and rode ahead, we could find one and bring him back—"

"Emma, it's almost full dark."

"In the morning, then," she insisted. "Nathan—" She only realized she'd used his name when Ben's frown deepened. "Mr. Reed's symptoms are not the same as the children's."

Now Ben crossed his arms over his chest. How could she convince her brother of the danger Nathan was in?

"He has measles. He's broken out in the rash. But his unnatural fever and now his cough—those aren't from the measles."

"If he's developed some other disease, you shouldn't be around him," Ben said, worry now creasing his brow. He started toward the wagon, taking a step and then pausing. Likely he'd just remembered his fiancée was the one in the wagon with Nathan.

"I doubt he's contagious," she said, and hoped with all her might that it was true. "But he needs doctoring— more than I know how to do."

After all, she was just a woman. Not even trained to be a nurse.

She could feel Ben's perusal and she didn't know if he could see her expression as it was falling dark around them. As it was, it took all her might to maintain a calm facade when she wanted to demand him to understand and *listen* to her.

"If he isn't better in the morning, I'll consider it."

It wasn't enough. But it was something. "Thank you. I'll relieve Abby. I'm sure you want to say good-night."

Nathan's condition hadn't changed when she changed places with Abby in the wagon bed.

She prayed over him as she settled into the wagon. Her heart was fluttering, pulse thrumming.

He moaned again, his head turning toward her. Was he rousing?

His eyes didn't open. But his lips formed a word. "Beth..."

Nathan burned. Had he died and now was being punished for his sins?

His entire body was weighted down as though he'd been buried in a rock slide.

He rolled his head to the side, seeking some relief. The movement seemed to seep all of his energy away. And it didn't help. The oppressive heat and darkness remained.

From far away—a memory, or reality?—he heard a laugh. It sounded like Beth.

"Beth!" he called out for her, but in his weakness he couldn't be sure if anything emerged from his mouth at all.

A memory flickered through his consciousness, a remembrance of her as a teen, looking over her shoulder and laughing. Probably at him. He'd always been able to make his sister laugh. Until the end.

Another memory flitted through him, but this one stuck. The awful moment when he'd found her crumpled in a pool of her own blood. One hand protectively clutching her stomach—he hadn't found out until later that she'd been trying to protect the babe in her womb from the violent blows its father had delivered.

She'd asked Nathan for help earlier, asked him for money to buy a train ticket. She'd been desperate for escape, willing to go anywhere.

"Beth," he cried out again, the name ripped from his lips, from his very soul.

She had been the only good thing in his life.

And he'd failed her.

If this was the end of him, he deserved this torture, the all-consuming darkness. Why hadn't he taken Beth away himself? He'd been younger, but he still could've protected her from that brute who was her husband. But she'd been afraid, too afraid to stay close. She'd wanted distance.

And with no education and no connections to recommend him, jobs were scarce. He hadn't been able to round up funds in time to save her.

She'd died because of him.

"Forgive me..."

But she'd gone, or her memory had, and only the darkness remained.

What would her son have been like? Or daughter? Beth had been full of life and laughter. She'd always known how to tease him out of a bad mood. She'd been the only one to tell him he didn't have to turn out like their father—a tyrant with an affinity for moonshine and a horrible temper—or the man she had married young to escape. She'd believed in Nathan.

And look what he'd done to her. He'd failed.

He burned hotter. Hotter. Until he felt as if he would incinerate from the inside out.

He just wanted the torment to end. Wanted to forget. Wanted blessed darkness.

Wanted to end this.

"I forgive you..."

He turned his head, searching for the source of the almost ethereal whisper.

"Beth?"

Had she come to ease his passing?

But then he felt something through the haze of darkness and heat. Soft fingers gripping his hand so hard he believed she could pull him back from the brink of death.

"I forgive you," the female voice said again. Not Beth. The cadence was wrong.

But something inside him responded, opening like a flower to the sun. Some of the weight—not all—on his chest eased. No one had ever forgiven him before.

The first rays of sunlight burst over the horizon as Nathan's fever broke and he became drenched in sweat.

Emma would never know what woke her in that darkest part of night. She hadn't meant to fall asleep at all, but exhaustion and worry had overcome her. She'd woken with a cramp in her neck from being bent at a wrong angle. Her left foot had been completely asleep.

But those small pains had disappeared instantly when she realized that his fever must have spiked. His breath had gone shallow, with a rasp that frightened her.

He'd murmured a woman's name—Beth—several times, finally begging for forgiveness in a tortured whisper.

She'd been afraid he was on the verge of death. Not knowing what else to do, she had grabbed his hand and told him she forgave him.

And his fever had broken.

Now she found a dry cloth and mopped the moisture on his brow.

When her hand passed over his face, in the growing light she watched as his eyes opened.

"Hello," she whispered, almost afraid that she was dreaming this moment.

"Seems like you'd have given up on me by now, Miss Hewitt." His voice was raspy and she fumbled for a cup of water even as that awful racking cough took him.

She held his shoulders until it had passed, helped him

to take a few sips of water, mopped his brow because the effort had made sweat bead there again.

When he'd settled again, she looked him straight in the face.

"I never give up." She let the gravity of the moment hold in a pregnant pause and then said, "And after all that's passed between us in the last days, I think we're beyond using each other's surnames, Nathan."

One corner of his lips twitched, the closest she'd seen him come to smiling. "Yes, ma'am," he said meekly.

Or maybe she imagined the meekness as his illness forced him to whisper.

"Good."

And it was good. She hadn't lost this man, who'd become more than an acquaintance. Did she dare to call him a friend?

Chapter Four

Later that morning, Emma was able to leave the wagon and assist Rachel with the breakfast preparations. Her fears had been unfounded. Nathan had revived.

"You're humming," Rachel observed.

Emma looked up from where she flipped bacon in the fry pan. "Was I?"

"Yes. You were." Rachel's pointed gaze seemed to demand Emma admit to something, but she couldn't imagine what.

She let her eyes linger on the landscape of tall, brown summer grasses before she returned her eyes to the pot. Did even the sunlight seem brighter this morning? "I suppose I am relieved that Mr. Reed is faring better."

"He is?" Ben's voice rang out as he joined them.

"His fever broke just before dawn," Emma told her brother.

"Good." Ben reached for the plate Rachel extended to him. "I won't have to send someone riding after a doctor."

"His cough still worries me."

"Sally Littleton said she's seen pneumonia develop from measles," Rachel said. The thirtysomething mother was one of their neighbors in the wagon train and had been friendly since they'd left Independence.

Pneumonia. The word silenced the three of them. At the end, Papa had contracted pneumonia and never recovered.

"We'll pray it isn't that." Ben's voice remained grave. "I can't spare any men to ride out. We need everyone on guard against the thief." The last was said quietly, as if to keep the words from prying ears.

Emma set aside her spoon. "It isn't Mr. Reed." She had no evidence, but somehow she didn't believe the man who'd been compassionate enough to comfort her through her fears of the storm could do such a thing. "I think Mr. Reed must have had a difficult life. But I don't believe he is a thief."

Nathan sat upright in the Hewitts' wagon bed, bracing his hands against the sideboard, panting from just that little exertion.

And completely floored by Emma's quiet, resolute statement, by her faith in him.

He'd done nothing to deserve it. In the face of her unexpected…friendship, he was ashamed of how he'd acted before this illness, brushing off and ignoring her attempts at kindness.

How long had it been since he'd known someone he counted as a friend? His childhood, twenty years ago. Or more.

And she was wrong. He'd done his share of thieving. When his pa had drunk away any money they would have used for food. As an adult, when his belly had been so empty he'd had actual pangs of hunger.

Having Emma's faith in him, even if it lasted only for this moment and no longer, made him feel as though he could face whatever punishment the wagon train committee deemed necessary. It made him feel as if maybe there was a chance that he could really be forgiven. Be redeemed.

And that was dangerous thinking. He, more than any other, knew how black his soul was. And that good things didn't come his way.

But then he heard Ben Hewitt's next words through his swirling thoughts. "Someone stole a wad of cash out of the Ericksons' wagon the night of the storm, during the fire."

"It couldn't have been Mr. Reed," Emma's sister chimed in. "You were with him in the wagon."

"Yes," Emma agreed.

"Whoever did it is sly," Hewitt said. "Every able-bodied man was working the bucket brigade—or so we thought. Mr. Erickson didn't notice the cash was missing until this morning. He thought his wife had it—she thought her husband had hidden it in their belongings. But it's definitely missing."

"How awful for them."

The three siblings kept talking, but their voices faded out of Nathan's head as he tried to scoot toward the tailgate.

If he was cleared, then he might still have a paying gig driving the Binghams' wagon to Oregon. He'd taken the chance of joining up with the wagon train, knowing that if he could earn enough for a stake, he might get the fresh start he needed when the caravan arrived at its destination.

He could drive…if he could get his bearings. His head was swimming. He felt off-kilter, a little afraid he was going to fall out of the wagon if he got too close to the edge.

And then his hopes for a silent getaway went up in smoke as he started coughing. And couldn't stop.

When he finally got his breath back, he was gripping one of the bows that supported the canvas, and Emma and her brother stood watching him from just outside the back flap.

"What do you think you're doing?" Emma asked, her words more like a demand. Or those of a concerned sister.

"I thought I would—" A cough surprised him and cut off his sentence, though thankfully this one didn't last long. "Head back to the Binghams' wagon. Hitch up the oxen and get ready to pull out."

Emma's expression had turned into a thunderhead to rival what they'd seen the other day. Hewitt coughed, but when Nathan's gaze slid to the other man, Hewitt had his hat off and was hiding behind it. Was he…chuckling?

"I figured I'd get out of your way, now that I'm better."

Her frown only intensified.

"Better?" she echoed. The word sounded more disbelieving than questioning.

Maybe if he wasn't so dizzy, he could follow the conversation a little better. Although that wasn't a guarantee because he was awful rusty at talking to folks.

She stepped up onto a crate that must've been put in place to help her reach or get up into the wagon. She was muttering to herself, something that sounded suspiciously like, "If this is what your thinking gets you, I recommend you stop."

But that couldn't be right. He'd only ever heard Emma speak kind words, not sarcastic ones.

"Lie back down."

He balked at the order and this time he heard Hewitt laugh.

She blocked him from moving anywhere but backward, deeper into the wagon. She'd pulled her hair up in a severe style since he'd seen her at dawn, the sun breaking behind her and casting a halo of light around her mussed hair.

He sent a glare over her shoulder at Hewitt. The man only shrugged, leaving Nathan to wonder if she made a habit of bossing him, too.

"As far as I'm concerned, you're cleared of the thefts," Hewitt said. "I'll speak to the committee when I'm able."

Nathan nodded his thanks, unsmiling. If Hewitt would've investigated better, maybe Nathan wouldn't have been blamed in the first place.

But he knew better than to expect an apology for the unfounded accusation or the manhandling of his meager belongings as if they had had the right to do so.

They might've found him innocent, but Nathan knew he did not have the respect of most of the men.

But a sudden weakness took his limbs. He wavered, and for a moment wanted nothing more than to lie down like Emma had told him to.

"Get some rest," Hewitt said. "You can drive when you're up to it."

The man walked off and Nathan wanted nothing more than to be able to do the same, to find somewhere private to lick his wounds, as it were.

But he was still near face-to-face with Emma, who remained half in and half out of the wagon, waiting for him to lie back.

He acquiesced, only because he didn't think his legs would hold him if he tried to climb out of the wagon. He stared up at the white underside of the bonnet, unsure whether, if he looked at Emma, he would see her disappointed that he hadn't been more grateful to her brother.

He wasn't good at this, at being friendly with people.

"It's good you've been cleared," she said. He heard the clink of a fork against a plate and smelled something that had his gut twisting in a reminder that he hadn't eaten in two days.

But he still couldn't look at her.

"I imagine Stillwell was disappointed." Nathan was surprised that the words emerged so easily when he hadn't intended to say anything at all.

"Why?"

He wasn't going to answer, but she touched his forehead, a gentle brush of her fingertips, and his eyes flicked to her of their own accord.

Her gaze reflected only sincere curiosity and he found himself saying, "He seems to have it in for me."

He watched a tiny crease form between her eyebrows, just above the bridge of her nose.

But she didn't laugh at him, she didn't dismiss his statement out of hand.

"Are you certain you're not…" She hesitated.

Her voice trailed off, but he could guess what she'd been going to say.

"Imagining that he dislikes me?"

He couldn't hold her gaze and turned his head to stare at the opposite sideboard. His cheeks burned with embarrassment.

Was he imagining Stillwell's watchful, suspicious gazes? No. The man expressed more suspicion toward Nathan than most folks, who tended to simply avoid him.

When she spoke again, her voice sounded cheery, as if the previous conversation hadn't occurred. "The good news is you won't have to bear my company all day."

It was a relief. He didn't know how to act around her.

But he also felt a small twinge of disappointment.

It was better this way. Better not to learn to enjoy her company, even for a few hours.

"What am I supposed to do, confined to the wagon all day?" he asked.

"You could sing," she suggested.

"Sing?" he repeated.

"Sing. Rachel and I would be cheered if you were to serenade us as we walk."

He stared dumbly at her until her lips turned up in a smile and then she dissolved into giggles.

Her mirth was contagious—how long had it been since he'd made anyone smile?—but he prevailed against the urge to smile.

She finally controlled herself, hiding her remaining smile behind her hand. "I suppose you'll have to read to pass the time."

"Read?"

"You can't read?"

His education had been spotty at best. But he'd spent several years of his adult life teaching himself to read, not wanting to be cheated by those he traded with.

And it was a matter of pride for him. A man should know how to read.

"I can read," he told her.

And if there was a flash of admiration in her eyes, he didn't feel a responding flash of pride.

She rustled around in the belongings packed against the opposite sideboard. What must it be like to own so many things?

Even in Nathan's childhood, his family had scraped by. Never enough money for necessities—like food— and none at all for frivolities like books. The Hewitts were blessed.

"I'll need to help break camp, so I'll leave you to your

breakfast." She placed a dark green hardcover book at his knee, next to the plate of food. *Pilgrim's Progress*.

"Don't get up," she told him, face and voice grave. "You're too weak to bear it."

And his fleeting sense of pride dissipated completely.

Emma spent the morning with Rachel, attempting to gather fuel for their campfire. The terrain combined bluffs and rocky hills, sometimes passing over ledges that frightened her if she found herself looking down.

So she stopped looking and focused on two brothers playing chase through the wagons.

She and Rachel ranged off from the caravan, though not too far, and worked at gathering buffalo chips among the sparsely growing vegetation. It was not her preferred fuel—she did not appreciate the smell as it burned—but it was something.

Every time her apron filled and she passed close to the wagon to deposit her load in the fuel box, she felt caught in Nathan's glittering obsidian gaze. She'd never met anyone with eyes so dark.

He kept the book in hand, she could see the deep green spine against his worn shirt, but she couldn't get a sense whether he was really reading it or not. Maybe he didn't like Christian's story.

Once when she passed, he was dozing. When she dumped her load into the crate affixed to the side of the wagon, he started and roused, looking wildly around for a moment.

"Sorry," she apologized.

"Why should you be?" He asked the question almost belligerently, as if he didn't have a right to a simple apology. He softened the awkward, hard statement by adding, "I'm a passenger—you're working."

He appeared chagrined, his cheeks going pink above his beard.

Maybe she'd found the one specimen of the opposite sex who was as awkward as she.

It made her smile. "I am not working *that* hard."

His eyes flicked to her. "Walking so far is hard work."

She shrugged. "I've stopped noticing. It was difficult at first because I'd grown so used to being sedentary." Because of all the hours spent at her papa's bedside.

His eyes darkened with recognition. He remembered what she'd told him two nights ago.

"I'll try not to burden you with my care overlong," he said gravely.

"You'll stay in that wagon until you're fit to get down, and not a moment less," she retorted.

His chin jerked slightly at the familiarity of her statement and she blushed, heat filling her cheeks.

It didn't stop her from saying, "I think it must've been a long time since someone looked after you, Nathan."

"You are the first in a great while." He didn't seem happy to admit it to her. His jaw clenched and he turned his head to one side, no longer looking at her.

Had she irritated him with her bossiness?

"Well, I'm honored to be your first friend this decade." She'd meant the words to be teasing, but he didn't look back at her. Had she offended him?

She slowed her steps, picked her way over the rocky terrain as her feet carried her back toward Rachel. How she missed their ranch, with its gently rolling hills!

What was it about the rugged outsider that put her at ease, allowed her to speak as she couldn't with anyone else of the male persuasion?

Beneath his gruff exterior—the man she'd avoided because he'd hurt her feelings—there was a living breathing person.

Was it simply because she'd prayed so deeply, from the pit of her soul, on his behalf? Because they'd been in close confines for that day and a half? Because the man carried such an air of loneliness?

Or perhaps it was because she saw in him an echo of the loneliness she felt.

How many nights of whispered conversations beneath the covers with Rachel had she missed because she'd been at Papa's side? While it had been hard for her to watch her father decline, it had been difficult for her siblings even to visit the sickroom.

By the time Papa had passed, she'd felt isolated, as if she didn't even know her own brother and sister. Grayson she only knew from his letters.

She hadn't been comfortable enough to tell them she didn't want to be uprooted and travel to Oregon.

"What's the matter?" Rachel asked, wandering closer to Emma. Her apron was half-full of the chips.

"Nothing," Emma answered. She put on a smile.

"Were you thinking of Tristan McCullough?"

The sound of the man's name startled her, and Rachel must have seen it. "I suppose not, then." She laughed.

What did that mean? Stung, Emma said, "Perhaps you're the one thinking of Tristan McCullough too much."

Rachel's lips parted in a gasp, but her cheeks also pinked. As if Emma's guess had been on the mark.

She hadn't meant to snap at her sister. It wasn't Rachel's fault that she felt ill at ease, uncomfortable in her own skin. As if she was drifting with no real destination.

"I'm sorry," Emma said. "Nights of little sleep must be making me grumpy."

Rachel considered her with her cheeks still flushed. "Hmm. I forgive you. I think we're all weary of the journey."

It was so much more than that. And they had a long way to go.

Chapter Five

Evening had fallen and Nathan stood in the shadows behind the wagon, knowing that right on the other side was the circle of light. The Hewitts were over there. He could hear them laughing, talking, the clink of pots, the crackle of the cookfire.

Behind him was the quiet chirping of night insects, the darkness outside the camp.

He couldn't make himself cross into that circle of light.

As the afternoon had passed, he'd quickly grown weary of being confined in the wagon.

Or maybe he was weary of the pinpricks of awareness he felt whenever Emma came near.

She'd said she was his friend. She'd called him Nathan. More than once.

She'd loaned him her book. It was a small act of friendship, but more than anyone had given him in so very long.

He couldn't let himself get used to it. Everything good in his life had been ripped away.

Even now he told himself to sneak away and find his

bedroll. Bed down beneath the Binghams' wagon where he should be sleeping.

It was better to keep himself isolated. Protected from when she decided he wasn't friend material.

His boots might be on the ground but he clung to the sideboard, trying to judge whether his wobbly legs would hold him.

He'd grudgingly admitted to himself that she'd been right about his weakened state. Every time he coughed, his weakness intensified.

He was still ashamed that she'd found him asleep. He was used to physical labor, to ignoring the pangs of hunger or illness and pushing through.

But there was no ignoring that he was like a newborn babe, dependent on the kindness of this family.

He hated it.

And then it was too late to sneak away. A head of golden hair ducked around the side of the wagon; her face was turned down to the ground. She didn't see him until she was about to run into him and then she drew up short.

"What are you doing up?" she asked.

As if he was a kid instead of a grown man. To his chagrin, heat slipped up into his cheeks. Maybe the shadows and his beard would hide it.

"Needed to stretch my legs," he said. "You gonna keep me from visitin' the trees over yonder to do my private business?"

Her nose wrinkled, but she didn't speak.

"She might try."

Ben Hewitt's voice came from behind her and then he joined them beside the wagon. Watching over his sister? Or watching Nathan?

"I'll walk with you," Hewitt said. "Make sure you don't need any help."

"I won't."

But the other man followed Nathan, anyway.

Past the circle of wagons, outside the noise and bustle and people, it was quiet. A whip-poor-will called. Another answered. The breeze clicked the tree branches together. Stars peeped in from above through the canopy of leaves and branches.

Nathan didn't reply to Hewitt. What was there to say? *Thanks for carting me like a bag of flour all day?*

The short hike out to find a moment of privacy had him trembling, wondering how he was gonna get back to the wagon.

Hewitt stayed near the edge of the woods, giving Nathan a moment of privacy. He should probably be thankful for that, but the fact that he was still under watch put a taste of bitterness in his throat.

Nathan had turned back toward the wagons but paused, still under the cover of trees and brush, supporting himself with one hand on a nearby tree trunk.

A cough overtook him, and kept hold of him until he almost thought he would suffocate. When he could finally catch his breath, he was as limp as a wet washcloth.

"Reed, you all right?"

Nathan jerked and the unexpected movement sent him into another fit of coughing.

"You surprised—" cough "—me," he told Hewitt.

Anger fired. He was so weak and distracted by his condition that the other man had snuck up on him. If Hewitt had had nefarious intentions, Nathan could have been dead.

He didn't like being caught unawares.

"You need to lean on me to get back to the wagon?"

"No," Nathan said shortly.

He pushed away from the tree, and tottered. Hewitt

took one step toward him, but Nathan waved the other man off.

"Don't like accepting help, do ya?" Hewitt trailed him as Nathan stumbled toward the distant light of campfires past the ring of wagons.

The other man must be a couple years younger than Nathan and didn't have Nathan's bulk. If he'd been at full strength, he might've gotten in Ben's face and told him to leave off.

But he was so tired, he couldn't even manage that.

So he didn't answer.

The glow of light around the canvas wagon bonnet got brighter. Almost there.

"Reed."

Nathan stopped at the commanding tone in Hewitt's voice. He didn't want to turn around, but he did. They stood in the darkness just outside the ring of wagons. He didn't look at Hewitt, though he sensed the other man glancing around them.

But there was nothing out here except darkness and the backside of the wagons. Nathan looked up into the night sky, the thousands of stars, pinpricks of diamond light against the midnight blue sky.

"I want to talk to you about Emma," Hewitt said, voice low. "She told me she's worried for you. Our pa—" he cleared his throat, before continuing "—died of pneumonia, at the last."

Nathan stood there in the dark with a man who wasn't a friend but hadn't been unkind to him, not really. Some long-lost sense of propriety pushed Nathan to say, "I'm sorry."

Hewitt nodded. "Just don't be deliberately cruel with my sister. She's more sensitive than she lets on."

Heat prickled up Nathan's neck. He didn't acknowledge Hewitt's words.

He wanted to make some retort about Hewitt not even noticing his sister's fear of thunderstorms, but he didn't. Emma had trusted Nathan with the fear in confidence and he wouldn't break it.

And some tiny part, deep inside him, liked that they shared something that no one else knew about.

He turned back toward the wagons and saw a figure move to stand in the open—backlit by firelight, Emma's long-limbed form her golden hair haloed.

"There you are," she said.

For a moment, he let himself pretend she was looking after him. Waiting for him. Imagining that someone cared about his welfare was like a fist tightening his gut.

Dangerous, pretending was.

"Worried about me?" Hewitt asked, bussing her cheek with a kiss as he neared.

"Abby was." Something passed between the two siblings, some wordless communication that Nathan couldn't decipher.

Was Hewitt's fiancée worried about him being with Nathan, alone outside the protection of the wagons? Or was there something else?

Then Hewitt passed her with a squeeze of her elbow.

Nathan hesitated.

Exhaustion weighed him down. He should get back in the wagon. Stay isolated.

Then he registered that she held a plate of food in her hands and his stomach rumbled loudly in the quiet.

"Figured you must be hungry."

And what he'd been pretending suddenly became very real.

* * *

In the flickering firelight, Emma saw Nathan's hesitation.

He took the plate from her with a nod and turned his back to her, using the nearby wagon to shield him from the others, she supposed. What had happened in his past that made him wary of even a small act of kindness?

He held the plate up close to his face and began shoveling food into his mouth with his fingers.

She'd watched him do the same on another occasion, when he'd refused to eat at their fire. Eating quickly, like an animal might, devouring the food in moments.

Or as if there had been a time in his life that he'd been starved. And now he was afraid he'd lose his chance to eat if he didn't gobble it down.

She swallowed back the emotion that rose at the thought of such a history and cleared her throat.

He looked over his shoulder at her, clearly in midchew.

"Nathan, we're friends now. I won't have you going back to hiding in the shadows. Come sit at the fire."

His eyes widened and she thought he would refuse, so she stepped forward and took him by the elbow as if he were a child and pulled him with her.

Perhaps she'd surprised him into compliance, but he didn't resist her.

At the fire, she sat down, and since she already had hold of his arm, she tugged him down to sit at her side, and then let go.

He kept his head down, and his inky hair was long enough that it hid most of his face from view. But she still saw him snatch glances up at the group congregated around the fire.

Ben and Abby sat off to one side, a little apart from

everyone else, whispering to each other. Which left Emma and Nathan with Rachel and Mr. Bingham for company.

"The Littletons already retired," she told Nathan. "My sister, Rachel."

Rachel watched him with unabashed curiosity. "I'm glad you're feeling somewhat better."

Nathan looked up and nodded briefly, then back down to his plate.

A wiggling ball of fur approached from behind and stuck his nose right up under Nathan's elbow.

The moment slowed as Nathan looked down on the dog. The man was at times irascible and the way he'd almost hoarded his food moments ago made her wonder if he would be unkind to the dog. She and Rachel had taken turns feeding it scraps over the past two days that Nathan had been confined in the wagon.

The dog whined and Nathan sighed, then picked up a morsel from his plate and fed it to the dog. The animal licked his fingers.

Emma let go the breath she hadn't known she'd been holding and the dog ducked out of Nathan's space and turned to her.

"Hello, Scamp," she said, laughing as the dog propped its small paws on her knee. She scratched it beneath its chin and its lips parted in a great doggie grin, tongue lolling.

"I see he's moved on and found a new friend," Nathan said quietly.

The dog stretched up and swiped his tongue across Emma's chin. "No, never!" she said, still laughing, as she pushed the dog away.

It sat in the small space between Emma and Nathan,

looking between them with an expression of joy that only a dog could make, its tail sweeping the ground behind it.

"What is his name?" Emma asked, hoping to draw Nathan into conversation. "I've been calling him Scamp, as I didn't know what you'd called him."

Rachel looked on curiously. Ben and Abby had their heads bent together, whispering furiously, and Mr. Bingham was nodding off above his plate.

"Didn't give him one." Nathan returned to his supper. His plate was almost empty now.

"A dog *has* to have a name," she protested.

Nathan shrugged. "It's just a mutt."

"Emma has an affinity for abandoned animals," Rachel put in.

Nathan's eyes came to rest on her and heat flooded Emma's cheeks. But he didn't ask, so she said, "It's true, I'm afraid. We had a dog when I was very young—"

"And the kittens," Rachel interrupted. "Not to mention the squirrel, two baby birds and once a rabbit…"

"And now a man," Nathan murmured.

She didn't know if he meant her to hear the words. He'd gone after the last few bites of his plate, again with his head down and face hidden behind the curtains of his long, dark hair.

Did he think she pitied him? That wasn't it at all. She believed he deserved to be treated fairly, that was all. Just like everyone did. No one should have to eat their supper alone in the dark, like an outcast. No one should be accused without evidence, as Nathan had.

And everyone deserved a friend, right?

A moving shadow between the two wagons caught Emma's eye. She recognized Clara as the disguised woman did her best to blend into the darkness. Clara usually ate with the Morrisons, but if she was here, she might need something.

How could Emma extricate herself from the campfire to check on her friend?

Unfortunately, Nathan's head came up and his focus went to Clara with the precision of the tracker that he was.

"That's my friend Clar-ence." Emma stumbled slightly over the name. She pushed up from her seat, dusting off her skirt and hoping her companions would blame the fire for the brightness in her cheeks. She was uncomfortable covering up the ruse Clara had concocted. "I'll just see what he wants."

She felt the intensity of both Nathan's and Ben's gazes as she hurried over to her friend. She was careful to stand just so, blocking Clara from their sight.

"Is something the matter?"

"I've torn my last shirt," Clara whispered.

Emma squinted in the shadowed darkness. Sure enough, beneath the slicker Clara wore, she appeared to be wearing a nightshirt with her trousers.

"I can stitch it up, but it's a pretty bad rip. And I need to borrow something to wear tomorrow…"

Emma's eyebrows went up as she comprehended her friend's predicament, but before she could offer a solution, Clara's hand tightened on her wrist. Emma looked over her shoulder to see Nathan approaching, his empty plate dangling from his fingers.

Was he ready to retire for the night?

She was stuck there between Nathan's sharp eyes and Clara, who seemed to want to shrink into the shadows, when a voice rang out.

"Hewitt, I need to talk to you."

Both Nathan and Clara went still.

James Stillwell joined their circle, nodding to Rachel and Bingham, who had roused at his loud greeting. Mr. Stillwell's glittering gaze swept over Nathan, Emma and Clara and held for a moment too long. Clara panted softly in Emma's ear, while Nathan stood stiff, shoulders rigid.

Was Nathan right? Did Stillwell have a grudge against him in particular? She'd intended to argue on Stillwell's behalf until she'd remembered when he'd slapped Nathan across the face when Nathan had collapsed. It had seemed unkind to her.

"You got a minute, Ben?" Stillwell asked, finally turning away from where the three of them stood. "There's a problem…"

Ben stood, leaving Abby to her father's care.

"I suppose its time to clean up, anyway," Rachel said, the words more a complaint than an acknowledgment as she stood.

Emma was afraid Nathan would disappear into the darkness. She knew his cough lingered and didn't want him sleeping out in the cool night air, not yet.

"I'll bring you something of Ben's in the morning," Emma told Clara quickly, then moved to intercept Nathan.

As Emma turned away, Clara was left in the glow of the firelight, and her coat flapped open on one side, revealing the girth of her stomach. She quickly strode away into the darkness, but as Emma took a step toward Nathan, his pensive gaze remained on the spot where the other woman had disappeared.

Surely he couldn't have seen through Clara's disguise in that one moment, could he? Nathan was intelligent and watchful. She could well imagine that he might notice Clara's condition when the Morrisons and Emma's own family hadn't.

"Are you ready to retire?" Emma asked, her words tumbling one over another in her haste to distract his attention from thoughts of Clara. "You'll bed down in the wagon again."

He didn't grumble, as Ben might've, but accepted her demand without argument. Which perhaps told her more about his condition than he would ever say aloud.

Sleep was a long time coming after she had joined Rachel and Ben in the family tent near the wagon. That moment in the shadowed darkness repeated in her mind.

Had Nathan seen through Clara's disguise?

Nathan startled awake to an unfamiliar sound, his breathing harsh in the early-morning stillness.

What was it?

His chest burned, and the fiery poker stabbing him with each inhale brought him to full awareness. He was in the Hewitts' wagon, its white canvas cover gray above him in the darkness. A corner of a crate poked into his lower back. Smells of coffee and flour roused him. His illness lingered; he could feel it in the heaviness in his limbs, the fire in his chest.

It was light enough he could see his breath puff out above him in a white cloud. Cold in the not-quite-dawn, he was grateful to be tucked in warm with the quilted blanket Emma had forced on him last night.

Emma.

The sound came again, and he sat up, careful not to rustle the blanket too much and scare off whoever was outside the wagon.

It sounded like bells tinkling, or a long-forgotten hymn he'd heard sung from inside a church when he'd been a very young boy, hiding outside the structure on a bright Sunday morning.

It sounded like joy.

Someone was humming.

The back flap had been closed for the night, and he hooked one finger around the quarter-size opening and tugged, ever so slightly. The canvas gave, the opening widened. Not all the way. Just enough for him to see Emma's profile in the predawn light.

Her head was bent toward the ground, her golden hair spilling down over her shoulders, down her back.

He swallowed. Hard.

She ran a brush through her silky locks, still humming a tune he could almost recognize, unaware that he watched her.

Against the darker silhouettes of scrub brush and prairie in the distance, she was so beautiful that it made him ache from the inside out. Her features, her form... her heart.

Anybody could see it. Why else would she have offered someone like him—an outcast—kindness, as she had done? Why would she have befriended Clarence—whom Nathan had some suspicions about—if not for her kind heart? Why help all the overburdened young mothers with sick children?

Why tell him he could be forgiven?

He'd never met anyone like her. Or rather...women like her stayed far, far away from the likes of him.

She made him remember things, want things that he hadn't thought about in years. Watching her with her brother and sister, the easy camaraderie they shared, how well they knew each other, and loved each other...

He missed Beth with the same intensity as when she'd just passed.

He should make some kind of noise. Let Emma know he was awake.

Who was he kidding? He should get down out of the wagon and walk away, never look back.

But something held him immobile as he watched her separate the waterfall of her hair into three parts and slowly tuck the parts into a long plait.

With the fall of her hair out of his way, his sharp tracker's eyes picked up the straight line of her jaw, the slope of her cheek and little upturn at the end of her nose. Her eyes were downcast, the curl of her dark lashes shadowing her cheek, hiding the clear blue depths.

Depths that didn't throw accusation or revulsion or derision when she looked at him. Only a gentle friendship that he didn't know what to do with.

He wasn't the man she thought he was. Yesterday, he'd overheard her defend him to her brother, but what she thought about him wasn't true. He had plenty of dark things in his past. Things he wasn't proud of.

Things that Beth would be ashamed to know he'd done.

A sudden fit of coughing took him and he ducked away from the canvas, deeper into the wagon.

He heard movement from outside the wagon, the rustling of clothes. Probably Emma's dress.

He went hot. Would she figure out he'd been watching her?

He couldn't stop coughing, even when it felt as if an entire lung lodged in his throat. Then Emma was there, undoing the canvas cover from the outside and thrusting a dipper of cool water into his hand.

He took a breath and a sip. The icy water soothed his throat enough that he stopped coughing, at least for the moment.

The concern on her expression made the poker of fire in his chest burn hotter. The sky behind her turned blue and it made her eyes—and whatever was in their depths—shine brighter.

"Woke up to ice on the water bucket this morning," was all she said. Then, "Are you still fevering? Your cheeks are flushed…"

She stepped up onto a crate on the ground at the foot of the wagon bed and reached up to touch his forehead with the back of her wrist.

He flinched away, unable to keep himself from shrinking at the innocent touch.

He didn't have a fever. He was embarrassed that she'd caught—or almost caught—him spying on her.

"I'm fine," he said, a touch too sharply.

Emma watched for a clue to Nathan's condition in his expression. His face revealed nothing, only stern lines and handsome planes.

But his eyes were another matter entirely. Several unreadable emotions flickered through the onyx depths before he lowered his gaze and cut off her view.

"I'm fine," he said gruffly.

When it was plain as day from the pallor beneath his flushed cheeks and his hacking cough that he was anything but.

He swung one massive, booted foot over the wagon bed and she moved out of his way as he clambered down.

"I hope you'll use the sense that God gave you and ride in the wagon again today." She wasn't sure where that stern, bossy tone had come from. She would never have dared speak to one of Ben's friends that way. But it was still clear to see that Nathan was ill, gravely so.

He didn't respond, only slid her a sideways look as he stalked off between the wagons and outside the circle.

When he returned, white-faced and bracing himself

against the wagon with one hand, as if he'd suffered another coughing spell, she was bent over a young girl who'd suffered a serious cut on her hand.

The little girl sat on her mother's lap and cried out as Emma tried to pry her fist open and get a look at her palm. She began struggling in her mother's arms and Emma was forced to sit back as the mother whispered for the girl to behave while she wrestled her to stillness in her lap.

By the fire, Rachel had finished frying up the salt pork and eggs and was ready to dish them out, though Mr. Bingham and Abby hadn't made an appearance yet. Familiar noises from nearby meant that Ben was likely tearing down the family tent and stowing it away.

"Sit and eat," Emma told Nathan. Ordered.

His clenched jaw and stormy dark eyes told her he wanted to protest, but he silently strode to the fire and accepted the plate Rachel extended him.

He sent Emma a baleful glance as he did so.

"You'd just as soon give over," Rachel said quietly, but not so quietly that Emma couldn't hear her as she went back to doctoring the girl. "When Emma gets her mind set on something, she's stubborn."

From the corner of her eye, she saw the inscrutable look he threw in her direction, and her cheeks heated. She bent over the little girl's hand with renewed attention. The girl finally opened her hand and Emma got a look at the angry red line that scored her palm.

It was true. Hadn't she told him so herself, when she'd said she never gave up?

But something had changed between them since that first dark night he'd passed in their wagon. A friendship had been forged, but it was more than that. At least for her. She'd seen a glimpse of the lonely, intelligent man beneath Nathan's harsh exterior. She hated that he had been cast to the fringes of the caravan. It wasn't fair to him.

The little girl cried out again as Emma attempted to clean out her cut with a washrag soaked with antiseptic.

"I know it stings," Emma said softly. "But it's important to clean out your cut."

Terribly important. The danger of infection out in the wilds like this was serious.

But the little girl didn't listen. She snatched her hand back with a loud, "No!"

Scamp, the little dog she'd named last night, sidled up to Nathan with a hopeful doggy smile turned up to the man.

The girl's eyes flicked in that direction. Nathan's face was turned down to his plate, shoulders hunched as if he was trying to make himself invisible. Had he even noticed the girl's interest?

The girl's mother continued to whisper to her, insisting she sit still while Emma worked on her hand. The girl sniffled, her eyes still on the dog. Emma waited.

The dog whined, a piteous sound.

Then Emma thought she heard Nathan whisper something and the dog dropped to the ground, its paw extended toward the man as if to play. Had Nathan told the dog to do so?

The little girl's chin turned toward the pair and Emma used the opportunity to grasp her wrist and bathe the cut with the antiseptic.

The girl flinched and opened her mouth as if she were ready to cry out again, but at the same moment Nathan tossed a piece of pork and the dog leaped into the air and caught it.

This time Emma was sure she heard Nathan give the

dog a command. She heard a flurry of movement, but she kept her gaze on her task and wrapped the girl's hand in a clean, white cloth and tied it off. Nathan and Scamp had distracted her now-giggling patient enough for Emma to finish the job.

Even Rachel giggled, but Emma looked up too late to see what had happened.

Nathan ducked his head and kept his gaze on his empty plate. The dog sat at his feet, tail sweeping the ground.

"All done," Emma said to the girl and her mother. She gave instructions and tried to impart the importance of keeping the wound from becoming infected. The bugle blew as they left the Hewitts' campfire. It was time to pack up. The wagon train was moving out again.

"Thank you," Emma said aside to Nathan as she picked up the cloth and antiseptic bottle. She was careful with their medical supplies, hoping she wouldn't need most of them before they reached Oregon.

He shrugged, his head still down.

But she knew what he had done. Even if he wouldn't admit to it.

Spotting Clara at the Morrisons' wagon, Emma couldn't help but notice her friend's white complexion beneath the hat mashed on her head. She hadn't been like that when Emma had rushed through the camp before dawn to deliver one of Ben's shirts to Clara.

Had Clara been sick again this morning? She was well into her second trimester, well past the time when she should be getting so violently ill. But then, she was taking the trail all on her own steam. It was grueling travel, and then caring for the animals on top of it all.

Conscious of Nathan's presence nearby, Emma knew she didn't dare go and check on her friend. While Rachel might be caught up in chattering with Abby, Emma knew that her actions wouldn't go unnoticed by the trapper.

Emma determined to check on her friend later.

When Emma glanced at Nathan, his gaze was also fixed on Clara.

Finally, Ben peered around the front edge of the wagon. "Ready, sisters?"

"Just about," Emma replied.

"Reed, Emma says you're in the wagon again."

Nathan didn't argue. He looked fatigued just from sitting up to eat.

He said nothing, but stood and strode to the wagon. His little dog had disappeared.

Emma accepted the breakfast skillet from Rachel, who waggled her eyebrows, and took it to the wagon to stow it inside for the day's journey.

Nathan was already inside, staring into the canvas. His clenched jaw made him seem angry.

In fact, he didn't acknowledge her at all.

Had she offended him somehow? They'd barely spoken this morning. She'd been worried over his flushed cheeks when she'd first seen him, but she didn't think his fever had returned.

"Is there anything you need? More reading material?"

He still didn't look at her, but shook his head minutely.

What had happened? Moments ago, he'd been charming a little girl, helping Emma by distracting her. Now suddenly he was aloof. Even uncomfortable.

He blew out a breath, rubbed a hand across his bearded jaw. "Look, Emma—Miss Hewitt."

She went back on her heel as he changed the salutation to the more formal surname.

"I appreciate you taking care of me, but there's something you should know…"

His voice trailed off, but then his jaw came up and his shoulders straightened as if he'd come to some kind of decision.

His face turned toward her and his onyx eyes met her gaze. They were filled with determination, but behind that, shadowed.

"I heard what you said to your family yesterday. About me."

She flushed, remembering how she'd come to his defense. If it had been anyone else, she likely would have kept her opinions to herself. Her natural shyness often prevented her from speaking her mind in the company of others, as evidenced by what had happened the morning Nathan had collapsed.

"I'm not the kind of man you think I am."

Nathan's quiet words drew her out of herself, out of her thoughts and self-deprecation.

His jaw had tightened and a muscle ticked in his cheek. What was he trying to tell her that was making him so serious?

"What kind of man are you?" she asked.

"A thief."

She flinched at the unexpected words.

"I mightn't have taken your hair combs, or anything else on this trip, but I have done so in the past. I've done my share of poaching and fistfighting. And other things I'm not proud of."

He stared at her, his expression hard.

She didn't know what to make of his unexpected confession. There was a reason he was telling her this, but she couldn't fathom what it might be. Her breaths were coming short and her stomach had tightened painfully.

And then she saw his hand, half-hidden behind his thigh. Trembling.

Something more *was* going on here. She must tread carefully.

"To what purpose were your crimes?"

"What?" His sharp question was laced with surprise. Had he not understood her?

"Why did you do those things?"

"Does it matter?" he demanded, voice gone slightly rough. "I did them. I'm a criminal."

"Emma!" Ben's voice called from the front of the wagon. "We've got to pull out, can you put up the tailgate?"

"Yes," she called back, but she didn't let her gaze waiver from Nathan's face.

"What I said the other night remains," she said softly. "*I forgive you.* Perhaps you need to seek God's forgiveness. And forgive yourself."

She stepped off the crate she'd been using to gain a better height and lifted the heavy tailgate, carefully latching it into place. Nathan watched her, his brow heavily wrinkled, as if in consternation.

She lifted the empty crate and hung it on its peg on the back corner of the wagon. But she had one more thing to say.

She stood on tiptoes, clasping the top of the tailgate to steady herself. "No matter your past, I still believe you need a friend, Nathan Reed. And I aim to be just that."

She left him sitting in the wagon bed as Ben commanded the oxen into motion.

Chapter Six

If Nathan expected Emma to heed his warning about his character and avoid him, he was surprised.

She checked on him throughout the day, as sweet and kind as ever. He couldn't understand why. Hadn't she heard what he'd told her about his criminal past?

From inside the wagon, he'd watched the landscape change from the rocky bluffs to a marshy bottom where the wagon's wheels had slogged through and the oxen had attempted to slow and graze as they'd pulled. He'd often heard Ben's deep voice from outside and in front of the wagon, urging the animals forward.

Then out of the marsh, they'd traveled along a creek bottom, mostly covered with grass.

He'd split his attention between watching the landscape pass and reading. Neither the book Emma had lent him nor the land kept his attention overlong—his thoughts kept tracking back to the woman, time and again.

He felt slightly better, able to sit up for periods of time, but he had little hope of being out of the wagon tomorrow. His cough acted up when he took the slightest effort, whether it was standing or walking. He would never be able to control the oxen, and his fatigue persisted.

The bugle sounded as twilight fell and Nathan was able to disembark the wagon after Ben had pulled it into the familiar circle, the circle that protected their caravan and its animals.

It was a relief to stretch to his full height, unencumbered by the wagon bonnet or the jumble of the Hewitts' belongings.

He lingered as long as he could, taking care of his personal needs. It was full dark when he returned to the Hewitts' camp, the night sky sparkling with stars too numerous to count.

His stomach rumbled with hunger, but he considered ducking back into the wagon. If Emma came after him, he could feign sleep.

He didn't need food as much as he needed to keep his distance.

A soft bark greeted him as he neared the wagon. *Scamp.* He'd heard Emma use the affectionate name and figured it was as good as any.

But he didn't want the little rascal announcing his presence to the entire company.

Too late.

A shadow separated from the wagon. Emma. Waiting on him again.

"Are you all right?"

She didn't seem to consider whether he might've been doing something he oughtn't. She only asked about his well-being.

And something inside him rose up in response. He tried to cram it back down into the darkness inside him, but there was some part of him that liked it that she cared enough, as a friend, to ask.

He nodded, when he'd intended to brush by her and clamber back up into the wagon. He looked down on the dog at his feet, wagging his whole rear end in silent joy at seeing Nathan.

"Supper's on," she said softly. "Join us."

He hesitated and she must've known it, because she cajoled, "Please, Nathan."

And somehow he found himself settling beside her on a blanket spread near the fire, accepting a plate of food, the dog at his side.

The food smelled so good—a gamey meat, biscuits, some kind of floury gravy—that he was desperately tempted to begin shoveling it in his mouth with his fingers.

But he'd felt how she'd watched him the past times he'd eaten at their fire. He knew he didn't have any manners, that he was as good as a wild animal.

But he wasn't an animal. And someone as fine as Emma deserved politeness at her table, such as it was.

So he forced himself to use the fork that felt unfamiliar in his clumsy fingers. Forced himself to eat slow, chew his food.

Her sister, the one who chattered all the time, sat across the fire with Ben and his fiancée and Mr. Bingham. Pressman was nowhere in sight and not for the first time, Nathan wondered at the friendship between Emma and the other man, whose unusual behavior had caught Nathan's interest.

"Are you feeling better?"

He startled when a female voice sounded from Emma's other side, the question directed at him.

He'd seen Sally Littleton around their camp but never had reason to speak to her. She held a baby on her lap, who cooed and drooled and waved a chubby hand in the air.

He swallowed the hunk of meat in his mouth and

nearly choked on it. "Somewhat," he finally answered, gruffer than he had intended.

"Emma is a good nurse. She's helped doctor Johnny twice, hasn't she, little one?"

Nathan wasn't sure if the woman's words required a response since her tone had changed at the end of her sentence so that she was cooing at the baby.

"I'm sure the orphanage would have discovered your nursing skills before long, if you hadn't left," Sally continued, now speaking to Emma.

"Orphanage?" he echoed, because he'd lost the conversational thread.

Emma cleared her throat. "After Papa passed, I became involved with a local orphanage. Doing some cooking on occasion. Sewing clothing for the children."

"So that's what you left behind," he said softly.

Emma's eyes flicked up and met his, shadows dancing in their depths. Or maybe it was just the reflection of flickering flames playing tricks on him.

"Not a suitor?" He wasn't even sure where the words came from, but they were out of his mouth before he could call them back.

"No." He could be mistaken, but he thought he saw her cheeks go pink before she ducked her head.

"Well, it's off to bed for this strapping boy," Sally Littleton said as she stood and gathered her things in one hand while she held the baby in the other.

"Good night," Emma offered quietly.

And then their neighbor was gone and he was alone with Emma on the quilt. Her sister had disappeared, along with Mr. Bingham, and only Ben and Abby sat across the fire from them, whispering to each other and not paying any attention to Nathan and Emma.

"What about you?" she asked. "What did you leave behind to come West?"

"Nothing."

She wrinkled her nose at his simple statement, but he wasn't putting her off. It was true.

"No family?" she pressed.

He shook his head. Beth was gone, as was his mother, and he'd left his pa behind and counted it a blessing.

"What about Beth?" she asked, her words going so quiet that he almost didn't hear his sister's name.

His jaw tightened, his back teeth ground together. He shook his head. He didn't—couldn't talk about Beth. What had happened, his guilt, was too painful.

But Emma was not offended that he didn't answer.

"Where did you grow up?" she asked, voice still friendly and open. Scamp lay down between them on the blanket and she scratched between his shoulders, which just enticed the dog to roll over and offer her his belly. She scratched that, too.

"Arkansas," Nathan answered with abruptness. "On a farm."

"Oh. We have that in common."

She sounded so pleased about it that his stomach curdled. "Hardly. We were dirt poor. I doubt you've ever known hunger such that your belly turns into a little stone inside of you."

"No, but my family lost much in the Panic," she said.

He'd forgotten. He knew she must've had a difficult time with her father ill and then passing. But he doubted she knew what it was like to not know where your next meal would come from—or if it even would.

He went silent. Afraid to say the wrong thing again. Afraid she would get up off the blanket and leave. When he should've been the one escaping back to the wagon.

"I think you must've overcome much to become the man you are today, Nathan."

And then in the wake of those words, she did stand up, brushing off her skirt.

"Prickly or not, I like you."

Her simple words kept him awake long into the night, long past the time when campfires had gone out and murmurs had quieted throughout the camp.

She couldn't mean it.

Two days later, Nathan chafed at the forced confinement of the wagon. Outside the canvas cover, life went on. Children laughed and played. Women talked and gossiped. Men drove the oxen.

But Nathan was stuck where he was.

He was much stronger than before. His fever had never returned, but his hacking cough persisted. Each time he had a coughing fit, he ended up as weak and limp as a finely tanned rabbit's fur. Ben and Emma had insisted he remain in the wagon one more day, but he wanted away.

He was used to being a loner. Being on his own.

After eating supper together these past nights, and the forced intimacy of their close confines, Nathan knew how very dangerous being around Emma could be.

He didn't understand her.

How could she state that she wanted to be his friend after what he'd told her? He'd expected revulsion, rejection when he'd told her that he was a thief. Or at least for her to turn cold, treat him like the cur he was.

She'd done none of those things.

Her continued acceptance made him want to take the friendship she was offering.

But it was dangerous to want. He'd learned it the hard

way, growing up. Whether it was a toy or food for his always-empty stomach, during his childhood the chances were that he'd get a smack if he'd told his pa he wanted something.

His family had been constantly on the edge of poverty.

As to wanting a friend, he'd given up on that after he'd failed Beth. He didn't deserve a friend.

Which was why Emma's continued kindness in the face of his confession baffled him.

Worried him.

What expectations did she have of him?

If she couldn't see it now, when would she figure out that he wasn't friend material?

Her dazzling smiles made him uncomfortable, more so because he knew he didn't deserve them.

And the thought that burned a hole in his gut…what if he failed her like he'd failed Beth?

He slammed the thick book Emma had lent him closed, frustrated that he'd become distracted by thoughts of the beautiful woman. Again.

He attempted to stretch out his legs, but there just wasn't *room* among the jumble of the Hewitts' belongings.

The forced inactivity wore upon him, more so because without something to distract him, his thoughts circled back to Emma like a hawk hunting prey. Over and over again. With alarming frequency.

He wanted out of this wagon.

He growled, a low sound of frustration ripping from his chest.

"Well, hello to you, too."

His head whipped up and he chastised himself for being lost in his thoughts because the very woman he'd been thinking about had approached and was walking close behind the wagon, peering up at him.

Afternoon sunlight turned her hair to gold and the cloudless sky made her blue eyes seem even brighter. Behind her, in the distance, the sparkling water of the big Bear River shone in the sunlight—almost as dazzling as her smile.

"Are you bored with the book?" she asked.

"The book is fine," he said shortly. It was he who was distracted.

He'd come to a decision earlier, after she'd told him she would continue to be his friend. No matter how kind she was to him, he would turn away her offers of friendship until he could escape the wagon or until she realized he wasn't friend material.

"I was wondering if you could help me with something."

Suspicion rose but was quickly disregarded. Emma was so open and trusting—possibly to her own detriment—that whatever task she'd brought him wasn't to his harm.

She tossed a burlap sack into the wagon bed. It landed heavily against his legs.

"What is this?" he asked, but curiosity had him unfurling the top of the bag before she'd answered.

Inside was a tangle of ropes.

"One of the young boys has been collecting pieces of rope. Some of them are in decent shape and could be spliced together to make a longer piece. Restore their usefulness."

He didn't know what to think about such a task. It was busywork, something to keep his hands occupied. Wasn't that what he wanted?

He met her gaze squarely and she looked at him with

no guile. "I think we'll find the rope still has use left in it."

There was something, some message, underneath her words. He was an expert tracker and could name the prints of dozens of animals, but he couldn't decipher her deeper meaning.

He thought to refuse her, in keeping with his plan to make her believe he wasn't friend material, but then she added a soft, "Please."

She was too good to have to beg someone like him.

He nodded.

Her answering smile was brilliant and lit her face. He forced himself to look away, to stare at the level sandy plain, covered with sage. Anywhere but at her.

Chapter Seven

That same afternoon the bugler called for a halt after only five miles, for which Emma was grateful. Her stomach grumbled for sustenance, although she felt she'd ingested several buckets' worth of dust. The oxen and wagons kicked up much into the air on this stretch of plain.

She was also grateful for the short day because she suspected Nathan must be climbing the walls inside the wagon. She'd given him the rope-splicing task, hoping it would keep him busy enough that his attitude wouldn't suffer. The task was childish, something an eleven- or twelve-year-old could've done, but he'd accepted it without complaint.

Without saying much of anything.

That was one of the challenges plaguing her. Nathan had been a loner for so long, it seemed that either he didn't know how to converse or he didn't want to.

But she knew he *must* want a friend. Her assumption was sparked by the hint of vulnerability she'd seen— or thought she'd seen—when he'd tried to scare her off days ago.

She'd finally figured out his intentions. Mostly because she'd pored over the conversation mentally since it had happened.

But the question remained—*why*? Why did he want her to stay distant from him?

She'd thought that what they'd shared as he'd been in the throes of sickness had cemented a friendship somehow because with Nathan, she didn't feel the same awkwardness that intruded on every other relationship, even acquaintanceship, with the opposite sex.

But what if he was only being polite and bearing her presence because she'd cared for him?

The thought made her stomach plunge and she steadied herself with a firm internal rap. She needed a friend. Nathan needed a friend.

And until he told her outright to leave him alone, she would be that friend for him.

"Is there anything wrong? We stopped early," she asked Ben as she approached where he was unharnessing the oxen. The wagons had circled a ways off from a beautiful, sparkling stream. It was the only beautiful thing in this barren, sandy stretch of land beneath the clear blue sky.

"The animals are exhausted. That's all."

"We're all exhausted," she said and he smiled, but was obviously distracted by his task.

Her stomach demanded food and she rounded the wagon, meeting Nathan as he clambered down from the wagon bed. And Rachel, who approached from another direction, having been visiting with a friend near another wagon during the morning hours.

"Are you hungry?"

She included both of them in her query, but Nathan ducked around the side of the wagon and disappeared.

She pulled a face at the spot where he'd gone and Rachel laughed. "Can I take it the man isn't following your nurse's orders as closely as you would like?"

Emma shrugged, unwilling to admit to her sister that it was friendship and not her doctoring that was causing the conflict between them. "He's been in the wagon for four days. You'd be anxious to stretch your legs, too," was all she said.

"Did I hear correctly that we're stopping for the day?"

Emma nodded, distracted. She was on a mission to find food. Where were the biscuits left from this morning's breakfast? She rifled through the open crate where she thought they would be. She muttered to herself.

"Do you think Mr. Reed will go back to eating alone?"

"What?" Emma said, still with her mind only half on her sister's conversation. "Why would he?"

"He doesn't seem to like us much. With his glares and foul temperament, I can imagine you'll be excited to be rid of him after we reach the Oregon Territory. He's horrid."

This time Emma bumped her head she turned to Rachel so quickly. "Nathan is not horrid!"

Rachel's brows went up. "Nathan, is it?"

Emma's chin hiked up. "We're friends, of a sort. He might be prickly, but he's never been rude to me. I think he's just lonely."

One corner of Rachel's mouth twitched and Emma instantly understood her sister had been baiting her.

Emma's reaction was telling. Maybe too much so.

She put her hands against suddenly hot cheeks. "We're just friends," she said with some vehemence. Her heart pounded against her sternum.

"I know," Rachel said simply. "I actually think Mr. Reed—Nathan," she amended with a waggle of her eyebrows, "is good for you. You don't seem uncomfortable with him. Or Clarence, either. Perhaps the trip is what has made the difference for you. Getting away from the memories," she suggested.

The mention of Clarence had given Emma pause. She wasn't good at hiding things from Rachel, but had so far been able to keep Clara's secret. But Rachel's blithe statement that the trip had been good for her had her clamping her jaw shut at the same time she forced a smile.

She would never tell Rachel that she hadn't wanted to go West, that every day brought new fears.

And she was so tired of walking.

But she didn't have to think of some way to distract Rachel from the mention of Clarence. Her sister wasn't done yet. "I suppose Tristan McCullough will be glad of the changes, as well."

Rachel's casual statement held Emma frozen in place. *Tristan.*

She hadn't thought of him or their possible match since the last time Rachel had spoken of him. That had been days ago. Had she been so wrapped up in her concerns about Nathan that she'd behaved inappropriately?

"You don't think Mr. McCullough would find fault with my behavior, do you?" she asked after a pause.

"How could he?" Rachel returned. "If you are only friends?"

Emma's mind spun as she gathered some eggs they'd traded for from another traveler and reached for the biscuits that had been left from breakfast. Not there.

Had Rachel meant to warn her about her behavior, her friendship with Nathan?

Rachel was so outspoken that Emma couldn't imagine her giving such a veiled warning.

But the warning had been imparted just the same.

Grayson and Ben thought the match would be good for Emma. She'd given her word to consider the match.

Her heart had been with the orphans back home. She still wondered if God was sending her to the McCullough family. Was this to be her new purpose?

She didn't know. And thinking about it tied her stomach in knots.

She had given her word. And so she must be careful of her actions with Nathan. If she did decide to go through with a courtship and marriage with Tristan McCullough, her actions must be blameless.

Then as she boosted herself in the wagon to look further for the leftover biscuits, she saw the most unexpected thing.

Several bundles of rope, neatly coiled, arranged in an orderly row.

Nathan didn't know where he was going, only knew he had to get away from the wagon. And Emma.

Nearby, a wide swath of trees broke up the emptiness of the plain and he aimed to reach its privacy. But he'd barely rounded the empty yoke when Ben called out to him. "The committee wants to see you."

Nathan's hackles went up. What did they want with him now? To make more accusations against him? He couldn't remember...hadn't Ben said something about Nathan being cleared of the accusations against him? He'd been so violently ill those first days that his memories were a muddle.

But there was no escaping, not with Ben waiting expectantly a few feet away.

Nathan fell into step with the other man as they moved through the chaotic mass of women readying cookfires, men mending belongings and children running through.

His stomach was tight but he forced his hands to hang loose at his sides. Better not to show a reaction.

This, *this* was the reason he distanced himself from Emma's friendship. Because if she was friends with him, she would be touched by the judgmental attitudes against him. And even though he recognized that he deserved it, she didn't.

The men had gathered outside the circle of wagons, already closed off in a tight-knit group. Would they push Nathan into the center?

His gut twisted even tighter.

Ben walked right into the circle, and it opened for him. Nathan hung back, until Ben jerked his chin, indicating Nathan should join him.

The sun beat down on his head and shoulders as he moved into their circle. Next to him, Ernie Jones shifted uncomfortably. Jones wasn't a committeeman, but perhaps he'd been asked here since he was the one who'd brought the accusation against Nathan.

No one seemed to want to speak. No one seemed to want to meet his eyes. The grass smelled sweet, but this situation stank.

Finally, the preacher cleared his throat. "It seems I owe you an apology for my accusation against you."

Nathan was so shocked by the man's words that he was sure his mouth dropped open. An apology?

But the other men still weren't speaking, or looking at him. What was this?

"I still don't trust him," Stillwell muttered from a few paces away.

Ernie Jones lifted his chin and said belligerently, "Just because he don't have them hair combs on him don't mean he didn't take them."

Nathan tensed at their suspicion and dislike, though he

tried not to show any reaction. The glaring sunlight—or maybe the tension in the gathering—shoved pinpricks of pain behind Nathan's eyes.

He was surprised when Ben spoke up from next to him. "He was sick in the wagon when the next theft occurred. It couldn't have been him."

"How do we know your sister wasn't just covering for him?" Ernie demanded.

"Watch what you say about Miss Hewitt," he snapped, surprised at himself even as the words flew out of his mouth.

"She could've fallen prey to his charms," Stillwell added, turning to the men next to him. They didn't appear to know whether to nod and agree or what to believe, most of them wearing uncertain expressions.

Nathan snorted. He exchanged a serious glance with Ben. What charms? He had none to speak of.

Ben cleared his throat and the rumbling men around him went silent, including Stillwell. "You'll want to remember that's my sister you're speaking of. She's a woman of integrity, her character is impeccable. Many of your wives would tell you the same, as she's doctored your children back to health."

Several of the men looked down or away, chagrined expressions on their faces. Good for Ben. No one should be allowed to speak badly of Emma. She was too pure, too good.

Jones spat on the ground. "He's been lazing about in the wagon, taking charity instead of driving. Eating your supplies." He pointed at Ben, as if all those things were Ben's fault.

Nathan inhaled, but kept his mouth wired shut. He didn't have to defend himself, though he wanted to argue he'd been so sick he hadn't been able to sit upright.

"I still say we should still throw him out of the caravan," Jones said.

Nathan forced the breath out of his nose in a long exhale, a low ache still remaining from the sickness. Anger boiled beneath his breastbone.

He'd driven Mr. Bingham's oxen nearly halfway to their destination. He was planning on the payment Bingham had promised to make a new start for himself. Counting on it.

He had to get to the Oregon Territory.

And he didn't owe them any explanation. "I'll drive the oxen tomorrow," he said.

Stillwell opened his mouth again and Nathan braced for the next argument as to why he couldn't be trusted, but Ben spoke, cutting off anything the other man might've said.

"We called this meeting to let Mr. Reed know he's been cleared of all charges. He's as innocent as you and me, unless proven otherwise."

Stillwell's face went crimson, but he remained silent, as did the blustery Ernie Jones, for once.

"Anyone else like to apologize for our unfounded accusations?" Ben asked.

The group remained dead silent. Unsurprising, but Nathan felt a pinch in his gut.

Or maybe it was because Ben had stood up for him. Nathan couldn't believe the other man had done it. How long had it been since someone else had stuck their neck out for him? Long enough that he didn't remember it.

He stood frozen as the group dispersed, most of the men avoiding his gaze, though Ernie Jones glared at him as he passed.

Ben stood at his side, tall as the stone landmark they'd passed a week ago.

When they were the only ones left, Nathan cleared his throat. "Thank you."

The words felt rusty on his tongue, uncomfortable enough to make him want to shift his feet, though he didn't show the sign of weakness.

Ben's brow creased as he watched the other men disappear into the circle of wagons. "Emma was right," he said under his breath.

Nathan waited, and Ben's gaze came to meet his. "She said all along you hadn't been treated fairly when you were accused. But I was too distracted by all their blustering to see it."

"So that…was for Emma?"

"That was because I believe a man deserves a fair chance." Ben clapped him on the shoulder, as if they had somehow become friends. "And because you defended my sister."

Nathan didn't know how to respond.

"I've got to check on Abby and her father. I'll see you back at the campfire?"

The other man held Nathan's gaze expectantly, until finally Nathan gave in with a nod.

He stood, alone in the bright afternoon sun, outside the circle of wagons. On one side of the wagons, the landscape was brown and sandy, with the sparkling river in the distance. On the other side, wild sage and the woodsy area beckoned. A hint of frost, the barest bite of cold remaining in the air even though the afternoon had warmed.

He felt a stirring of some emotion he couldn't name. Maybe hope.

Emma wanted to befriend him. Ben had stood up for him.

Was it possible he didn't have to live in such deep isolation? Could he have friends? If he could find a way to keep a careful distance. They couldn't be bosom friends, but perhaps he could share their campfire until they arrived in the Oregon Territory.

And he wouldn't be so lonely.

He started toward the wagons, unsure of whether he would to go find Emma or see if he could assist the Binghams, but before he'd reached the ring of conveyances, a tall shadow separated from the near wagon.

Stillwell.

Nathan's hands curled into fists, but the other man didn't approach, just stood still and silent, watching Nathan.

Like many of the other men, he wore a weapon at his waist and his hand rested at his hip, just above the butt of the pistol. A threat?

Nathan knew that trying to talk to the other man was liable to get him into trouble. Stillwell clearly didn't trust him, even after Ben's assurances to the committee.

Turning, Nathan stalked off, rounding the outer edge of the wagons. His mind spun as he hurried around the tightly circled camp. Around the campfires, there was chatter and noise, sounds of families together, pans rattling, singing, whistling, the bark of a dog.

But out here, there was only him. No noise, no laughter. No one but him.

The pride and hope he'd felt moments ago after Ben's actions had shriveled away. Though Emma and her brother and the Littletons had been kind to Nathan, how could he forget that most other folks in the caravan saw him the same way Stillwell did?

A criminal. A threat. Someone to be avoided or gotten rid of.

Most folks saw him for what he was.

Not Emma.

He should stay away from her. Surely after a couple of days apart, she'd forget him completely.

But he kind of liked the man he'd seen through her eyes. Someone who could have a second chance.

Maybe he didn't deserve a second chance, not after he'd failed Beth all those years ago.

But Emma said he could be forgiven. Her words had stuck with him all these days and *still* wouldn't leave him alone

He retrieved his satchel from the wagon, holding his breath in hopes that no one would notice him. Scamp did, the little mutt following as Nathan snuck away from the campsite toward the distant river.

He followed its edge far enough that he lost sight of the caravan, until he couldn't hear it anymore. The dog ranged in front of Nathan, following unseen trails left by some other animal, rustling in the rushes at the water's edge, then up into the brown grasses farther up the creek bed.

The water was beautiful and clear, spreading wide over its pebble-covered bottom. Fish darted in the water, and if he had a pole, he could have brought Emma something fresh for supper.

But that wasn't his purpose right at the moment. He needed washing up. Badly. The stench of sickness still clung to him. He didn't have a spare shirt, and so he took his off and scrubbed it as best he could, and laid it out over a boulder to dry in the sun.

Then he dunked himself, the icy water cool and refreshing. Scamp followed him into the water up to his chest, but refused to swim, even when Nathan beckoned him into the water.

All the while, his thoughts spun.

He knew the safer way would be to reject the tentative friendship Emma and Ben had extended to him.

But a part of him wanted to accept what they offered. Even though he *knew* they would eventually dismiss him. Everyone left him. He'd grown to expect it.

He still hadn't made up his mind what to do, but he used his straightedge to shave off the disreputable beard he'd grown over the past months. It hadn't mattered when he'd been content to stay on the fringes. Maybe he shouldn't have let it go until now.

Finally, he sat on the rocks, near his shirt for a long while, pondering. The sun beat down on his head and water trickled from his wet hair down his back. The dog lay out on his side on the riverbank, content to be warmed in the sun.

He knew what he wanted. He wanted the tentative friendships he'd formed. But he also knew that wanting was dangerous. A body didn't always get what they wanted, or sometimes it was taken from them, like Beth had been.

But was he going to let Stillwell's mistrust scare him off, when Emma and Ben had offered their friendship?

Finally, the sun began to wane in the sky. The dog roused, shaking out his fur and looking over his shoulder at Nathan as if to ask, *Shouldn't we be going back now?*

Nathan shook himself from his immobile state. He donned his shirt. It was mostly dry and smelled of the sun-drenched boulder. A major improvement.

How had Emma stood being cooped up in the wagon bed with him stinking like that?

He returned to the camp just as the shadows began to lengthen. Just behind the Hewitts' wagon, he hesitated, breath caught hard in his chest. Could he really do this?

Several female voices chattered. Every once in a while he picked up Emma's distinct, sweet tones.

And then a ruckus erupted. A chorus of high-pitched children's voices joined the women's.

He couldn't resist a peek around the wagon. A ragtag bunch of children crowded around the Emma, Rachel and Abby, taking over their entire campfire.

Emma looked up, her gaze landing right on him. Her blue eyes smiled even before her lips parted in a welcoming grin.

She waved him toward her, as if inviting him to join their group.

He rose on the balls of his feet, and the moment lengthened, laden with anticipation.

And he took a step forward.

Chapter Eight

Emma and Rachel had used the rare afternoon in camp to catch up on the chores that seemed to snowball as they traveled. All of the linens and their clothing had been washed down at the river.

They'd reorganized few crates that comprised the mobile pantry, such as it was. They would reach Fort Bridger in several days. Although they'd heard that the fort would overinflate prices for the goods the travelers would require, if they needed supplies then they must buy them.

She was mending a pair of Ben's trousers, with several more items of clothing in a basket at her feet. They'd noticed the tears and worn patches during the wash.

Smoke from the caravan's campfires filled the cooler evening air. Rachel and Abby chatted about the supper preparations, leaving Emma to her mending, when a horde of children descended on them.

She recognized most of them from helping their mothers treat them during the measles epidemic that had hit their caravan.

"Miss Emma!" Four-year-old Prudence ran up to her,

raising grubby hands as if she wanted to be lifted into Emma's lap.

With a laugh, Emma carefully poked her needle into the fabric and set aside the trousers to oblige the little girl.

As she straightened with Prudence on her lap, she became aware of a presence behind the family wagon. Nathan.

She could see his right shoulder and one boot, and when their gazes connected, she waved him forward. He belonged at the campsite with the group.

Something crossed his face, an expression she couldn't decipher, but he stepped toward her, first with one hesitant movement and then another.

When he crossed from outside the circle of wagons toward her, she got a good look at him and her mouth dried out.

"You shaved," she said. She'd meant the words to be quiet, but the children had gone silent, all of them staring at Nathan.

"Hmm," Rachel hummed at her elbow, but Emma scarcely heard her.

She couldn't tear her eyes away from the handsome angle of Nathan's jaw, the full lower lip that begged to be seen in a smile.

Color crept into his cheeks and it crossed her mind that she was staring, but she couldn't seem to tear her gaze away. He was completely changed by just a shave. His hair still hung long at his collar, but shone in the firelight as if freshly washed. The strong planes of his face had been hidden beneath the bushy, unkempt beard.

"That's the mean man," one of the children whispered, breaking through her focus, breaking her gaze.

She looked across the group of frozen faces, some

painted with uncertainty, some with fear written on the small expressions.

And a glance back at Nathan revealed him at a standstill just beside their wagon, an expression of helplessness on his face.

Emma didn't want him to rush away into the darkness.

"Did you know," Emma said conversationally, "that Mr. Nathan was sick with the measles, just like you, Prudence." Emma looked down on the little girl, who looked back up in avid interest.

Several of the children's faces turned toward Emma.

Rachel seemed to catch on and added, "Miss Emma nursed him just like she nursed you, Josh."

The boy in question, all of eight, wrinkled his nose in skepticism. "That true?"

Nathan nodded gravely. "Miss Emma is a good nurse."

She was surprised he'd entered into the conversation, when he'd been so taciturn on many occasions. Hope rose within her, filling her throat with emotion.

"Miss Emma gave me willow bark tea—"

"She made me take some awful medicine!" another little voice called out.

"She put a stinky poultice on my chest," a third put in.

While some of the children had been quick to converse, others watched warily.

Nathan nodded, his expression a little astonished as he attempted to follow the conversation. Was he surprised to find such easy acceptance among children?

Jeremiah, little Prudence's older brother, evidently became bored with the attempts to outdo each other because he came to stand at Emma's elbow. "We came to hear you read some more. We gotta find out what happens with the wicked stepmother."

Nathan raised one fine black brow.

"It was hard keeping the children confined to bed, so I made a habit of reading to them," she explained to him. "But I'm afraid I've got to finish mending these clothes," she told the children.

"And it's almost time to start supper preparations," Rachel added.

"Aww!" a chorus of disappointed voices rang out. She loved the noise. And she missed her little band of orphans from home. Missed them desperately.

Nathan caught her eye. Maybe she imagined the compassionate gleam in his dark eyes.

"But perhaps we could convince Mr. Nathan to continue our reading," Emma suggested.

Several cheers erupted as an expression of pure panic crossed his face, such that Emma couldn't contain a soft laugh.

She let Prudence slip out of her lap and stood. He had opened his mouth as if he would protest.

She took his elbow and turned him toward the wagon. The strength of his arm beneath her fingertips sent a thrill down her spine.

Around the side of the wagon it was quieter, the children's noise slightly muted, though she was aware of their presence.

"They'll be distraught if you refuse," she said. Somehow she knew that telling him the children would like him more if he read to them would not move him.

He looked down on her, his handsome face new with no beard to hide behind. His frown and drawn eyebrows expressed his consternation. "I should be taking care of the livestock or helping your brother."

"Ben checked on the oxen earlier. He told Abby he

would be by momentarily to take a walk. The chores are finished."

He looked as if he would protest again.

"There is no shame in using this time to rest. Ben told us you would drive the Binghams' wagon tomorrow. You should save your strength."

That statement did not ease him. His frown deepened.

"It would be a help to me if I could finish the mending," she said. Perhaps it wasn't kind of her to manipulate him into it, but understanding glinted in his eyes.

And then an amazing thing happened. His lips stretched into the tiniest of smiles.

Responding joy thrilled through her. She used the crate to see into the back of the wagon and reached for the book that she'd been reading to the children. It had been jammed into a cranny as she and Rachel had reorganized earlier, and she couldn't quite get it—

It came loose at all once, and she lost her balance, wobbling precariously.

Nathan steadied her with a warm hand at her waist. Her free hand came to rest naturally on his shoulder, slightly lower with the additional height the crate gave her.

He was so close that her skirts brushed against his trousers. That if she swayed forward slightly, they would be in an embrace.

"All right?" he asked in the silence, breaking the moment of connection.

She pushed the book into his hands, trembling slightly from the intensity of the previous moment.

But she smiled tremulously up at him just before they rejoined the others. "I'm glad you've decided to join us," she whispered.

* * *

By midmorning the next day, Nathan was having difficulty breathing.

Maybe more than that.

Each breath seared him like a hot knife.

Emma had warned him he might not be ready to drive the Binghams' oxen. She was probably right.

He took another breath that sawed through him. His legs felt like molasses as he trudged beside the oxen.

She was definitely right.

He suppressed the cough, not wanting to spook the animals and endanger the other wagons, knowing that if he started coughing, he likely wouldn't stop.

He couldn't afford another day riding in a wagon, couldn't afford to show weakness, not when Stillwell was still sniffing around, searching for any evidence that Nathan wasn't acting appropriately. Ernie Jones's accusation that Nathan was being lazy still rankled.

And there was a small part of him that desperately wanted to prove Emma wrong. She had seen him at his weakest. Watched him fight for his life.

Fought for him, in the form of cooling his fever, putting water to his lips...

He wanted her to see him strong.

But he didn't feel strong.

The breeze coming off the distant, craggy peaks was enough to relieve the worst of the heat spreading through his chest.

They'd only just gotten started and the day looked to be a long, difficult one.

His booted feet dragged through the long, moist grasses and a cough hovered just beneath his breastbone, waiting for him to take the next deep breath...

"Hello, Mr. Nathan!"

The high voice filled with childish delight startled him out of his concentration. Nathan began to cough.

The placid oxen didn't bolt, which was a pleasant surprise, but he'd been right about being unable to stop coughing once he'd started.

He staggered, still on his feet, but the oxen quickly outpaced him and wandered to the right as his cough racked his body.

"Gee!" The young voice gave the command to move forward and the oxen obliged at the same moment a slender arm snaked through the crook of his elbow, steadying him.

Emma, and her young blond friend, a boy named Georgie. She must be checking on him.

The small burst of pleasure was swallowed up by bitterness that she was seeing his weakness once again

He wanted to tell her he was fine, but he couldn't draw breath. Stars swam before his eyes as he hunched over, his body attempting to expel whatever liquid threatened his lungs.

And Emma's steady presence remained.

He finally straightened with a last shudder, his face hot from his body's efforts and not a little embarrassment.

He'd fallen several paces behind the oxen, but the eight-year-old boy had kept them in line. Nathan lengthened his strides to catch up to where he should have been, boots rustling in the tall grasses.

Would Emma point out his weakness, attempt to cajole him into getting back in the wagon? He couldn't bear it if she did.

But she stayed silent as he hurried back to the oxen.

"Didja see me helping with the oxen, Miss Emma?" the boy asked, his face bright and innocent.

Nathan had noticed the boy last night, reading by the fire. He'd remained at Emma's elbow throughout most of the evening and been one of the last to return to his family's wagon. The boy's reluctance to leave had been noticeable, but Nathan didn't know if it was the story that drew him, or Emma's attention.

Emma hadn't answered Georgie yet when another child, a little girl, scampered up, calling out, "Miss Emma!"

He reacted instinctively, moving away from Emma's hold and putting himself between the small girl and the oxen's dangerous hooves.

"Don't startle the oxen," he warned.

The child looked up at him with wide eyes and then her lower lip began to tremble.

Nathan glanced away, ostensibly to watch the oxen but not before he saw Emma's gentle hand come to rest on the girl's shoulder.

He hadn't meant to bark at the girl, but what if she'd run beneath the oxen's feet?

"Stay away from the oxen," he said gruffly, but what he really meant was *stay away from me*. Even as he should've been kind in the face of Emma's attempt to help him.

But Emma didn't seem to be bothered by the lack of a thank-you or his gruff manner. She only spoke softly to the girl about the dangers of being trampled.

The two females lagged behind slightly as Emma and the little girl made a game of looking for buffalo chips among the grass. Not far enough for Nathan's awareness of Emma to dissipate.

The boy remained in Nathan's periphery, casting curious glances in his direction, but Nathan returned his focus to suppressing the next cough that he felt building in his throat.

And then a group of five other children descended on them, siblings from their white-blond hair and the matching pattern of the three girls' dresses. They were stair steps, each several inches shorter than the other, close in age.

The girls flocked to Emma and her first little friend, while two boys of eleven or twelve approached Georgie. And they didn't look particularly friendly, as one of them shoved the smaller boy's shoulder.

Georgie didn't say anything, only kept walking, but color rose in his cheeks.

Nathan pretended not to notice. His job was driving the oxen. Nothing else.

But even as he kept his focus on the animals, he could hear one of the boys mutter, "What're you doing, *cousin?*"

They had the look of bullies, both of them larger than the younger boy, with a hard, angry light in their eyes.

He easily recognized it, as he'd lived with a bully for a pa his entire childhood.

He tensed, even as he told himself to ignore whatever altercation was coming.

"Nothing," Georgie mumbled. "Just walking. Always walking."

Nathan heard the slightly mocking tone in the boy's voice and no doubt his older cousins did, as well.

"With him?" the second cousin asked. "Ain't you heard he's a bad egg? Everybody's talking 'bout him 'n' how he's tricked the Hewitts 'n' Binghams into liking him."

The words eviscerated Nathan, but he kept his expression neutral and blank, staring at the wagon out in front of him, eyes focused over the lead oxen's ears.

"Miss Emma is smart," Georgie argued. "She ain't gonna get the wool pulled over her by some confidence man."

Nathan remembered telling her about thieving and poaching—and she still trusted him, or so she said.

"If she's so smart, why's she letting *you* hang around?"

The words were delivered with another shove, this one that sent the boy sprawling in the dust.

He jackknifed up spitting and red-faced, spoiling for a fight, but somehow Nathan had gotten between the bigger boys and Georgie. How had he come to walk away from the oxen?

"Leave off," he said, the words just popping out of his mouth.

What was happening to him? Somehow Emma and her ideals were spouting from his mouth.

Georgie pushed to his feet, slightly behind Nathan, and Nathan instinctively knew the boy was going to go after them and possibly get himself in a fight he couldn't win, not being smaller and against two boys. Nathan held out a hand to stop him.

But the two older boys were already running off, hooting and hollering.

Nathan looked down on Georgie, with his mussed hair, dirt-smudged face and tears standing in his eyes, and something pulsed painfully beneath his breastbone.

He reached out, not knowing if he meant to pat the boy's shoulder or what, but the boy shied away just as Emma overtook them, panting and with her skirts above her ankles as she ran.

"Georgie, what happened?"

"Nothin'." The boy shot an almost-belligerent look at

Nathan before stomping off to the giggles of the girls, who Nathan had to assume were also his cousins.

Nathan stared after his retreating back for a long moment before he returned to the oxen, thankful they hadn't wandered as he'd walked off for several tense moments.

He was unprepared for Emma to join him.

He'd thought she would stay with the children but when he looked back, they had all disappeared.

"It looked like Georgie was pushed. Did you see what happened?" she asked.

He should've known better than to think she would leave it be.

If she'd put up a fuss about him being mistreated, how much more would she fight for a child? Something settled in him with the knowledge that Emma could probably do much more for the kid than he ever could.

He shrugged.

She waited.

He expected she might walk off, but she just sighed softly and kept pace beside him. "It was good you stepped in."

He snorted. He couldn't help it. "Maybe. Or maybe they'll just pound him later since they lost their chance now."

Her brow wrinkled and his stomach curdled.

He didn't meant to be harsh, didn't mean to put that little wrinkle above her nose, but it was the reality the kid lived with, probably every day.

"Perhaps I should speak to Georgie's aunt and uncle," she said, voice soft and eyes far-off.

"He doesn't have parents?" He shook his head even as the unintended words slipped out. It wasn't his business.

But Emma's expression softened as she considered

him. "They are deceased. His aunt and uncle have charge of him."

"And five children of their own?"

"And five children of their own," she confirmed.

He swallowed back suspicions that Georgie was being bullied by his older cousins. It was likely that this wasn't the first time the two had ganged up on their younger cousin.

He had no right to get involved. Their words, aimed at both Nathan and Georgie, had held a note of authority. Likely they'd heard their parents speaking ill of Nathan. How could *he* help the boy?

And the glittering, angry gaze he'd received from the boy before Georgie had run off had told him plain enough that his help wasn't welcome.

"You're coddling Reed."

Emma's head came up at her brother's soft-spoken reprimand.

The caravan was preparing for the bugler to sound his call for moving out after the noon meal, most families packed and oxen hitched. They'd circled the wagons loosely on the flat, sandy banks of the river. Even now the gurgle and rush of its water lulled them in the bright noontime sunshine.

Nathan hadn't shown his face for the noon meal. There was a chance he was avoiding her.

Had she seemed like a busybody, worrying about Georgie?

When he hadn't appeared for lunch, Emma had prepared a plate for the missing man.

And now Ben had confronted her.

"I'm not coddling Nathan," she defended herself. As if

their prickly acquaintance would allow it. Nathan barely tolerated any of her friendly overtures.

Ben raised one expressive eyebrow.

"All right. Maybe I'm attempting to *take care of* Nathan, but it isn't as if he has anyone else."

"He isn't a stray puppy," Ben said.

She knew that. She was perfectly aware that Nathan was a man. A virile, rugged man.

Who was probably enough like her brothers that he wouldn't appreciate her concern or might even see it as interference.

And the concern in Ben's furrowed brows was unmistakable. The last thing she wanted was for Ben to forbid her from seeing Nathan. There was nothing inappropriate between them, only friendship. The barest of friendships.

And she knew, with a strange certainty deep inside, that Nathan needed a friend. Whether he admitted it or not.

"It's only a bit of lunch," she said, affecting a casual manner. "I'll come right back to the wagon after I deliver it."

Ben still didn't appear convinced.

"You can't expect him to keep his precarious health without sustenance," she pushed, hoping that Ben would feel some level of compassion for the other man.

Finally, Ben nodded, though his frown remained.

Emma bussed his cheek before scurrying off to the Binghams' wagon to look for Nathan.

She found him sleeping in the shade of the wagon, oblivious to the bustle of people around camp getting ready to pull out.

He'd curled on one side with one muscular arm pillowing his head, his back to the wagon's frame.

The position was telling about how guarded he was in general.

The little dog lay at his back, head raised and alert, as if he was guarding Nathan.

She stepped closer, hesitating, and found she could see the side of his face slack with exhaustion.

Her entire being softened toward him. How hard had he pushed himself, driving those oxen today?

No wonder he hadn't appeared for the noon meal, if he'd fallen to sleep.

He'd recovered from the measles, but his cough and weakness remained. But she could guess that he was as stubborn as her brothers and that if she suggested he rest in the wagon, he would refuse.

She would have to settle for feeding him.

"Nathan," she said softly. The bugler would call for pulling out at any moment.

She saw his small start, the exact moment he came to consciousness, though he didn't immediately move.

She took one step back, conscious that she had invaded his space.

He rolled over, one hand moving to rub down his face. The exhaustion she'd noticed as he slept remained and she bit her tongue to keep from asking after him.

"I brought you something to eat," she said instead.

He squinted up at her, as if he couldn't understand her motives. Or perhaps it was simply the sun at her back blinding him.

"You'll need to keep up your strength," she said, and thrust the plate at him.

The dog whined in welcome.

And Nathan smiled. A tired, half bit of a smile, but it was there.

Chapter Nine

Two days later, Emma counted Nathan as much improved. His cough had lessened, although it remained a concern. He'd become a fixture in their camp of the evenings, reading to the children at her urging, instead of remaining in the background.

The children continued to treat him with awe and some fear. She'd hoped that with time, both Nathan and the children would grow used to each other, but that hadn't transpired as of yet.

The land had changed yet again, this morning bringing them to a series of high, rocky bluffs that led the wagons in a snaking line along the banks of the river. The imposing cliffs, some hundreds of feet high, made her dizzy to look up their perpendicular edges to the cedars that looked so small at their tops.

It had rained much of the night, a soft, driving patter, and the ground remained wet. Emma's skirt quickly became sodden and heavy, chilling her.

And she wished to be home. Would she find a new home in the West, in the Oregon Territory? With Tristan McCullough?

Bright morning sunlight streamed over her head,

warming her and at least starting to dry her skirt as she trudged alongside Rachel, who had been quiet and pensive these past days.

The cliffs grew closer to the riverbed, and the wagon wheels began sinking into the soft, muddy bank. The men pushed the oxen harder, so they wouldn't become stuck.

And then there was a sound like a huge, rushing waterfall, only it wasn't water tumbling down the mountain, it was the bluff itself, a hundred yards in front of Emma.

She and Rachel watched in frozen horror as three wagons were swept away beneath the flood of earth and rocks, several more were knocked to the side, animals scrambled for purchase, and men and children ran for safety. Women screamed. Children cried.

It seemed like forever, though it must've only been moments.

And then Emma ran forward to the wagon, blessedly far enough that it was safe. Ben was safe, though the oxen shifted nervously in their traces.

"My bag," she said, to no one, as Rachel flew past her toward the wreckage.

Precious moments were lost as Emma rifled through the wagon, finally coming up with the satchel that held her medical supplies.

Where was Nathan? Her thoughts ran to the enigmatic man, but she was sure the Binghams' wagon had been behind the Hewitts'.

She didn't have time to dwell on her intense relief at that realization, not with fellow travelers hurt or worse…

As she neared the rockslide, she saw a small boy sitting alone, wailing, his forehead cut and bleeding.

Farther along, Ben and several other men dug with

shovels and pickaxes where the bonnet of a wagon could barely be seen above the mass of earth and rock.

Emma knelt next to the boy, attempting to calm his loud cries. Were his parents buried there?

She could overhear clearly, as Nathan rushed forward to join the men, a man she didn't recognize grunt, "We've got enough hands here."

She gasped as she took his meaning. The wagon was still buried, yet the man was turning away Nathan's help?

But Nathan didn't argue, just walked off in silence. She watched him pick his way over the edge of the rockslide, farther along the river's edge, farther away from the majority of their caravan, the wagons trapped back here.

Then a young woman rushed up toward Emma, sobbing, claiming the young boy. She was rumpled and dirty as if she'd been tumbled end over end by the rockslide, but she appeared whole.

And when Emma looked back up, Nathan was gone.

What had he thought? That just because Emma and her family had reluctantly accepted him at their campfire that he would be welcomed by other families?

Seething with anger at the rejection—at himself for the stinging feeling in his chest—Nathan stalked along the edge of the rockslide, picking his way carefully over the slippery rocks and moist earth.

Water rushed in the river just behind him, trickling in a musical way over rocks and the streambed. A shock of beauty against the horror of the moments before.

The truth was, he hadn't thought. Some long-buried part of himself had called for him to help, to rescue. To be a part of the community. Ha.

He'd long passed the bustle of the activity, where the

other travelers had worked like busy ants. Where he hadn't been welcome.

He didn't know what he was doing. Looking for someone isolated out here who might need help? Or licking his wounds?

The bright sunlight didn't illuminate anything out of place. No swath of fabric, no person driven this way by the rockslide.

Then he heard a small sound. A cry.

Was it a child? This far from the rest of the wagon train?

He spun in a slow circle, ears attuned to every small sound, listening for the cry to come again.

Crickets chirped. Far back at the caravan, voices called and a shovel struck rock. Wind rustled leaves in the nearby aspens.

And there. The weak cry came again.

He found it trapped beneath several rocks the size of bread loaves, weak and whining.

A wolf cub, with only its gray snout and one white paw visible beneath the rocks.

It was small, so young that its eyes were barely open. Not a newborn, but close. Had its den been dislodged in the rockslide?

He glanced around for its mother, just in case.

And saw instead, Georgie's towheaded form standing a piece off. Watching him.

"Whatchu got there, Mr. Nathan?"

Georgie's words were curious but wary. He had come to the campfire reading last night, but kept his distance from Nathan, though he hadn't been able to hide a bruise on his cheek. Courtesy of his cousins?

Now the boy scrambled closer before Nathan could

tell him to go away. He scampered so close that he stood next to Nathan in moments.

"A baby wolf," the boy breathed.

"Stay back," Nathan warned, but Georgie wasn't paying him any mind. He squatted over the injured animal, reaching out.

"Don't—" Nathan knew the danger an injured animal could pose and reached for the boy. Too late.

The pup licked Georgie's hand.

The boy inhaled hard. Then looked up at Nathan in a way that no one had since Beth, his eyes pleading.

"We gotta help him."

Nathan exhaled, the sound harsh in the stillness around them.

He couldn't let the boy get his hopes up.

"He's hurt pretty bad."

Nathan didn't have to dig the pup out to know the extent of his injuries. With such a small body, he must've been crushed beneath rocks larger than he was. Probably the kindest thing to do would be to put the animal out of its misery.

"He probably isn't gonna make it. Look how he's been crushed by the rocks."

Maybe Nathan should've softened the words—though he had no idea what to say or how—but the boy needed to know the truth.

"We can't just let him die, Mr. Nathan."

The undeserved trust the boy placed in Nathan made him hesitate, when he should've insisted they put the animal out of its misery.

"Please, we gotta help him."

Nathan knew the folks in the wagon train wouldn't welcome a wolf in their midst. He also knew the wolf wouldn't survive.

Looking down on the boy's earnest countenance, the expression trusting that Nathan would do the right thing, pleading...

Nathan couldn't forget that Georgie had no one except his bullying cousins and a possibly negligent aunt and uncle.

He didn't answer the boy but he did kneel and carefully begin drawing the rocks away from the wolf cub.

Emma was exhausted, drained from treating the injured.

After the disaster earlier, the wagon master had called a halt. Sam Weston had ridden out and determined that there were no other passable trails and this pass would have to be dug through.

They'd circled the wagons, even though it was early afternoon, as the men worked and women tended to those injured.

They'd lost two people who had been suffocated by the dirt and rocks before the others could dig them out. Emma hadn't known them, or their names, but she remained shaken and upset even as the camp settled.

The trail, the land had turned vicious. It seemed to wait, lulling its travelers into a sense of safety, but days like this made survival a question that thrummed through her deeply, wounding her spirit.

How could God allow this to happen? Tear apart two families by unexpected deaths, leave children without their parents...

There were no answers.

Only her anxieties, and the knowledge that months of travel remained, and ceaseless prayers.

A twinge of relief burst through her as she saw Nathan trudge into camp. He carried a small bundle in his large hands, and was that…? Georgie strode at his side, looking up at the man and speaking with animation.

Ben called out to Nathan as he passed the area where the men worked. Nathan nodded tightly, but kept moving toward Emma.

Rachel and Abby were deep in conversation and didn't notice as Emma went to meet the two males.

Nathan's expression was pinched, frowning, though he seemed to be listening to the boy at his side.

She met them behind the family wagon, where there was some semblance of privacy from prying eyes. Nathan's little dog appeared from under the conveyance, where he must've been resting, and stood at her side.

Nathan's expression softened to concern as she drew near.

"Are you all right?" he asked, voice low.

Georgie's head came up, those bright eyes assessing her. "You hurt, Miss Emma?"

Their concern brought hot tears to her eyes unbidden, and she shook her head and blinked them away.

"I'm fine." Physically, at least. Emotionally, she didn't know when she would feel settled again.

Above Georgie's head, she met Nathan's eye. His glance examined her more closely than she would've liked. He knew. Knew she was discomfited and upset.

But he didn't say anything about her fragile emotional state.

"Miss Emma, lookit. We found him buried under some rocks."

Georgie's subdued excitement had her sending a questioning glance at Nathan.

He opened his hands slightly toward her and she saw the small dog cupped in his palms.

At her side, Scamp growled. The little animal's pointed ear twitched.

No, not a dog.

"Is that a—"

"Wolf cub," Nathan said.

Worry spiraled through her. "The committee—"

Nathan cut her off with a sharp shake of his head.

"Georgie, I've got an old towel in my satchel, tucked in the box on the front of Binghams' wagon. Fetch it for me."

Nathan's comment was more of an order but Georgie ran off without argument.

"You can't have a wolf in camp," she rasped. The committee would never allow a wild animal among their group.

"I couldn't tell him no." Nathan seemed frustrated as the words flew out of his mouth.

He untucked the pup from where it was wrapped in the tail of his shirt. Scamp growled again until Nathan gave a command that had the grown dog hiding beneath the wagon again.

The wolf cub barely moved its head, panting, its chest heaving with each breath.

"It won't last the night," he said softly, looking to make sure Georgie wasn't returning. "It was crushed beneath large rocks—its insides must be crushed."

He shook his head, looking down on the animal.

"I should've put it down."

He sounded confounded, utterly confused as to why he hadn't.

And her heart turned over in her chest.

He'd spared the boy's feelings—must've spent time digging out the pup and bringing him here, all for Georgie.

"All I could think was getting him back here, but

it isn't going to change anything…" He looked so uncertain.

Ben shouted Nathan's surname and his head came up. "They want me to work."

His frown reminded her that another man from the wagon train had rejected his help earlier in the day.

Georgie rounded the wagon, waving a ratty piece of toweling.

And she found herself reaching for the injured pup even as her emotions expanded toward the man himself. "I'll take care of him until you're finished for the day."

Nathan returned to camp well after dark, trailing the other men. They'd dug through the worst of the rockslide, leaving enough room between the bluff and the river that their wagons should be able to pass in the morn.

He'd loitered at the river's edge after washing up, wasting as much time as he could.

He didn't know what he would face when he returned to camp. Would Emma have told others about the cub? Would he face more judgment from the caravan?

And that was if the pup lived.

The fires had burned down by the time Nathan slipped around the Hewitts' wagon into their campsite proper. Ben and Abby were nowhere to be seen and Rachel ducked into the family tent as he approached, looking as if she was bedding down for the night.

Emma and Georgie sat together near the dying fire, their heads bent over the tiny bundle of cloth between them, their profiles throwing long shadows that met at his feet.

Nathan hesitated, but he'd done this. He'd brought back the wolf pup, knowing it didn't have a chance, knowing the boy would face this sorrow. It was his responsibility—he wouldn't leave Emma to face it alone.

They must've heard the scrape of his boot against the ground because both looked over their shoulders at the same moment.

He nodded his hello, stepping closer.

In the light thrown by the fire, he saw Emma's face was wet with silver tears. Georgie's lower lip trembled.

Nathan crouched near them, between them but slightly behind. "Did it…"

Emma nodded quickly, reaching out and squeezing Georgie's shoulder. "We made him as comfortable as possible, kept him warm here by the fire."

Georgie scrubbed at his face with his palms. "Thanks for helping me rescue him, Mr. Nathan."

An unfamiliar hot knot rose in Nathan's throat. He should never have allowed the boy to bring the wolf pup back to camp.

"What should we do now?" Georgie asked.

"I'll take care of it." Nathan had just put down his shovel. He could easily pick it back up.

"You sure?"

Nathan's heart lurched at the boy's whispered words. He'd suspected the boy had a soft heart, a good heart, when he'd seen him being bullied before. The fact that he was owning up to the responsibility of taking care of the animal tightened something in Nathan's chest.

He cleared his throat. "I'm sure."

"I'll walk you back to your uncle's campsite," Emma offered to the boy.

They left Nathan with the bundle of deceased animal and cloth and Nathan scooped it up, grabbing the shovel he'd just tucked up against the wagon and walking out into the night.

The cub was tiny and it didn't take long to dig a hole large enough that scavengers would leave it alone.

Nathan filled in the hole and stood leaning on the shovel, staring up into the night sky for a long time.

When he returned to the caravan, he felt the need to wash up again and was thankful he'd left water in a bucket near the Binghams' wagon, where he'd roll out his bedroll.

He scrubbed his hands and forearms and then splashed his face before he realized he'd given the boy his only towel for the pup earlier. It was now buried with the animal.

He used the tail of his shirt to dry off, though it wasn't entirely clean.

"You all right?" Emma's voice came out of the darkness, startling him. He rose from his crouch, looking around.

The camp was still active, campfires burning and folks not abed yet even at the late hour. Likely folks were as unsettled as he was by everything that had transpired today. He and Emma weren't entirely alone, and it wasn't inappropriate. No one seemed to be paying them any mind.

"That was a kind thing you did for Georgie," she said, clinging to the wagon bonnet with one hand.

He couldn't make out her expression, nor the nuance of her emotion with only the light from the stars and a flickering fire too far away to be of any help.

He bared his teeth in a self-deprecating snarl. "Real kind to let the animal suffer."

And the boy. He had a feeling he'd done worse for the boy than if he'd insisted on putting the animal out of its misery in the first place. Why couldn't he choose correctly? He could skin a rabbit in minutes but his skills when dealing with people were as rusty as a knife left out in the elements.

"Don't be cruel," she said softly. "You told him the truth, that the animal wasn't likely to survive. You allowed him to say goodbye."

Her voice dimmed to huskiness with emotion and he knew she must be thinking of those who had passed when the rockslide had surprised everyone.

Something deep inside made him want to reach for her, comfort her, but he remained still, his arms hanging at his sides. He'd thought everything soft in him had died with Beth.

But after today, he didn't know what to think. What had possessed him to attempt kindness toward the boy?

He didn't know what to say to comfort her, didn't know what to do with the emotion rioting through him, he only knew that he didn't want a part in any of it.

Hadn't things been simpler when he'd been on his own, before he'd gotten caught up in Emma's desire for friendship? He wasn't any kind of friend, and didn't this prove it?

But she didn't seem angry at him.

She wiped her face with the back of her wrist and then *she* reached for *him*. Her small, cool hand closed around his palm, blistered as it was from working the shovel all day.

"Georgie knows about facing hard things. He's lost his parents already."

He could feel her trembling, with exhaustion or emotion, he didn't know.

But she wasn't done. "You did a kind thing," she said again.

He shook his head but she squeezed his hand and he

froze, everything inside him attuned to that one point of contact.

And then she turned and disappeared into the night.

He remained unsettled as he rolled out his bedroll and the mutt dog appeared, sniffing him over good before settling at his shoulder as the night cooled around them.

Nathan didn't know what to do about the boy, or about Emma. She deserved a far sight better than a friend like him, but she seemed to want his company.

And he was coming to crave hers.

Chapter Ten

Twelve days later, Nathan worked at unhitching the Binghams' oxen from their wagon.

They'd traveled nearly three hundred exhausting miles under the challenging wagon master. The country had become exceedingly mountainous. Tonight they were camped on the banks of the Bear River. Mountains rose on both sides of this valley, snowcapped peaks glinting gold in the last rays of sunlight, for as far as the eye could see. Quaking aspens grew at their base, in the far distance, and along the river, cedar and sour-berry bushes grew.

The basin valley would be good grazing for the oxen, Nathan was sure of it.

Nathan had exulted at being able to do his job again. Bingham would still pay him at the end of their journey. He'd grown hale again, his muscles remembering the strain of work, his cough finally subsiding.

He'd enjoyed the routine they'd fallen into, even though he constantly told himself it couldn't last. It had been two weeks of Emma's smiles. Two weeks of quiet breakfasts with her family, and boisterous evenings with the children who wandered into their camp and were never turned away.

The children's parents hadn't softened toward Nathan. Mostly, they watched him with wariness, if not outright suspicion. He left them alone and they rarely spoke to him.

Which suited him fine.

"Mister, can you fix this?"

Nathan startled at the childish voice, bumping the nearest oxen with his hip to entice it to move forward after he'd released its yoke.

Supporting the weight of the wagon tongue, Nathan looked down on the towheaded boy at his side. Georgie. The eight-year-old kid held a toy soldier up for Nathan's inspection, clearly unmindful of the danger he'd been in moments ago.

"Where'd you come from?" he gruffed.

Heart still pounding, he didn't wait for an answer, but rushed on, "Don't get close until I've got the rest of the oxen away, all right? It's dangerous."

Georgie's eyes widened. He looked up at Nathan.

Nathan was aware of the boy standing in his shadow as he turned out the other three oxen. If he had been underfoot, he could've been trampled.

Nathan didn't know whether to reprimand the boy again or if his previous warning had been enough. So he didn't say anything as he settled the tongue on the grass and made sure everything was ready for hitching up in the morning.

Scamp ran up, somehow knowing to stay away from the oxen, barking joyously at seeing Georgie. The boy laughed, dropping to the ground to allow the dog to put its paws on his shoulders and lick his face.

"Hi, Scamp!"

Finally, Nathan cleared his throat. "Let me see what you've got," Nathan said grudgingly.

Georgie stood, and the dog returned to having all four paws on the ground. He circled the boy, sniffing at his trousers as if trying to discover all the adventures he'd been on this day. Georgie handed Nathan the wooden soldier, only a few inches tall. Broken in half.

He had appeared every evening since Emma had cajoled Nathan into reading for the kids. After multiple nights of putting up with the kid, Nathan couldn't fathom why he sought out a grump like him instead of someone more personable, like Ben. It was clear Emma had a soft spot in her heart for the boy. For all of the children, in fact.

And Georgie seemed lonely, even with a family like he had. So Nathan didn't turn him away, even though he probably should.

When the weather in the evenings was clear, the children appeared. Somehow, she'd coaxed Nathan to read to them by candlelight before they had to return to their families and bed.

He'd read until he was hoarse, with her pressed to his side, holding a candle so he could see the pages.

He'd memorized the sweet smell of her hair, felt the nudge of her upper arm against his, relished her soft gasps as the story had surprised her, just like the children.

He was more aware of her than a simple friendship should allow, but he didn't know what to do about it.

"I'm sorry," Nathan told the boy now. "I don't think I can fix it." The break was clean, but he didn't have glue.

The boy shrugged and didn't attempt to take the trinket back. Nathan stuck it in his pocket, wondering if Emma would later have a solution to put it back together.

"Look what I found today."

The boy dug in his shirt pocket and produced a bit of a robin's blue eggshell that he cupped carefully in his grubby palm.

Nathan nodded, not sure how to react to such a find.

He wasn't sure how to relate to the boy at all, but that hadn't stopped Georgie from following him around.

Scamp sat at their feet, nose lifted as if he was listening to everything they said.

"I've got to tend to the wagon," Nathan said, but if he'd hoped the boy would understand the hint and leave him alone, he was disappointed.

"I'll watch."

The boy chattered on, something about his cousins and a rabbit, while Nathan examined a good-size crack in the front corner of the wagon box.

He'd heard it happen close to the time the wagon master had called a halt for the day. The rough terrain was hard on the wagons and it didn't help that Bingham had overfilled his.

He was good at tracking, setting traps, skinning animals. Not so good at woodworking, and the only tool he owned was his pocketknife. At least he could tell Ben about it.

"Miss Emma!" Georgie suddenly piped and Nathan's head came up.

She was there wearing a light blue dress, her hair windblown into little wisps around her face. And of course, her ever-present smile.

To his consternation, he couldn't help himself from smiling back, though his gut tightened. Was today the day she would realize the kind of man he was and walk away from their friendship?

Both boy and dog jumped and bounced around her in a circle until she laughed.

"I should've known I would find you with Mr. Nathan," she said to the boy, but her gaze quickly came back to him, radiating approval.

Uncomfortable under the undeserved emotion, Nathan rubbed one hand over the shadow of whiskers on his jaw. He'd attempted to shave daily, but there wasn't always time with the bustle of readying the wagons for the day's travels, especially not if the oxen had ranged afar as they grazed. Today he probably looked the disreputable pirate they'd been reading about in Emma's storybook.

"We're looking at the wagon," Georgie explained.

"Hmm…? Oh." She caught sight of the cracked wagon bed. "That can't be good. Can it be fixed?"

Nathan shrugged. "I'll have to get Ben and Mr. Bingham to look at it."

"Look what I found today!" Georgie lifted the piece of robin's egg in his grubby palm and Emma bent over the boy, her hands on her thighs.

"That's very lovely."

"It's the same color as your eyes!" The boy was so excited by the find he was fairly dancing in place. "Ain't it, Mr. Nathan?"

Emma's face turned up to him, her cheeks a lovely pink.

He swallowed hard. "An exact match."

The color in her face got even darker.

She stood to her full height. Looked at him, looked back at the boy. She seemed uncomfortable and the muscles in his shoulders tightened.

"Umm…"

"Miss Emma, we gonna read the end of our book

tonight?" Georgie interrupted before she could get out whatever it was she was going to say.

I can't be your friend anymore.

He'd cherished every night sitting around the fire with her family and the others. Mostly her. He'd started looking forward to it by the time he got out of the wagon for the day.

But no one could call him personable. He'd been waiting for this to happen, for her to say she'd had enough. To go back to being acquaintances.

"Well, Georgie, I don't know..."

"Aww. Why not?" The kid seemed genuinely disappointed.

No storybook tonight. The thought dropped like a ball of lead in his stomach.

She looked up at him again and there was something on her face, some emotion he didn't recognize.

His hands fisted at his sides of their own accord.

Her eyes flashed to the kid again. Whatever it was, she didn't want to say it in front of Georgie.

That was okay with Nathan. He didn't want to hear her tell him to leave her alone with an audience, either.

"Don't you have somewhere else to be?" Nathan asked. "Something to do?" Maybe the words weren't polite, but they the best he could do.

"I'm helping you," Georgie replied, as if the answer was obvious.

Emma's lips twitched as if she was fighting off a smile. But the seriousness behind her gaze remained.

She bent to the boy's level again. "The truth is, a group of adults are getting together for some music tonight, over near the Larsons' wagon. And I'd like to go."

Her blue eyes came to Nathan again, but he couldn't understand what she was trying to say. She wanted to go be with people her own age. She didn't want to do the reading.

Oxen lowed in the distance, the sound hanging in the awkward silence between the three.

"But will we read tomorrow? We're almost to the end," Georgie asked.

"Yes," Emma said with a laugh.

A little of the tension left Nathan's shoulders. They would read again tomorrow. She wasn't telling him to leave her alone. He wasn't sure why it even mattered so much to him, only that it did.

"Don't you think Mr. Nathan should go with me?" Emma asked Georgie.

And Nathan's tension ratcheted back up. "What?" he asked sharply.

Georgie looked between the two of them, lips pursed as if he was thinking hard.

"I don't think that's a good idea," Nathan said to Emma. He'd do anything to keep the travelers' dislike of him from rubbing off on Emma.

Georgie was still looking between them, and Nathan grew uncomfortable under the boy's scrutiny. Maybe this discomfort was what Emma had felt before she blurted out her invitation.

"Why not?" she asked. "It's just a group of friends getting together. With the music playing, you won't even have to talk to anyone."

A group that he wasn't a part of. He shook his head.

"You should go with Miss Emma," Georgie pronounced. He stepped closer to Nathan and cupped one of his hands in front of his mouth, as if he wanted to share a confidence.

Nathan stared at him.

With the other hand, the boy motioned Nathan closer.

Reluctantly, Nathan bent at the waist.

Georgie's breath was uncomfortably hot on his jaw as the boy whispered. "Miss Emma is right pretty. And you'd get to sit next to her."

His whisper had been loud enough that Nathan was sure Emma had heard it, but she maintained a straight face.

His face heated as he stood to his full height.

Georgie looked at him expectantly.

What he'd said was true. Emma was the most beautiful woman traveling with their caravan. A man would have to be an idiot not to see that.

But she wasn't for him.

"I don't—" He started to protest, but with both of them watching him so expectantly...he gave in. "Fine."

Emma's face lit with joy.

Georgie whooped.

He just wished he could believe it would all end happily.

Later that night, Emma nervously smoothed her skirt and tucked a fallen lock of hair back into its pins.

Where was Nathan?

He'd agreed—reluctantly—to accompany her to the informal musical gathering. Ben and Abby had already walked over, and she'd insisted Rachel go with them.

But Nathan hadn't shown up for supper, and now as the sun's last rays were slipping over the horizon, he still hadn't come for her. Had he changed his mind?

Her hands shook and she attempted to calm herself by gazing up at the star-filled twilight sky. The sun's last rays had disappeared behind the mountain range and left only a slight glow, highlighting its monstrous proportions.

She was glad of the event. She'd known the trip would be arduous, but after the difficulties of the measles outbreak and the rockslide that had taken two lives... It would be nice to sit and enjoy the music and take her mind off all the things that could go wrong out here.

Perhaps she'd crossed the line of ladylike behavior when she'd extended the invitation to Nathan earlier. Was that why he delayed?

Something about Nathan put her at ease. She'd told him about the orphans she had left behind and now missed terribly. About her mother, memories from before Mama had passed. With Nathan, she was more herself than with any other male, but asking the question had been difficult for her. It was akin to asking him to come courting.

Maybe her forwardness had put him off.

She paced around the side of the wagon. The Millers' fire several wagons over glowed in the near-darkness, but there was no sign of a tall, broad-shouldered figure striding toward her.

She would be too embarrassed to attend without Nathan at her side, especially since her siblings and Abby knew about the invitation. Maybe she should just go to bed...

No.

He'd said he would come, and one thing she was learning about Nathan was that he kept his word. And he never said no to her.

His cough had improved, though it still occasionally caught him unaware in a fit. Had he possibly fallen ill again?

She set out to find him. She checked the Binghams' wagon first, knowing he usually slept nearby. She called out softly, but only Scamp appeared with a small *woof* of welcome. No Nathan.

At the edge of their wagon, she peered out into the darkness beyond the circled caravan. She couldn't go traipsing out in the wilderness to find him, not alone.

Then she thought she heard a deep voice from out in the darkness.

"Nathan?" she called softly. If it wasn't Nathan, she didn't want to attract notice.

Something moved out in the shadows beyond the wagons. Grasses rustled.

And then a darker shadow separated from the night, moving closer to where she stood. She made out a head and shoulders and her stomach jumped once in fear. Was it…?

"Nathan?" she asked again.

"It's me," came his familiar voice. "I need help."

Her pulse quickened. Something *was* wrong. She took a step toward him, and her movement allowed firelight from the camp behind her to spill out into the darkness. He was carrying something.

Someone.

As he neared her, flickering light illuminated Clara's pale face as Nathan supported her in his arms.

"Clara!" Worry for her friend sent her rushing forward, and the name spilled from her lips without thinking. "I mean—Clarence," she amended as she drew near to Nathan.

"It's a little late for pretense," Nathan said. "I know about the ruse."

"Put me down," Clara murmured. Perhaps the demand would have been stronger if Clara had been able to do more than toss her head from side to side.

The fact that she was allowing Nathan to carry her must mean Emma's friend was ill indeed.

"What happened?" Emma asked.

"Help me get her to her campsite."

"I'm fine," Clara muttered. But her eyes remained closed.

Emma and Nathan shared a look over the other woman's head. She was obviously in no condition to walk.

Emma started to lead Nathan toward the opening between two wagons but froze when Clara cried out, "Not that way!"

Then she did start to struggle against Nathan's hold. He shifted her in his arms. Emma knew his burden couldn't be light, not with Clara being as far along as she was.

"She won't want to be seen like this," he muttered. "Been fighting me the whole way."

Ah. They were supposed to sneak Clara to her tent. Emma counted it a blessing that many of the people from the nearby wagons had gone to attend the music playing.

"I don't want to attract attention!" Clara's bellyaching had become louder now.

"Your loud complaints are sure to do so," Nathan retorted.

After looking around carefully, Emma changed course and made her way carefully around the outer ring of wagons, picking her way slowly through the grasses.

"I was washing up," Nathan said, his voice coming out of the darkness behind her. "For the…" He trailed off. The music. "And I was on my way back and found her down by the spring. Looked like she'd been pretty sick before I found her."

"Clara! Why didn't you come to me for help?" Emma

drew up near the Morrisons' wagon and peeked through the break in the wagons. There was no one around.

"I'll be fine in the morning," the prone woman said. "It's just the baby."

"You shouldn't be pushing yourself so hard," Emma returned. "The lack of proper nutrition out here isn't helping," she muttered beneath her breath.

Nathan came alongside her just in front of Clara's tent. His grim smile told her he must have heard her words. And was likely remembering her many complaints and fears about life on the trail.

Emma threw back the tent flap and Nathan knelt with some difficulty, laying Clara atop the bedroll inside.

"Go away!" Clara barked.

He was quick to back away, giving them a modicum of privacy as Emma helped loosen her friend's clothing.

Emma touched her wrist to Clara's forehead, but the other woman was cool to the touch. No fever. That was a blessing.

Clara turned her head sharply to the side, avoiding looking at Emma. "You, too. Go on, now."

"I'll fetch some water," Nathan said from behind Emma, outside the tent.

"I'll stay with you," Emma told Clara. "I'm concerned that you're still having morning sickness so late in the pregnancy." She was scared for her friend. What if Clara had contracted something else? Dysentery? Or cholera?

"Morning, noon and night sickness," the other woman said, voice raspy. "My mama said she was the same way. I'll be all right."

Emma pulled a blanket up over her friend. "Regardless, I'll stay."

"No," Clara said, a soft vehemence in the words. "Go

on to listen to the music, like you planned. I'll be fine. I just need some sleep, is all."

Worry for her friend had Emma taking a breath in preparation to argue, but a soft touch on her shoulder stopped her.

Nathan. He stood at her elbow with a tin cup in his large hand.

She took it with a grateful smile and put it on the ground inside the tent, next to Clara.

Her friend's eyes had already closed, but tears showed silver on her cheeks. Was she missing her husband? Afraid, out on the trail alone?

How could Emma go and have fun, knowing Clara was alone in her tent? She couldn't.

"Go," Clara whispered. "Please." But then she gripped Emma's wrist, hard. "Wait. Will he tell?"

Emma didn't follow the change in conversation immediately and had to run over Clara's words in her mind again before she understood. Her friend was asking if Nathan would reveal her deception.

"I don't think so," Emma whispered. "He's trustworthy."

"You've got to make him promise," Clara demanded, slightly stronger now, or maybe just her fear made her voice rise.

Emma didn't want her friend's upset making her discomfort worse. "Fine," she agreed.

It took a span of several minutes and an unkind word from Clara to get Emma to leave the tent. She and Nathan moved several paces away, but still within seeing distance of the tent. Emma stood with her hands on her hips.

"She's so stubborn," Emma grumbled under her breath.

Nathan's eyebrows went up and Emma wrinkled her nose at him.

"I'm only trying to help," she argued softly, though he hadn't said a word.

"Maybe she doesn't want help, not tonight." There was something dark in his eyes as he said the words.

She had to concede. He was right. She couldn't help her friend if Clara refused.

She lowered her shoulders, let her head fall. She rubbed her forehead, where tension seemed to gather.

"Do you still want to go to your music thing?" he asked, his voice low. "I'll walk you over."

She'd almost forgotten her impatience and anticipation from before. If she didn't show up, her siblings and Abby might ask questions. Questions that she didn't need, because she wouldn't lie to them.

"*We* should go."

He blew out an extended breath but didn't argue with her. Small blessings.

They picked their way carefully through the campsites now that it had gone dark. His hand steadied her beneath her elbow—his presence beside her was a comfort. What would have happened to Clara if he hadn't been there, hadn't discovered her? Would her friend have suffered alone in the darkness all night?

How long would it have been until someone realized she wasn't with the others in the morning? Emma was so grateful for Nathan that she squeezed his hand where it rested beneath her arm.

She knew the music could go on long into the night. It was a way for the travelers to express that they could get back to doing things they enjoyed, like socials and dances, once this ordeal was over. A way to relieve some of the drudgery of the constant walking and driving.

"I'm guessing your family doesn't know about...is it Clara?"

"It is. I suppose there wasn't time for formal introductions when you found her," Emma responded. "And no, I'm the only one who knows her true identity. And her condition."

The first trickle of music, a fiddle, reached their ears as they continued toward the sound. Clara's demand that Emma make Nathan promise to keep her secret bounced through her mind.

"I had my suspicions even before this," he admitted.

She'd worried that others would be able to see through the baggy clothes and the feminine motions that Clara hadn't been able to totally do away with. Clara had managed so far. And Nathan was more observant than others.

"Will you keep Clara's secret?"

He exhaled sharply, the sound almost a snort. "Who would I tell? Although if folks knew about it, they might help her."

Sudden apprehension went through her. "Or they might throw her out of the train. At least, that's what she has told me she fears."

He shook his head. "I can't see your brother letting that happen to a woman alone."

She stopped, surprising him, and he missed a step. She turned toward him, put her hand on his forearm. "Ben is just one of many. You know how some of the men can be swayed."

His jaw tightened and she had to wonder if he was thinking of the time he'd been judged by the committee.

"Please, Nathan." She hadn't meant for her voice to have such an edge of emotion, but it was there in the huskiness.

He nodded, and she knew she could trust his word.

Music and voices from behind her reminded her they weren't in a private place. If they wanted to avoid suspicion, they would do well to join the others.

He seemed to realize it, too, because he muttered, "Come on," and ushered her forward.

A crowd had gathered, listening to the fiddle, guitar and harmonica play in harmony.

She saw Ben, Abby and Rachel sitting on a spread blanket toward the front of the gathered crowd. The Littletons were nearby, the baby attempting to crawl out of Sally's lap. Grant and Amos Sinclair whooped and danced not far away, drawing attention to themselves.

Emma knew that Nathan wouldn't want folks to see them making their way up to join her siblings.

He already seemed uncomfortable, the tense set of his shoulders betraying the emotion.

"Let's stand back here," she said. "I can hear just fine."

He nodded, but his expression didn't lift.

The stars unfolded above them like a blanket of diamonds in the sky. The mountains rose on both sides of their camp, majestic even in the darkness, their darker, inky blackness obscuring the night sky to the heights.

She lost herself in the music for several moments, conscious of the man beside her, of the way her shoulder brushed his biceps. Then he took a half step away and she became distracted from her enjoyment of the music.

She considered their friendship settled, but why had he drawn away? Did he not want to be here? With her?

The thought made her stomach ache.

She was starting to feel more than friendship for Nathan. Watching his bumbling, gentle ways with the children, seeing how he'd helped Clara without judging her for her deception… She was starting to admire him.

His hand beneath her elbow distracted her from the music and a low voice—*not Nathan's*—broke her concentration entirely.

"What are you doing here, Reed?"

She recognized the voice as James Stillwell's, but couldn't see the man past Nathan's broad shoulders. He had surreptitiously shifted her behind him, out of the other man's line of sight, though several other folks could easily see her if they turned away from the music.

"I ain't looking for trouble," Nathan replied. His hand remained on her elbow, as if willing her to stay out of it.

Maybe that was a blessing because her mouth had gone as dry as the desert plains they'd traveled through weeks ago.

"Funny how it seems to follow you around." Stillwell's voice had risen and heads turned toward them.

Nathan shifted again, still blocking her from curious eyes.

Protecting her.

Part of her wanted, desperately, to step to the side and demand Stillwell treat Nathan with common decency.

But her legs were shaking with the thought of how many people would be watching her if she did. She could imagine their eyes boring into her.

And her tongue cleaved to the roof of her mouth.

Someone from the crowd muttered, but she couldn't see who.

"Why don't you just get along." Stillwell didn't speak overly loudly, but his voice carried enough menace that heads turned toward them. "No one wants you here."

I do. Emma wanted to shout the words, but she was frozen from head to toe.

How had this happened? She'd had the best intentions bringing Nathan for an evening to relax and enjoy the music.

"What's going on?" Ben's welcome voice joined the group.

Abby and Rachel crowded around and Nathan let go of her arm.

Cold rushed in where the warmth of his hand had been.

With her heart pounding in her ears, she had never been so glad to see her brother.

"What's going on?" Ben asked again, putting himself between Stillwell and Nathan.

"Just a little conversation, Hewitt."

Nathan turned halfway to her. Fear of being the center of attention still held her immobile, and the apology stuck in her throat. She'd wanted to stand up for him. Wanted it so badly. Tried to convey it in her gaze.

His eyes were unreadable, black in the semidarkness.

"Nathan," she started to whisper, but he was already gone, abandoning her to Ben's, Abby's and Rachel's company.

Rachel sidled up to her, and must've seen the upset in her expression.

"I was done listening, anyway." She pulled Emma away and through the darkness toward their wagon as Ben began to argue with Stillwell in low tones.

"What happened?" Rachel asked.

Emma had to swallow tears that blocked her throat before she could speak. "We were listening to the music and Mr. Stillwell started making trouble for Nathan."

Why had he done so? As far as she knew, Nathan hadn't done anything to the other man.

Rachel huffed. "Why would he do that?"

"I don't know. Nathan mentioned something before

about Stillwell holding a grudge... I should've defended him!" she burst out. "My voice caught in my throat, and there were people watching..."

Rachel put a hand to Emma's arm. "It's all right—"

But Emma wasn't to be appeased. "It's not all right. I'm Nathan's friend and I let my shyness get in the way of defending him."

Her steam expelled, there was only a strange emptiness left inside.

She felt more than friendship for Nathan. Her protectiveness proved it.

Rachel was silent at her side.

"I've let myself get too attached," Emma admitted to Rachel.

"That's not a bad thing," her sister said.

Except for the man her brothers thought she should marry.

"But what of Tristan?"

Rachel shrugged. "You've never even met the man."

"But Gray thinks—"

"Do you really want Grayson in charge of your courtships? We haven't seen him since he went West. He might think he knows what's best for you, but does he really?"

Emma shook her head; she just didn't know.

Rachel was the outspoken one. She could get away with not deferring to their older brothers. Emma had never made a practice of standing up for herself. What was she to do?

Her protectiveness for Nathan had surged so strongly— how had she come to care about him so much in such a short time?

Rachel squeezed her arm where they were linked together. "Don't be afraid to explore where things could go with your Nathan. Your friendship has grown. I've seen you stop worrying so much about every possible danger because you've been counting the minutes until you can see him again."

She'd noticed all of that? Had her sister noticed Emma's despair over the journey, as well? Her approval of Nathan warmed Emma, but she remained unsure of the right course of action. She'd believed being Nathan's friend had been a purpose, small though it was.

Would Nathan even want to be her friend anymore after she hadn't come to his defense?

Chapter Eleven

The morning after the fiasco with Stillwell, Nathan sat immobile in the early-morning stillness. Ben had woken him early for watch duty and that was fine with him. He'd been unable to sleep for most of the night.

Dawn hadn't broken yet, but fingers of fog stretched over the valley, obscuring where he knew the river to be. His nose and ears were cold, but he still didn't move.

The worst thing that could've happened last night had happened. Emma had almost been touched by her association with him.

He'd sensed her shrinking behind him once Stillwell had started spouting his vileness.

He hadn't blamed her for not wanting to be seen once heads had started turning, but it had still cut him deeply.

He'd wanted to protect her, but maybe he should've protected her better by refusing to accompany her. Why should she be tainted by a friendship with him?

Dawn's first rays began sliding over the horizon, lighting the landscape. The fog began to dissipate. Ben had assigned Nathan near the horses, grouped together for protection against predators.

And in the early light Nathan saw something that

didn't belong. At first he thought it was a dog, but the silver fur and long, pointed snout disabused that notion quickly.

A wolf. Sitting quietly among the horses.

And they tolerated him.

Was this the animal that had been serenading them all night? What did he want?

Years of being a trapper and experience in the wild gave him the knowledge that this wasn't hunting behavior. If the wolf was hunting, it would be slinking around the periphery of the horses, not sitting right in the middle, plain as day. The horses weren't reacting to the predator. Did they sense that it wasn't a danger to them?

Wolves, at least those that he'd come across before, usually hunted in packs. Why was this one alone? It didn't have any of the hallmarks of a rabid animal.

Did he not have a pack? Had he been abandoned or left of his own accord?

As if it sensed his perusal, the animal took a long slow look at Nathan.

His questions about the wolf swirled back around to Nathan himself.

He didn't belong here, either, in this wagon train. Last night's altercation proved it. In the beginning, he'd been looking for a way to earn the funds to get to Oregon, to find a fresh start that he desperately needed.

A way to leave his guilt over Beth and the past behind.

He had to remember why he was doing this. The money. If he forgot that, then the lack of trust, of community, could hurt.

If he didn't care about them, about being a part of their community, their rejection couldn't hurt him.

But that left Emma. Who both liked and trusted him. She believed they could have a friendship.

And maybe they could, if there were only the two of them in the world. He cared about her too much to let her be hurt by an association with him.

He was like this wolf. A loner.

Maybe it was meant to be that way.

His entire being quaked thinking of turning Emma away. She was the one good thing in his life. Seeing her and being in her presence were the best moments of his day.

He had to. If he didn't start distancing himself now, it would only be harder to bear when they arrived in Oregon and went their separate ways.

His mind was made up

"What is that?"

Emma's soft voice startled him out of his thoughts. She appeared out of the near-darkness, and her movements startled the wolf, as well. It disappeared through the horses. None of the animals even noticed.

"It was a wolf." Nathan stood, his muscles stiff from disuse.

Her presence raised the hair on his arms and sent prickles of awareness down his back, caused a roaring in his ears like rushing rapids. His chest cinched tight.

"Here," she said quietly. She extended him a mug with steam curling out of the top and he smelled the coffee hot in the cool morning air.

It wasn't fair for her to appear, looking like an apparition and bearing coffee.

He thought of refusing it, but couldn't quite make himself do it. He accepted it without a word.

"I wanted to apologize for…last night." Her words were spoken so softly they almost seemed to scatter on the light breeze.

He shrugged, not quite looking at her. "It wasn't your

fault." It was his, just like Stillwell said. He was a mag-
net for trouble, and he deserved whatever found him.
She didn't.

"Ben said we'll reach Fort Hall later today. Rachel and
I wanted to know if you would accompany us to the fort."

He heard the slight undertone of vulnerability in her
voice, even though he kept his eyes on the horses.

"No."

His forced the word out through his teeth with his entire core tight. There would be a lot of people in the fort,
not just from their caravan. Other caravans. People who
lived at the fort. Soldiers, who would likely look at him
the same suspicious way Stillwell did. The acquaintances
back at Fort Laramie who might've upheld his honor—
might've—were far behind. Emma would be better off
in her brother's company than his.

"But—"

"I said *no*," he barked. He pressed the coffee cup back
into her hands. He hadn't even taken a sip, but couldn't
stomach it now.

He threaded one hand into his hair as he turned his
back on her, but he sensed that she hadn't gone away.
What could he tell her that would show her that he wasn't
the heroic man she'd conjured up in her imagination? To
get her to stay away?

And then he knew.

He whirled, before he could lose his nerve. "I let down
the one person I should have protected," he said, making his voice as hard as he could. "My sister, Beth. She
died, and it was my fault."

He saw her face crumple in recognition and emotion.
But she stayed where she was.

He feared now that he had opened the door, she would

press him for information, details he couldn't bear to share.

"I as good as killed her, do you understand? That's why you should stay away from me."

She still wasn't leaving, so he marched off, the sight of the compassion filling her eyes and how pale her face had gone branding itself into his mind.

But it was for the best, wasn't it?

The afternoon waned as Nathan unloaded goods from the Morrisons' order from the low adobe building—Fort Hall—in the distance. The store had delivered the goods out to the Morrisons' wagon and he'd found Clara trying to unload. Not only should she not be lifting the fifty-pound bags of flour in her condition, but the store had sent a boy of twelve to drive the delivery cart out to the wagon. Which left Nathan to unload for her, since the boy was too small to do it.

Nathan had a bag of sugar—a treat that Clara must've saved for—over his shoulder when he caught sight of Emma's honey-colored hair several hundred feet away, moving toward the wagon train. She was walking with Rachel and they were flanked by two men in uniform.

He turned his back and hefted the goods into Clara's wagon, but as he returned to the delivery cart, couldn't help noticing how Emma's face was turned up at the soldier beside her. She said something to him and he smiled down on her.

And something ugly broke loose inside Nathan. Hot emotion poured through him.

He wanted to hit something, but made himself reach for a short, stodgy barrel marked…pickles?

He forced himself to keep his head down as he unloaded more items, leaving the heavy flour sack for last.

The delivery cart shifted as the horse hitched to it decided he'd had enough of standing still and moved.

The boy at the horse's head steadied it, but seemed to be distracted by a young lady several wagons over. Nathan kept working. The sooner he unloaded the last of Clara's goods, the sooner he could escape seeing Emma with the soldier.

Nathan didn't have any right to Emma. He wasn't her beau. He probably wasn't even her friend after how he'd treated her this morning. She could walk and talk with, and smile at any man she wanted.

And he needed to remember she had a man waiting on her in Oregon, the one her brothers were pushing her to marry.

But none of that stopped his stomach from rioting inside his midsection or his hot, sticky throat.

He couldn't be…he wasn't…jealous?

He didn't have any right to Emma, but it didn't stop him from wanting her.

And hadn't he told himself all along that wanting was dangerous?

Their voices grew louder as the small group neared. He worked at keeping his head down, at not being noticed, but of course it didn't work.

"Hello, Nathan."

He couldn't keep his head from tipping up at Emma's soft greeting, though heat speared through his cheeks and he wanted to disappear into the ground.

He nodded because he wasn't real sure he could force words through his suddenly dry lips.

"We've delivered ya. Guess we'd better head back," one of the soldiers said.

"Thank you for the escort," Rachel said.

She and Emma passed, stopping to talk to Clara,

though Nathan couldn't help noticing how Emma distanced herself from her friend. Probably fearful of giving something away.

He reached for the last parcel, the heavy flour sack, just as a high-pitched voice from his hip exclaimed, "Hi, Mr. Nathan!"

Everything seemed to happen at once.

Nathan glimpsed Georgie at his elbow. Scamp appeared from nowhere and barked in delirious happiness at seeing the boy.

The horse startled from the unexpected noise, rearing, which pushed the cart back.

Georgie was right in its path.

The teenaged delivery boy couldn't stop the horse.

Nathan let the flour fall back into the cart in time to bend and push Georgie out of the way of the cart's wheel, but his shoulder bore the brunt of the conveyance's weight.

He bit back a cry as he stumbled forward and went to his knees.

"Are you all right?"

"What happened?"

Emma and Rachel rushed in, Rachel kneeling to check on the boy sprawled out in the dirt.

Nathan saw the delivery boy had calmed the horse and the wagon was stationary, for now.

Emma reached out for him, but Nathan shied away from her touch, clamping his right hand over the injured left shoulder. He couldn't bear her kindness, not with the emotions boiling through him.

His joint hadn't come out of socket, but the pain radiating down his back meant there would likely be a nasty bruise forming.

"That was a close one, Mr. Nathan," Georgie said, still laid flat out in the dirt.

The boy had almost been hurt. If Nathan hadn't moved in time, the wagon wheel could have crushed a leg or if he'd fallen, crushed the boy himself.

The fear of what could have happened coiled inside him like a snake ready to strike—

And he did.

"I told you to stay out of my way," he snapped at Georgie.

The boy's face scrunched up as if he was getting ready to cry.

He brushed off Emma's quiet, "Nathan," and the hand she reached out toward him and whirled away, stalking off from the campsite, out into the wilderness, where he knew she wouldn't follow.

She was scared out here, after all.

And maybe now she was scared of him, too.

Emma waited near the Binghams' wagon all evening for Nathan to return. Huddled on the ground, leaning back against the wagon wheel, with Scamp snuggled into her side, keeping her company, she waited.

Long into the night. The moon had set hours ago, leaving only the blanket of the night sky filled with stars. Campfires had dimmed and voices slowly died out until only the noises of crickets chirping and the light breeze blowing surrounded her.

If she'd realized his temper—which she knew really hid his fear over what had almost happened to young Georgie—would have taken so long to cool off, she wouldn't have skipped her supper to wait here for him.

Or maybe she would've.

She cared about him.

And knowing what he'd been through with his sister, she could easily guess that he blamed himself for the almost accident.

And she wanted to give him comfort, even if he couldn't forgive her for her behavior when she'd let Stillwell say those awful things about him.

His refusal to accept her apology had hurt.

If she could ease Nathan's mind, just a small bit, she would be happy. Mostly.

But first he had to come back.

It was well after dark and she was starting to worry. Had it really taken him that long to calm down?

Had he abandoned the wagon train, had he been that upset by what had transpired?

Had something happened to him?

The more her worries swirled around her, the more she began to shake.

And then Scamp gave a soft whine and Nathan finally emerged from the darkness, the small amount of firelight from within the circled wagons illuminating his stony face as he approached.

She saw the moment he realized she was there, saw the surprise in his expression before his face shuttered.

She pushed Scamp off her lap and stood up, brushing loose grasses from her skirt before she could look at him.

"What are you doing out here?" he asked.

"Waiting for you."

"Why would you do such a fool thing?" he burst out. He spun away, one hand going up, his fingers spearing into his hair. Even in the dim starlight, she could see the play of muscles in his back beneath his shirt.

All right, so his temper was still simmering.

That was fine because she'd gotten a little riled herself, waiting up half the night for him.

She stomped around him because she didn't want him to hide from her. Until she could see right up into his face, his head backlit by the few remaining campfires that burned. She pointed her finger at him.

"What took you so long to come back?"

"Are you my keeper?" he asked with a sort of sneer.

"Maybe I should be," she fired back. "Maybe you need someone to watch over you."

"I don't need anyone," he gritted out.

And that just made her madder. She took a step forward, until they were almost face-to-face, and poked her finger into his massive chest. "Everyone needs someone to make sure they're all right. That's what I came here to do, to check up on you."

"I'm all right," he said with a stubborn lilt to his chin. "Now leave me alone."

The words cut straight to the quick, but she lifted her chin to keep him from knowing it. "Fine."

"Fine," he repeated.

She turned away, emotions rioting, worries unassuaged.

And then thought better of it.

She turned back to him, hiccuping a little sob. "No, it's not fine—"

And the raw emotion on his face, emotion he'd hidden until she'd turned away, drew her toward him. She couldn't *not* reach for him.

And he reached for her, too.

One of his arms came around her waist as both of hers went around his neck. She drew up on her tiptoes and he bent his head and captured her lips.

He kissed her with what she imagined was all his pent-up fury and hurt and hope—wild and passionate until she was dizzy and gasping.

His head came up, only enough that the starlight illuminated his dark, glittering eyes.

Her lips parted of their own accord and he groaned low in his chest, bending his head to kiss her again.

One of her hands went into the fine, soft hair at his nape and she felt a tremble go through him.

His right arm tightened at her waist and then he moved his left arm—

And gasped, breaking their kiss.

Nathan struggled to breathe through the blinding pain radiating through his shoulder.

And because he'd just been kissing Emma.

What had he done?

"What's the matter?" she whispered, panting.

"Shoulder," he bit out.

She didn't move from their embrace. She remained tucked against his chest, with his good arm around her waist. "How badly does it hurt?"

"Only when I move it," he answered hoarsely.

He should let her go.

He was going to let her go.

But his arm wouldn't loosen from around her.

If this was the only moment he had with her, like this, he wanted to make it last as long as possible.

"We shouldn't have done that—I shouldn't have done that," he whispered.

She remained silent, but didn't move away from him. His breath stirred the fine hairs at her temple.

"It wasn't right," he went on stubbornly, even as his arm remained tight around her. "You're supposed to marry what's-his-name in the Oregon Territory."

"I'm supposed to *meet* Tristan McCullough in the Oregon Territory," she corrected.

Tristan McCullough. He hated the name. Hated the man he'd never met in that moment.

Her breath was hot against his chest, through his shirt.

"We haven't exchanged any promises."

But that didn't mean someone like this McCullough wouldn't be infinitely better for her than Nathan was.

"I was jealous of the soldier—the kiss never should have happened."

But he still couldn't let her go.

"The soldier? Oh. They were just being kind and escorting us back."

No, they weren't. They'd found the prettiest girls in the party and walked with them.

"I know you were worried about Georgie," she whispered. "He's fine. He wasn't even shook-up."

A tremor passed through him at the remembrance of how close the boy had come to being crushed beneath the wagon wheel.

If he'd reacted a second later, the boy could've been injured or even died.

He couldn't risk being around Georgie. He'd already failed Beth.

He couldn't be responsible for failing a little boy, too.

Emma's arms tightened around his neck, and it was that moment of comfort that finally gave him the impetus to gently disengage their embrace.

"You should go back to your family's tent."

"And tomorrow?" she asked.

He spoke, the words the most difficult he'd ever said. "Tomorrow we pretend this never happened."

Chapter Twelve

Over the next eighteen days, the caravan traveled another two hundred miles, and things returned to a semblance of normal for Nathan.

Early on, he asked Ben for the first watch, which meant no more evenings reading by the campfire. When in camp on their rare rest days, he spent time helping Clara—much to the disguised woman's consternation.

And he barely saw Emma. When he did see her, she rarely spoke to him.

When she did, it was with a cool distance that hurt more than it should. He'd wanted to protect her from his reputation, but protecting her came with a price. He missed their friendly talks, missed hearing her tell about her day.

Part of him even missed the children.

The bruise on his back and shoulder had healed, first turning into an ugly purple-and-green mess, until it finally faded. But his growing feelings for Emma and for the children that gravitated toward her hadn't.

Maybe that's why he was here, in the early-morning stillness, carrying three wooden soldiers he'd carved.

Past the ring of wagons, a lone mountain rose out of

the plain, far distant. Several miles, at least. Between the mountain and their camp spread only flat ground, brown grasses and sage. All was quiet in the early-dawn sunlight.

Nathan's hands had been kept busy by the project when he'd sat alone in the shade of the Binghams' wagon at lunchtime, but not his mind.

He never should have kissed Emma. He couldn't get the memories of that night out of his head. Holding her. Tasting her.

Just the closeness he'd felt with her in his arms.

Something he didn't deserve. She was meant for the sheriff her brothers wanted her to marry. He'd heard the conversation between Ben and Rachel before he'd counted Emma as a friend, before his brush with the measles had brought him into their circle. The detail hadn't mattered to him back then.

But it mattered now.

He knew which wagon belonged to Georgie's family and crept toward it. The bugler had woken the camp minutes ago, but he might be able to sneak the gift into the boy's bedroll before anyone noticed him.

He saw Georgie's blond head on the edge of five other bedrolls, the farthest away from the family wagon. Nathan's heart lurched. The boy was an orphan—did his family keep him on the fringes, outside their existing family?

It wasn't fair. Georgie had a lot of love to give. He'd even attempted to befriend Nathan.

But then, life wasn't fair. Nathan knew it better than anyone, but he wished things could be different for Georgie.

He was suddenly fiercely glad that he'd carved the

soldiers for the boy. Maybe they would be the only thing that belonged to Georgie in his own right.

Nathan crept closer and deposited the three wooden men next to Georgie's hand atop the bedroll.

Before he could sneak away, Georgie twitched in his sleep and bumped the soldiers, rattling them together.

"Huh?" The boy's eyes popped open and he gave a sleepy yawn. "Mr. Nathan?"

Where another child might've been afraid at seeing Nathan's hulking form first thing upon waking up, Georgie simply looked confused.

Nathan looked over to where Georgie's cousins were stirring in their bedrolls, but none seemed upset that he'd appeared at their campsite at such an early hour. That might change if their ma saw him.

"What're you doing here?" The boy sat up, tousled hair catching the breeze and ruffling. His legs were still encased in the bedroll.

His hand knocked the soldiers again and he looked down. "What're these?"

Nathan finally found his tongue, rocking back on his heels. He cleared his throat. "I made 'em—carved 'em for you."

The boy's face lit. "Really?"

Nathan nodded. "I couldn't fix your other little soldier, but I thought you might like to have these. Sorta my way of saying…I'm sorry for shouting at you before."

Georgie looked down. "It's awright. I know I'm always getting in the way—at least that's what Uncle Ned says." Georgie idly ran one fingertip over the soldier nearest his knee.

Nathan's heart thrummed once, hard. The boy's uncle told him he was in the way, wasn't wanted?

Something unfamiliar and uncomfortable filled Na-

YOUR PARTICIPATION IS REQUESTED!

Dear Reader,

Since you are a lover of our books – we would like to get to know you!

Inside you will find a short Reader's Survey. Sharing your answers with us will help our editorial staff understand who you are and what activities you enjoy.

To thank you for your participation, we would like to send you 2 books and 2 gifts – **ABSOLUTELY FREE!**

Enjoy your gifts with our appreciation,

Pam Powers

SEE INSIDE FOR READER'S SURVEY

For Your Reading Pleasure...

FREE!

We'll send you 2 books and 2 gifts
ABSOLUTELY FREE
just for completing our Reader's Survey!

YOUR READER'S SURVEY
"THANK YOU" FREE GIFTS INCLUDE:
- ▶ **2 FREE books**
- ▶ **2 lovely surprise gifts**

PLEASE FILL IN THE CIRCLES COMPLETELY TO RESPOND

1) What type of fiction books do you enjoy reading? (Check all that apply)
- ○ Suspense/Thrillers ○ Action/Adventure ○ Modern-day Romances
- ○ Historical Romance ○ Humour ○ Paranormal Romance

2) What attracted you most to the last fiction book you purchased on impulse?
- ○ The Title   ○ The Cover   ○ The Author   ○ The Story

3) What is usually the greatest influencer when you <u>plan</u> to buy a book?
- ○ Advertising   ○ Referral   ○ Book Review

4) How often do you access the internet?
- ○ Daily ○ Weekly ○ Monthly ○ Rarely or never.

5) How many NEW paperback fiction novels have you purchased in the past 3 months?
- ○ 0 - 2   ○ 3 - 6   ○ 7 or more

YES! I have completed the Reader's Survey. Please send me the 2 FREE books and 2 FREE gifts (gifts are worth about $10) for which I qualify. I understand that I am under no obligation to purchase any books, as explained on the back of this card.

102/302 IDL GH6M

FIRST NAME	LAST NAME

ADDRESS

APT.#	CITY

STATE/PROV.	ZIP/POSTAL CODE

than's chest—something like camaraderie. He cleared his throat again.

"That wasn't why I shouted," he said gruffly. "I was afraid of you getting hurt. You're a…good kid." He hesitated over the words. He didn't know how to do this. But the memory of Georgie's downturned face made him keep going.

"I… If I would have been one second later, that cart could've crushed you. And it scared me. And that's why I shouted. But I shouldn't have lost my temper and I'm sorry."

The words expelled out of his mouth all in a rush.

Georgie looked up at him, hope and something else lit in his eyes and he smiled so beatifically that Nathan actually got a lump in his throat.

And then Georgie looked behind Nathan and raised his hand in a wild wave. "Miss Emma! Miss Emma!"

Nathan glanced over his shoulder to see Emma passing by, her skirt held slightly above the frost-wet grasses. She must've been returning from the small rivulet off the creek, adjacent to their campsite, having washed up.

She saw him. He saw the momentary hesitation that passed over her face and his gut twisted painfully.

"Look what Mr. Nathan made me!" Georgie called out.

And then she changed course and came toward them.

Emma knew she shouldn't join Nathan and Georgie. Over the past two and a half weeks, Nathan had kept his distance from her, taking his turn at the watch in the evenings instead of spending time with her and the children.

Once, she'd even seen him change direction and walk away when their paths would have intersected.

Obviously, she'd been too forward the night they had

kissed. He'd told her when he'd come out of the darkness that he hadn't wanted to see her. But her emotions had overtaken her and...

She'd thought his passionate kisses meant something, but maybe he'd only been expunging his emotion.

Because someone that cared about her enough to kiss her like *that* wouldn't have pushed her away, would he?

She couldn't help thinking that she'd done something wrong. Her naïveté and uncertainty about the opposite sex had rushed in the moment he'd spoken the words *tomorrow we pretend this never happened.*

She'd revealed her true feelings—that she felt more than friendship for him—and his immediate response was to push her away.

Obviously, she'd been the only one who felt as she did.

But she couldn't ignore Georgie's plea.

And some part of her sparked with curiosity. What had Nathan done for the boy?

She drew close and, to her surprise, Nathan didn't immediately get up and leave. She saw the shadows beneath his eyes and the shade of unshaven beard at his jaw, before she forced her eyes away. Who was taking care of Nathan now?

"What do we have here?" She knelt next to the man and boy.

"Mr. Nathan carved 'em for me."

Georgie deposited three wooden soldiers into her cupped palms and the proceeded to struggle free of his bedroll.

"Ain't they something?"

The craftsmanship was intricate. Obviously Nathan had spent hours on each one. To their tiny faces and shoes, they were carved in detail.

"They are wonderful," she said softly and the man at

her side inhaled slightly. "How did you learn to do such work? What tools do you use?"

"Pocketknife," responded his familiar voice.

She couldn't help the slight shiver that traveled through her as he spoke, but she didn't dare look up at him.

"I taught myself," he went on, voice low. "Lots of evenings alone during trapping season."

And now he spent his evenings alone here. He didn't have to. Emotion clogged her throat.

Georgie finished rolling up his bedroll and toted it toward his uncle's wagon.

Nathan stood, towering above her where she knelt, and she was afraid he would just stride off.

She stood, wobbling, and he placed a hand beneath her elbow, but quickly jerked back as if touching her burned him.

"It was kind of you to make these for Georgie."

He rubbed the back of his neck and shrugged. "I felt bad about yelling at him."

He looked off in the distance and squinted and she wondered if he was trying to figure out how to extricate himself from the situation.

But then he said, quietly, "I think Georgie's uncle might not be very kind to him."

She looked at the boy delivering his bedroll to his aunt, who looking down on him with a frown.

"What makes you say that?" she asked, just as softly as Nathan had spoken.

"Something he said. You told me he was an orphan. What if they're treating him like he doesn't really belong?"

Georgie started back toward them, his young face shining despite what Nathan had just told her.

She didn't think Nathan would say something without cause. He wasn't the kind of person to stick his nose in others' business. But…it also wasn't their place to interfere.

"Never mind," he muttered.

"Thanks for holding my soldiers!" Georgie bounced when she dropped the little men back into his hands. He hugged her around the waist and then hesitated next to Nathan, but then embraced the man.

And Nathan placed one hand gently on top of the boy's head. Only for a moment because Georgie was off and running, calling out to one of his cousins, leaving them behind.

And Nathan stood with an unreadable expression on his face. She would guess that he was almost…perplexed.

"That was kind of you," she said again.

He looked down on her, as though he'd almost forgotten she was standing next to him.

The vulnerable expression half-hidden deep in his eyes made her want to reach out to him. Her hand lifted at her side before his face shuttered and blanked of all emotion. Blocking her out.

Her stomach dipped as her hand fell back to her side.

She didn't understand him at all. But she wanted to.

He rubbed the back of his neck again. "I've got to go tend to the oxen."

"Nathan," she said, before he could escape.

He hesitated, but remained in profile to her, not looking at her.

"I—I've missed you."

His dark eyes flicked to her and then away, back at the ground. Maybe she shouldn't have said anything, but something inside responded to his vulnerability—unless she'd imagined it—and wouldn't let her stay silent.

"I know what happened—the kiss—"

His head came up and he glared at her and then glanced around, as if he was afraid someone would overhear her words.

"I know it changed things between us—" revealed her feelings, feelings he didn't return "—but I had hoped we could remain friends."

His forehead creased, his dark eyebrows lowering over stormy eyes.

Nathan had so much emotion bottled up inside. Why wouldn't he share some of it with her?

He shook his head slowly. "I can't be your friend, Emma."

And he turned and walked off. That was all.

No chance for her to argue or make her case. No sign of the vulnerability that had lit his face when he'd spoken of Georgie.

She saw just his back, as he walked away.

Blinded by tears, she began picking her way through the camp to their wagon. She must pull herself together before she returned to Rachel, or her sister would know something was wrong. Rachel had already been asking why Nathan avoided their camp, and Emma hadn't had a satisfactory answer to give her.

But if Rachel saw Emma in tears…she would discover how very much Emma felt for Nathan.

And Emma would have to reveal that Nathan felt nothing for her.

Chapter Thirteen

One week later, Nathan was at Clara's campsite, wrestling the Morrisons' ornery ox into the traces. He'd already hitched the Binghams' oxen and knew the bugler was going to call for pulling out anytime now. They were a day out from Fort Bois, roughly two-thirds of the way to their destination.

But he wasn't in a rush to get back to the Binghams' wagon, near as it was to the Hewitts' wagon. Helping Clara with her chores kept him away from Emma and the *wants* that plagued him.

Emma.

He'd seen hurt fill her face when he'd told her they couldn't be friends. The memory chilled him still, chipped at the ice around his heart. Being around her was too difficult. It made him feel things he shouldn't. Their kiss was evidence of that.

He had a sordid past. She was on her way to her future.

Georgie had been coming around more since Nathan had given him the wooden soldiers. Once he'd appeared with a red mark in the shape of a man's palm on his jaw. Nathan had asked about it, but Georgie had made excuses.

But Nathan remembered making his own excuses for his father. What should he do about the boy? He didn't know.

The only thing he knew to do was to help Clara, even though there was no friendship between them. She didn't want his help. And told him so repeatedly.

But she needed it, and so he gave it, like now when the Morrisons' oxen needed to be hitched up.

He was intensely aware of Emma trailing Clara back from her morning ablutions. He smelled her sweet scent on the breeze when she passed within a few feet of him.

"Morning," she murmured.

His face went hot and he was glad for the gray morning light since he no longer had his beard to hide a flushed face. He nodded his response.

Behind the wagon, he heard Emma and Clara arguing in low, tense voices. Something about Clara and an injury that had her bleeding…

Until he took their meaning and blocked out the rest of their words. Emma must be worried about her friend and the baby. She'd already been concerned when he'd found Clara sick and immobile all those weeks ago.

But it sounded as if Clara didn't want the extra attention or Emma's meddling.

Finally, Emma brushed by him and walked away, avoiding his gaze.

A hot flush of shame rushed up through his chest and neck, blinding him momentarily so that he almost pinched his fingers in the yoke.

He nearly stumbled over Clara when he turned around. He rubbed the constant ache at the back of his neck, hoping she didn't think he'd been eavesdropping on her.

"You need anything else?"

"No," she said shortly. "And don't come back tomorrow morning."

He ignored her rebuff and was about to step away when she said, "Did something happen between you and Emma?"

The heat returned to his face and he slapped one hand against his thigh in agitation. "What do you mean?"

"You two have been dancing around each other ever since the night you found me sick." They were the most words she'd ever spoken to him. Usually she avoided him in stony silence. And it was the one thing he most didn't want to talk about.

"It's nothing about you," he muttered, eyes on the ground. Why would he admit the kiss to her? She didn't even like him. They weren't friends.

"Your cheeks aren't red for nothing," she said.

His face flamed even hotter.

He gritted his teeth. He wouldn't lie to her. But he didn't have to admit to anything, either.

He didn't know what business it was of hers, but her next words flabbergasted him completely. "If you intend on courting her, you should speak to her brother."

"I don't intend anything of the sort." Saying the words twisted a knot in his gut. Courting Emma had never even crossed his mind. Well, maybe in his wildest imaginings.

She had *Tristan McCullough* waiting on her.

"Why not?"

Clara's frank question made his mouth drop open.

She laughed, a short, sharp sound. "You're a hard worker, Nathan Reed. A woman could do a lot worse in a husband."

The sharp pang of *want* cut like a hot knife through his belly, but he shook his head. Blundered, stumbled over his words.

And finally left, without a real answer for her. The momentary wild surge of hope that swirled through him at her words faded into emptiness. Emma was not for him.

His feet carried him toward the Hewitts' and Binghams' camp.

He was surprised to see a tall stranger standing near Ben, whose serious expression made Nathan want to detour to Hewitt's side and find out what was going on.

He made himself walk to the Binghams' wagon, though he loitered at the tailgate, pretending not to listen to Hewitt's conversation while he did just that.

Emma knelt nearby, loading several utensils into a large cast-iron skillet. Her movements were quick and the utensils clanked loudly against the skillet—she was working faster than just the threat of the bugle signaling them to move out.

"We need help," the stranger was saying. "We heard you had a nurse in your wagon."

A nurse? Was he talking about Emma?

Ben's jaw locked and Nathan felt a frisson of worry. What was going on?

"My sister has no formal training—"

"Word back at the fort is she nursed a bunch of kids with measles. I rode all night to catch up to your caravan. Please, my son is bad off—"

"She did nurse a bunch of kids, but—"

Emma stood to her full height, and both men stopped conversing to look at her. "I'll go," she said firmly.

"No," Nathan murmured.

She didn't act as if she'd heard him or even knew

he was standing there. Her attention remained on her brother and the stranger.

"Emma, you can't go away from the caravan alone," Ben said. He was a whole lot more patient than Nathan would've been if she was his sister.

The bugler blew a warning call. It was almost time to pull out.

But Nathan couldn't force his feet to move from the spot he occupied. He had to know what would happen.

"I promise, I'll bring her back once she doctors my son."

No! Nathan's internal shout rang through him like a musket shot. Ben couldn't let Emma ride off with this stranger. What they were talking about would put her a day or two behind the wagon train—and besides all that, what if something happened to her?

"Ben, if I can help this boy, I must go."

Drat the stranger for playing on Emma's sensitive heart. She would never hesitate to help a child.

And somehow Nathan found his feet moving toward the tableau in front of him. "You can't go," he told Emma, even though it wasn't his business and he'd fully intended to stay out of it.

Emma flicked a glance at him, but acted as if he hadn't spoken at all.

But Ben also looked up at Nathan, a realization coming to his expression.

Nathan took another step nearer, his heart thundering in his ears and his pulse racing. "Emma. It's too dangerous."

Now she did turn toward him, but her face remained curiously blank of emotion.

"Perhaps if you were my friend, your advice would

be appreciated. But since that is not the case, I'll thank you to keep your opinions to yourself."

He felt as if she'd punched him in the gut.

She turned her face away and maybe his expression had betrayed him.

But Ben was speaking to the stranger in low tones and then turned to the both of them.

"Reed, Emma, c'mere."

The siblings moved halfway behind the wagon, Nathan trailing behind.

"There's not a lot of time to decide," Ben said. "Emma, are you sure you want to leave the caravan?"

No!

But Nathan didn't get a chance to say anything as Emma nodded. There was the tiniest bit of fear beneath the stubborn tilt of her chin and he knew she must be thinking of all the dangers out there.

Why would she want to risk everything and leave the relative safety of their wagon just to tend to a kid?

"Fine. Reed, I'll find someone to drive the Binghams' oxen today. You can ride a horse, right?"

Stunned, Nathan nodded. Where was Hewitt going with this?

"I can't leave the wagon train. The committee is counting on me. But you could take her, Nathan."

Ben would trust him to look after his sister?

But Nathan didn't trust himself. What if he let something happen to her? Failed her?

"I can't—" Nathan started, but the bugle sounded again. It was time to pull out.

"There's no time for discussion. Either you take her or she'll go on her own."

Emma nodded, her chin set, arms crossed over her middle.

And Nathan suspected she would. She was a caring, giving person. And if a little one needed her, she would go.

He couldn't do it. He couldn't be responsible for her.

But he couldn't let her go on her own, either.

Emotions warred inside him but he found himself nodding reluctantly.

"Give me a few minutes. I'll round you up a horse."

Ben disappeared.

Emma stood on the crate and rustled around in the wagon, pulling things into a small satchel.

Was he the only one who didn't think this was a good idea?

"Emma, I don't think we should go."

"Quit worrying," Emma said, her attention still inside the wagon.

But he couldn't. His mind ran in circles, thinking of ways she could be hurt or even killed.

He met Ben just outside the circle of wagons as the man led a sorrel horse.

"I don't like this," Nathan said. Maybe the man could talk some sense into his sister.

"She's got a compassionate heart."

She was also afraid of so many things out in the wild, though her brother didn't know the depths of those fears.

"She'll go without one of us."

He was right. If Ben couldn't accompany her, then Nathan had no choice but to go.

How would he manage to keep his heart from wanting Emma when they were alone together?

Emma joined Nathan where he'd already mounted up on a large red horse.

He didn't smile at her. The tense set of his jaw betrayed what he wouldn't say.

Nerves fluttered in her belly. She'd been prepared to leave the caravan on her own—with only minor misgivings—but felt much safer in Nathan's company. No, it was nerves at being near the man that had her trembling.

He grasped her wrist and she stepped on his boot in the stirrup. He boosted her into the saddle behind him and kicked the horse into a walk before she'd even really got her arms around him.

They followed Mr. Harrison, their new acquaintance, through the predawn light. The man put his horse at a gallop and they followed, over the meandering hills they'd traversed yesterday. The mountain range to the southwest was familiar, as they'd traveled in its shadow most of yesterday afternoon.

Their caravan had crossed Snake River yesterday and she found the crossing slightly more harrowing on horseback, without the wagon to protect her from getting wet.

She clutched Nathan's waist a bit tighter until they'd crossed to the opposite side.

She knew he worried something would happen; his tense posture betrayed what he wouldn't say.

But he was intelligent and a good tracker. She trusted him to deliver her safely back to her brother, after she'd helped Mr. Harrison's little boy.

She didn't understand why he'd pushed her away, not really. He had helped Clara for weeks even though she refused it—although her refusals had become somewhat halfhearted of late.

She'd witnessed his patience with Georgie as the boy followed Nathan around whenever they were in camp.

She'd begun unobtrusively watching the boy's interactions with his family and feared Nathan might be right in his concerns. Georgie's cousins often left him out of their games, and his aunt and uncle didn't seem to have an inclination to draw him into the family events.

She thought perhaps Nathan cared about the boy because he'd experienced difficult times and neglect as a child. He had a softer heart than he let on.

He didn't want to be her friend. But he didn't want to let her go out of the caravan alone.

He was a mystery to her.

But one thing was true—her feelings for him, friendship and admiration, hadn't faded with the distance he'd instituted between them.

Hours later, a plume of dust appeared in the distance. The other wagon train was smaller, with fewer wagons than their caravan possessed. The young wagon master welcomed them into the train with a nod, but Emma felt his hard eyes following their progress as Harrison led them to a wagon midway back in the caravan.

A teenaged boy drove the wagon, his face pale and upset. He brightened the smallest amount when he caught sight of his father, but his expression quickly settled into drawn lines again.

With Harrison's help, the young man guided the wagon out of the snaking caravan line and to a stop.

Nathan pulled up several paces out from the wagon, where they weren't in danger of being trampled. He swung one leg over the saddle and slid down to the ground, then reached up for Emma.

She went into his arms easily, his hands spanned her waist as he set her gently on the ground. He looked down on her with stormy eyes. The moment stretched, awkward and uncertain between them until he let her go.

He glanced at the caravan, or maybe the Harrison family, uneasily, reaching one hand behind his neck to rub there.

"What am I supposed to do?" he asked, voice low.

She reached up for her satchel, tied behind the saddle. "Make friends?" she suggested with a smile over her shoulder.

She hadn't meant the words to sound flippant, but his face darkened like a thunderhead.

Harrison was talking to someone in the wagon as she approached, with Nathan a few steps behind.

And then a very pregnant woman lumbered out of the back of the wagon.

"This is my wife, Sarah."

She was followed out of the wagon by three, no—four children, near-identical with only a few inches between each, except for a gap between the youngest two.

Nathan made some sort of sound behind her as introductions were made. She half turned and extended her hand to him. He took a small step closer to her but stood out of reach. The same way he'd avoided her touch since they'd kissed. As if he thought if he got too close she would grab him and do it again.

"A friend, Mr. Nathan Reed."

The children all chimed a greeting and his brow creased, but he only gave a silent nod.

"Samuel is in the wagon," Sarah said.

"You'll have to examine him as we go," Harrison said. "It's too dangerous to separate from the caravan."

Nathan nodded agreement and Emma moved toward the wagon.

"Can I ride with you?" The boy who looked to be about five had gravitated toward Nathan, who shot Emma a sullen glare.

She hid a grin, shrugging at him.

"You'll have to walk like the rest of us," Sarah said to the little boy.

"Aww…"

"Perhaps later?" Emma offered.

"Whoohoo!" the boy crowed.

The relief that had taken over Nathan's expression disappeared, and he sent her a cross look, to which she laughed.

She felt sure his eyes bored a hole into her back as she made her way to the wagon. It felt good to tease him again.

But she wasn't laughing when she climbed into the wagon and saw three-year-old Samuel lying prone in a nest of blankets.

His eyes were wide and fearful when he saw her instead of his mother.

"Hello, Samuel. I'm Miss Emma," she said in a soft voice she hoped was comforting. "I'm here to help you."

From the front of the wagon, the teenaged boy leaned in to peek inside the bonnet.

"That's Chris," the pale boy whispered. "My brother."

The wagon pitched as Chris called the oxen to move, then rolled into the jostling motion Emma had grown so weary of as she'd cared for Nathan. Sarah's head appeared in the opening behind the wagon. She must be walking very close, to talk to Emma.

She settled as best she could against one wall of the wagon and reached for the blanket that covered the boy's legs.

"May I see what's wrong with your leg?"

Samuel winced as she drew back the worn quilt. Someone had bandaged his leg, but the cloth was dirty and bloodstained in spots. She bit back a wince at the sight and smell of infected flesh.

"I'm going to take this off…"

The boy cried out a little as she unwrapped the too-tight dressing.

She stopped what she was doing, hating the small cry that he had given.

Perhaps if she distracted him, it would help. "How did this happen?"

"Chris—"

She didn't know if he was calling for help or if his older brother had been involved, but when she glanced out the front of the wagon, she saw the young man jerk as if he'd been struck.

Sarah peered in the back of the wagon "It was an accident. Chris was skinning a rabbit and the knife got away from him. He didn't mean to catch Sam with the blade."

Emma had peeled back the bandage as best she could until finally she ripped it free of the wound. The boy cried out again, his head twisted on the pillow.

"I'm sorry, Sam," she said, brushing her hand over his forehead. He felt feverish and her worry escalated.

Her attempt at comfort didn't help, as he continued to whimper.

A glance out the rear of the wagon revealed they had rejoined the long caravan line, crawling along. Nathan walked next to his horse, his attention diverted by two of the children who walked next to his horse and appeared to be chattering at him.

He must have sensed her perusal because he looked up and his dark eyes met her gaze. His gaze turned questioning and she shook her head slightly. Harrison had been right. Sam was bad off.

He nodded grimly, acknowledging her. He glanced around, still reading the lay of the land, maybe even the people closest to them.

His protectiveness meant something her. Wasn't it a sign that he cared for her?

Was she the only one who couldn't forget about their kiss? She couldn't forget how safe she'd felt in Nathan's arms. How cherished.

She had shared secrets with Nathan that not even her family knew about.

But if he was too closed off to admit there was something between them...

Those thoughts were for another time. Samuel needed her attention now.

The children wouldn't leave Nathan alone. Emma had disappeared into the wagon and except for the occasional glimpse of her fair hair, he was out of communication with her.

They traveled through a fertile bottom land, good for grazing. He'd already seen it, walked it yesterday as their company traversed this path. Which meant his thoughts were free to go right back to Emma.

He hadn't been able to relax with her riding behind him, her arms clasping his waist. Part of him had wanted to apologize for his cruel words from before, *I can't be your friend*, but he knew that would just raise more questions, questions he didn't have good answers for. He only wanted to protect her.

His mind ran in circles, except the kids distracted him. Maybe they were a blessing in disguise.

Before he'd isolated himself, he'd grown accustomed to the kids around Emma's campfire. They treated him with the same watchfulness, wariness even, that their parents did.

These kids were different.

They cavorted around his horse until he was afraid

they'd either fall beneath it or start climbing the animal's legs.

They talked. They wouldn't stop talking.

He couldn't remember their names, not with the brief introductions and how much alike they looked. He called them by what he guessed their ages were. Five was a little boy, Seven and Eight girls with long, honey-colored pigtails down their backs. Similar enough to Emma's hair color that he swallowed hard.

They wouldn't stop talking. Asking him *what the horse's name was*—he had no idea—and *where was he from* and *did he want to know they were from Chicago?* until he'd lost the conversational thread completely.

And they didn't seem to notice. They just kept talking, looking up at him with wide, curious, open gazes as they walked.

Couldn't they tell he was…him? Rough, uncouth, unused to human company. Grumpy.

Maybe it was because no one had told them to avoid him or that he was a suspicious character. In their innocence, they believed he was a friend.

And he found he sort of…liked it.

Probably they wouldn't have had the same reaction to him if they'd meet him weeks ago, before he'd shaved off his beard and begun taking better care with his appearance.

Or had his entire attitude changed, as well? Did they find him more approachable, more gentle?

If they did, he knew whose doing it was. Not his. It was all Emma. Being around her made him want to be…more.

Made him want more.

Dangerous.

Even now, when he knew there was no hope for a relationship between them.

The fertile bottom quickly changed to sandy riverbank and the line of wagons slowed. They'd chosen a different crossing for Snake River than the Hewitts' caravan had used yesterday. Maybe their guide knew of a shortcut.

He'd thought the river slightly swollen this morning when they'd crossed on horseback. Maybe there had been rains in the night, upriver.

Now the wagons needed to stop to ford, when he'd pushed the Binghams' oxen across nearly dry banks.

Emma leaned out the back flap and he made his way toward the slow-moving wagon.

"I need time—and some boiling water—to wash out the wound. Harrison was right about it being infected and I'm afraid if we wait too long, Sam's blood could become poisoned." She spoke in a low voice, probably to keep the boy and his worried mother from overhearing.

Any delay was unwelcome, in his book.

The sun neared its zenith.

"Surely the wagon master will call for a stop after the crossing," he said.

She watched him with her hooded eyes, as if taking his measure. "Will you help me with Sam? I'm afraid his mama won't have the strength to hold him down if my actions bring him pain." The fact that she had hesitated before asking him burned a hole in his gut.

Her face remained creased in concern, as if she was afraid of asking him. When he would give her anything, if he could.

"Yes."

Relief crossed her expression and an answering emotion, something strong and whole, expanded in his mid-section.

"When we stop, could you get a fire going?"

He nodded.

They neared the body of water and Sarah and the children took moments to clamber up into the wagon, while Chris climbed on top of one of the oxen, as Nathan usually did when fording deep water.

Nathan mounted the horse, taking care to stay near the wagon. He'd lost sight of Emma, and there were six of them pressed into the small space.

Seven and Eight were in the back of the wagon, their golden heads visible over the tailgate.

The oxen pulled the wagon into the waters and he followed on horseback, several paces behind.

They were crossing the most dangerous part, the deep middle where the oxen didn't always have good footholds, and the wagon was afloat when it happened.

Something shifted in the weight of the wagon. There was a shout from the front, maybe from the teenaged boy. One side of the rear of the wagon dipped ominously.

And someone tumbled over the tailgate, out of the wagon, into the swirling waters. A female, in a heap of skirts going over the honey-colored head.

A woman's scream rang out and Nathan didn't think. He only reacted.

Emma!

Nathan's first thought, only thought, was the woman he cared about.

He urged the horse after the golden head that bobbed and sank in the swirling waters.

A familiar form leaned out of the back of the wagon. Emma, with a frantic glance at him.

So it must be one of the little girls in the water. Was it Seven? Or Eight?

He didn't even know their real names.

The horse was moving as quickly as it could get its footing in the waters, but time seemed to have slowed like spilled molasses and everything inside Nathan went tight and pulsed with emotion.

He couldn't let this little girl drown.

His horse plunged through the water, going deeper into the stream, and then a current caught Nathan and he was swept off the horse.

His boots instantly filled with water and threatened to drag him under, but he fought with everything in him to keep his head above the water.

Where was she? He struggled against the water that seemed to pull him in several directions at once, pulling his legs this way and his torso that.

If he could just keep his head above water, he could try to catch a glimpse of—

There!

She had traveled several yards downstream and he cut through the water, swimming with all his might.

He didn't know where his horse had gone, didn't have a sense how far they'd traveled downstream from the wagon train.

All he could think about was grabbing that girl.

And then he did. His stretching, reaching fingers grasped the sodden fabric of her dress and he dragged her against the current into his arms.

She rested limp against him and a silent scream released inside him, though he had no breath to do anything other than fight to stay afloat.

He held her against his shoulder, fighting against the

water, swimming with the water, until his feet found purchase on the muddy bank.

He'd gotten her to shore.

But was she alive?

Chapter Fourteen

Emma raced along the riverbank as fast as her jellylike legs would carry her. Her lungs burned with the exertion but it wasn't that pain that threatened to overwhelm her.

Nathan!

What if Nathan was lost?

God, protect him!

The prayer, the silent cry was the only thought in her entire being until she saw him crouched on the bank, dark against the greens and browns of the landscape.

He was kneeling over Ariella's prone form, and the moment she saw that Nathan had survived but Ariella wasn't moving, her prayer changed to *Don't let her die!*

Instantly, she knew that if the girl died, Nathan would be thrown back into the guilt and self-blame he'd borne when his sister had died. Emma had barely glimpsed it, barely understood how he'd cried out for Beth in his delirium, but some instinct deep within her knew that if this child was lost, Nathan would be lost to her, as well. As a friend...as the possibility of something deeper.

Her wordless prayer surged from the deepest part of her heart as she raced those last few yards to his side,

Harrison and Chris behind her, Sarah even farther behind them.

Heedless of mud or grass staining her skirts, she fell to her knees at Nathan's side. "Is she…?"

He'd rolled her onto her side and Emma witnessed how he pounded her back, none too gently.

But Ariella coughed, expelling dirty brown water from her nose and mouth and took a gasping, shaking breath.

And Nathan sat back on his heels as she supported Ariella's back and helped her sit as beautiful color, beautiful life filled her face.

Ariella began to sob, no doubt latent fear over the whole ordeal, and Emma gathered her close as Harrison and Chris neared, closing in behind Nathan.

But she couldn't look away from Nathan's face, from the stark fear still revealed in the planes of his face, the fire behind his eyes.

Somehow she knew the fear hadn't been for himself. He could have drowned. She'd read accounts of it happening.

He looked away from her, turning his head in profile to look back across the creek as Harrison ran up to them. As if to hide his emotion from her.

But it was too late. She'd seen the vulnerability in the man.

She surrendering the still-sobbing Ariella to her father's embrace and stood up, her legs still shaking from the adrenaline that had rushed through her and hadn't abated from the moment the wagon had lost control and Ariella had tumbled into the rushing waters until just now.

Nathan stood, and made as if to turn away, but she

reached out to him with both arms and he pulled her into his arms, burying his face in her hair.

Oh, Nathan.

He was soaking wet, and she could feel the cold radiating off him, but she didn't care.

He was here. He was whole. He hadn't drowned.

He shook, his entire body trembled against hers as he just held her.

"I'm so glad you're safe," she whispered into his shoulder. She didn't know if he could hear her, but she tried to telegraph the sentiment through the strength of her arms around his neck, through how tightly she held him.

"I thought it was you, at first."

His words didn't make sense, and then they did.

And if he held her a bit too tightly, that was all right. He *did* care about her.

When a sobbing Sarah finally reached them, Nathan gently released Emma.

Sarah held her daughter close, as close as she could with her very pregnant stomach between them, then moved toward Nathan.

Emma was likely the only one who saw his slight flinch as the other woman rounded on him. But the surprise written across his expression when Sarah flung herself at him was there for everyone to see.

He patted her back awkwardly through the unexpected hug.

"You saved our girl," Sarah said as her tears began to dry. "How can we ever thank you?"

She moved back from Nathan, placing a hand to her lower back.

The younger children, all except little Sam, ran up to them, followed by several other men from the caravan, though they stayed a little apart to give the family its privacy.

"That was the bravest thing I ever saw!" warbled Aaron, the second youngest at five years old. "I can't believe you jest jumped off your horse to save Ariella."

"Ariella," Nathan breathed beside her. Then said, "The horse."

One of the other men chimed in, "Elijah caught him downstream. Got him tethered up at the Harrisons' wagon."

Nathan blew out a breath. She knew that must be one worry off his mind.

But Emma couldn't forget the small boy waiting for news back at the family wagon. Nathan had saved Ariella. But what would happen if she couldn't treat Sam's infected leg? Would he lose it? Or worse, even lose his life?

Nathan felt the change in Emma and knew where her thoughts had gone.

Her blue eyes had gone dark with worry. For Sam.

He couldn't forget the moment of her embrace. The relief that she was safe and whole. The feeling, even for those few precious seconds, that she cared for him. He couldn't deny that he cared about her.

He knew she couldn't care as much as he'd begun to care for her—more than the bonds of friendship—but for those few precious seconds, he'd pretended that she felt just as strongly for him as he did for her.

He overheard some of the men talking of the short stop they would have for a quick mealtime and remembered that Emma wanted water boiled. There wouldn't be much time to attend to the tasks she needed done, not with the delay that his impromptu swim had caused.

He hurried back to the family wagon, his feet squelching inside his boots with every step. They'd settled a good distance from the creek. He was gratified to see Ben's horse tied off like the men had said.

He found a spade among the family's belongings and was halfway through a decent-size hole for the campfire when the family trudged up from the gathering on the creek bank.

"Thank you, Nathan," Emma said.

He made the mistake of looking at her. Something sparked between them, something that had been dormant until just now. Because of that embrace down by the river.

"Why don't you let me finish there," the teenaged boy offered. "I can make the fire." The young man's seriousness seemed to be his natural state. Nathan hadn't seen him smile even when he'd come running up to his sister.

Nathan relinquished the spade, intent on finding buckets to start hauling water for Emma.

He turned and almost ran smack-dab into Harrison.

"You've got to be uncomfortable with your duds soaked," the other man said. "They'll be too large around the waist, but these of mine should do for you until yours can dry out in the sun."

Nathan stared at the man's outstretched hand, holding a pile of clothing.

Offering it to Nathan.

He shook his head, bewildered. "You'd let me wear your clothes?"

Nathan couldn't wrap his mind around the offer. The folks in the Hewitts' caravan had been worried he would steal their belongings, but Harrison offered his up, just like that?

"You saved my daughter from drowning," Harrison

said, gravely serious. "I owe you a debt, far more than I'll ever be able to repay."

But you don't know me, Nathan wanted to say, but the words stuck in his throat.

He took the clothes, mostly because Harrison looked as if he would stand there holding them forever if Nathan didn't.

Nathan had suffered worse than wet clothes, but didn't refuse.

By the time he'd changed into the dry clothes—which *were* too wide in the waist!—the young man had a good-size fire going and water on to boil.

Emma knelt over a blanket laid out on the ground, where someone had moved Sam out of the wagon.

"Is it gonna hurt?" the little boy asked his mama, who was hovering close beside him.

Nathan hung back, ready to help when Emma needed him, but not wanting to be in the way.

The pregnant woman gasped a little and laid a hand over her stomach, her face going pale and lips pinching for a moment.

"Are you all right?" Emma asked.

"Just one of those pains that comes with bearing a little one," Sarah said.

Nathan didn't know much about childbearing, but her reaction seemed a little extreme for a common discomfort.

Seven—whose name he had found out was Anna—and Ariella knelt nearby with Aaron, their attention on their injured brother.

"His face is pretty white—like a slice of bread," Anna said.

Aaron contributed, "Chris did it."

"Aaron," Sarah chided.

Chris, the teenaged brother, was nowhere to be seen.

"Is he supposed to look like that?" Ariella asked. Her voice was slightly hoarse, and she was wrapped in a blanket with her hair wet and loose down her back.

"Will it hurt him?" Aaron asked, lower lip trembling on his brother's behalf.

And Emma sent Nathan a half amused, half exasperated glance. What did she expect *him* to do about the children that chattered like magpies?

A look at Sarah revealed a white face and perhaps even a sheen of sweat on her upper lip.

"Why don't you take the children on a short walk while I assist Miss Emma?" he suggested.

A chorus of *aww!* had a smile tickling the corner of his mouth, but he resisted. One crack in his expression and Emma would never be rid of the children.

"Are you certain?" Sarah asked, one hand resting on the mound of her stomach.

Emma nodded. "We'll manage."

The little boy whimpered when his siblings and his mama left.

Emma gently brushed his hair back from his forehead. "It'll be all right, Sam. They'll be back in a moment."

Nathan could imagine her gentle touch for her own children. For McCullough's children.

Imagining her with the other man and his family burned like a hot poker in Nathan's midsection.

He closed his eyes briefly against the image.

Sam was having none of Emma's comfort. He knew she wasn't his ma and the lip that had been trembling was suddenly open in a whimper.

Nathan joined her at the blanket. "What do you want me to do?"

The faster they helped him, the faster his ma could come back and comfort him.

"Keep him from thrashing about."

Nathan put his hands on the boy's shoulders but didn't apply pressure as the boy stilled. No doubt when it began to hurt worse, he would squirm, but Nathan didn't want to scare him.

Movement from the opposite side of the wagon drew Nathan's gaze beneath the conveyance, where he could see a pair of trousers and boots. Chris, he suspected. Curious, or something else? Maybe watching over his brother?

Beneath Emma's hands, Nathan caught glimpses of the angry red cut, several inches long, scoring Sam's shin.

"This will hurt, Sam. Can you be a brave boy?"

She'd lathered a washrag with soap and didn't give the boy time to anticipate the hurt, because she began scrubbing the cut even as she spoke.

Sam cried out and tried to break away from them. Nathan pinned him in place, using only as much strength as necessary to keep the weakened boy still.

"I'm sorry," Emma muttered, but she didn't stop using the soapy rag. "We've got to get it cleaned out—"

She'd pinned Sam's opposite leg with her elbow but as she worked on his injured leg, the good leg flailed upward.

"Don't—" Nathan ordered, but the boy was past the point of being rational, and Emma was the one torturing him—or so he must've thought.

His small boot caught her on the jaw. Nathan reached out a hand to press down on Sam's leg, but that left one of the boy's shoulders without an anchor and he clawed at Nathan's hand, raising scratches on the back of his wrist.

"Sam. Quit it!"

Nathan didn't look up at the voice, but knew it when Chris knelt near his brother's head.

The teenager wasn't here out of blatant curiosity, like his siblings had been. He wanted to help. Nathan had seen—recognized—the guilt in his face earlier, before he'd even overheard about the boy's part in his brother's injury.

"Can you hold his shoulders?" Nathan asked the boy.

"Nathan—" Emma began to protest, but Nathan flicked a resolute glance at her.

She might not want Chris to help, but Nathan wouldn't let her be hurt again. He could see the darker red mark on her jaw.

"You'll need my hands," he said simply. He moved next to her and pressed both of Sam's ankles into the blanket, gently. "You okay?"

She nodded, her attention not diverted from cleaning out the wound.

"I w-want Ma!" Sam cried, voice quivering.

"I know you do, but you know she can't stand the sight of blood with the baby coming," Chris explained quietly.

The young boy was not comforted by Chris's explanation. He wanted his ma.

Emma reached across Nathan for a pitcher of water, her shoulder brushing his. She washed out the wound, the soapsuds sliding away to reveal angry red skin.

Chris sucked in a breath and Nathan watched his face go pale.

Sam still cried soft sobs.

And Nathan caught sight of a single, silver tear, rolling down Emma's cheek.

She was such a tender heart—no doubt she disliked putting the boy in pain.

His gut twisted painfully tight. He had a moment of wondering exactly how he'd gotten here.

And he knew why.

Emma.

He couldn't stay away from her, couldn't resist her sincere request for help. Even when he knew better.

Because he was starting to fall in love with her. There would be time for reflecting on that later.

He wanted to ease this moment for her, for the boys. But what could he do?

Emma felt Nathan go still at her side and for a moment she wondered if both he and Chris would become sick at the sight of blood and whether she would be on her own doctoring the boy and avoiding his kicking foot at the same time.

Her jaw still throbbed from where he'd gotten in a good kick moments ago.

But Nathan surprised her by offering, "I once got lost in a snowstorm."

At first, his words didn't make sense to her.

But he'd gotten Chris's attention, and even Sam's sniffles quieted slightly.

Ah. He was telling a story. About himself.

"I'm ah…" He hesitated slightly and when she flicked a quick glance at him, she saw the red creeping into his cheeks. "I'm a trapper and I was out checking the lines and didn't realize a storm was brewing—it came on too quick."

Sam had ceased struggling—maybe that was because she had finished rinsing the wound—and both his and Chris's eyes were fixed on Nathan.

"I've got to expel the pus," she whispered to Nathan.

He nodded. And kept talking. "I was at least a mile

from the remote cabin I was staying in, and the snow came on so fast I knew there was no way I could make it back safely."

Emma used another clean washrag and her thumb to press against Sam's wound. The boy flinched, but otherwise remained still.

Bless you, Nathan, she thought. Both boys were so entranced by his story they'd almost forgotten she was working.

"I ducked into this cave I'd found while I'd been exploring, and prepared to hole up until the snow stopped."

"Bet it was cold," Chris said.

Nathan nodded. "So cold I could barely stand it. The cave was small—a real tight fit for me—and everything was quiet. Snow was building up in the mouth of the cave, making it dark…"

Emma thought she'd gotten the wound as clean as she could. But she didn't want to wrap it, not yet. It had been wrapped so tightly before that she believed the wound needed to dry out.

"I'm done, Sam," she interrupted.

Nathan and Chris both looked at her, surprise registering in their expressions.

"Can you sit up for me?" she prodded.

Nathan helped steady the boy as he struggled to sit up.

"I'd like to leave it unwrapped until we have to get back into the wagon, all right?"

"Then what happened?" Sam ignored her, directing his question at Nathan.

Nathan seemed surprised by the boy's interest. Chris hadn't moved off, either.

"Turns out I wasn't alone in the cave. About midway through the storm, I started hearing scratching and snuffling. I'd seen wolverine tracks in the area and I thought the worst..."

"What's a wolverine?" Sam asked.

Emma moved from her kneeling position on the blanket, picking up the washrags she'd used to spare Sarah from having to do it. She suspected there were more to Sarah's stomach pains than simple discomfort. She guessed the baby was coming soon.

And Sarah would have her baby out on the trail.

Emma shuddered. She knew women gave birth on the trail, but how awful an ordeal.

Nathan made as if to get up and help her, but Emma waved him back down.

Chris was explaining what a wolverine looked like to his younger brother. "...and they're real mean, ain't they?"

"I've seen a wolverine tangle with a black bear before and the wolverine chased the bigger bear out of his territory. All I could think was *what would happen to me if a wolverine got ahold of me?*"

Anna and Ariella and Aaron came running up, skidding to a halt behind their brothers, careful not to jostle Sam.

"What're you talking about?" Anna demanded.

"Mr. Nathan was in a cave with a snowstorm and there was some kind of animal..." Sam said.

It was obvious in his tone and his wide eyes that he'd assigned Nathan a place in the story as hero.

Good. Maybe it would do Nathan some good to see himself through different eyes than those he'd been around in the other caravan. He'd all but admitted to her that he'd kept to himself before joining the wagon train, hadn't given folks a chance to know the real Nathan at all.

Maybe being around the Harrisons, even for a short time, was a blessing for him.

Maybe he could learn that not everyone saw him as he saw himself.

"What happened?" Chris asked. "Was it a wolverine?"

"Well, I was afraid to go out in the snow, thought I might freeze to death. So I got out my hunting knife and…" Nathan paused.

Was he thinking of a way to make the story more child-friendly? Had he killed the animal?

Apparently, he'd been pausing for dramatic effect. So much for his storytelling skills being rusty.

"Nothing ever came out to get me," he concluded.

She released the breath she'd been holding.

"Whatever it was must've smelled me and decided not to come out and challenge me—which means it probably wasn't a wolverine because they are territorial. Maybe it was a fox. I'll never know."

The children didn't seem disappointed at the tame conclusion to the story.

Anna said, "Tell us another!"

And the others chimed their agreement.

Nathan seemed stunned by their effusive words. He stood up, rubbing the back of his neck, a sign that Emma was coming to recognize meant he was uncomfortable or nervous.

"I've got to help Miss Emma finish up. We've got to catch back up to our wagon train."

From the back corner of the wagon, she heard his words and the children's disappointed cries, but her focus went to Sarah, who stood in the shade behind the wagon, clutching her stomach, face white and drawn with pain.

Sarah looked up and their eyes met.
"You're in labor, aren't you?" Emma asked.
And Sarah nodded.

Chapter Fifteen

Nathan heard Emma's words as he left the children on the blanket and joined her near the wagon, but they didn't really register until he saw the white-faced woman, bent and clutching the wagon sideboard as if she could barely stand straight.

And then Sarah stood upright, color returning to her face as she released the breath she must've been holding.

Chris joined them. "Ma?"

"Can you fetch your father for me?" she asked.

Chris must've recognized the serious tone of his ma's voice because he scurried off toward the other wagons without another word.

Emma went to Sarah, while he remained frozen in place. A baby. Born out here? Would she expect Emma to help with the birthing?

And what of the other children?

"It'll be hours still," Sarah said, gently refusing Emma's offer to help her sit down. "Best thing is for me to keep moving until it's time."

Emma turned to him, her brows creased, just as Harrison came hurrying up, Chris on his heels. "The baby's coming?"

Nathan turned Emma with a hand beneath her elbow, moved her several paces away from the wagon and the shade where the children rested, out into the piercingly bright sunlight.

"We don't have time to stay for a birthing," he muttered. "It's already late."

Afternoon sunshine warmed their shoulders, but the hours before nightfall would slip away too fast as they tried to catch up to the caravan.

She looked up at him, her face not revealing disappointment in his declaration, but not revealing approval, either.

"Let the other women in the caravan help," he said. "Every hour that we delay, your family's wagon train moves farther and farther ahead. If we want to catch up to them by nightfall, we should leave now."

There was something in her blue eyes that he couldn't name. "I'm not worried about Sarah," she said softly. "I'm worried about Sam. I've cleaned out his leg but if the infection doesn't clear up, he could be in danger of amputation."

He shrugged helplessly. It wasn't that he didn't care about the boy—because somehow, strangely, he *did* care if the tyke worsened—but Ben had entrusted him with Emma's care and he'd promised to return her by nightfall.

"His ma will be indisposed for hours, maybe all night. And the girls aren't old enough to take care of him the way he needs."

"Chris—"

"Will probably be tasked with caring for the livestock and tending to chores."

He knew she was right, but he also knew how dangerous it was to continue on with the Harrisons. He should spirit her away this very moment.

And every second spent with those kids, with their wide, innocent eyes that believed he was friendly and… *good* made him want to stay longer. Made him want to believe he could be those things, too.

"We've got to get back to your family. The farther away the caravan gets, the more dangerous it will be for us to travel back to it alone."

It wasn't fair, playing on her fears. He hated himself a little for attempting the manipulation.

A shadow passed through her eyes, but she braved a smile up at him. "I know it isn't ideal. But we came for Sam, to help him. I won't leave until I'm certain his wound is healed."

He shook his head as she turned and returned to Harrison and Sarah.

Something tugged at his trouser leg and he looked down to find Aaron wearing an endearing grin on his dirt-smeared face. "You stayin'? Come tell us another story." The demand was spoken so sweetly, with such trust that Nathan would comply, that it felt as if someone had stuck a hot poker directly in his esophagus. Aaron took Nathan's huge paw in both his hands and gave a tug back toward the other children on the blanket.

"Not now, kid," Nathan grumbled. He tugged his hand out of the kid's grasp and stalked off, all the way into the woods, where maybe he could find a modicum of privacy.

Why was she doing this to him?

He knew why, and he couldn't fault her. Emma had a compassionate heart. It was what had drawn her to Nathan in the first place. She hadn't wanted him treated unfairly. Couldn't bear for him not to have treatment when he'd been down with the measles.

And now she wanted to take care of Sam.

But he couldn't sit and share a meal with the Harrisons. Seeing Emma with them, having them act so friendly toward him...

It made him want things that he knew weren't for him. A home.

A family.

Emma.

She'd told him once before he could be forgiven, but even if that was true, he would never be good enough for her. She had *Tristan McCullough* waiting on her in Oregon. Someone who'd never done the things Nathan had done.

Someone who was her match.

Someone *better*.

But the thought made his stomach churn until he thought he would be sick.

Emma waited for Nathan's return all afternoon. The wagon train had moved on until the evening faded.

Nathan had ridden alongside, far enough away to be a silhouette in the distance.

She'd walked alongside the wagon with Sarah and the children, checking on Sam inside every so often.

Had she pushed Nathan too far?

She felt she needed to stay for Sam, to ensure he got the care he needed, if only for a short time.

And she'd felt that Nathan needed the Harrisons. She'd seen the surprise and the poignant moment of joy in his quickly shuttered expression as the children had gathered around to hear his story.

She cared about him. As a friend, as...more. If she

could teach him that he didn't have to be an outcast, always on the outside, then perhaps she would have given him something. It was all she could do.

She'd felt his trembling when he'd said he'd thought it was her in the river.

Maybe he did care. But something held him back.

She kept her admiration for him as a secret wish, deep in her heart. Even if Nathan opened up, even if he wanted to be with her, there were still obstacles. Her brothers expected her to end up with Tristan McCullough. They still had mountains to cross before they reached the end of the trail.

And before there was room for any secret wish, Nathan had to return to the caravan and her company.

The bugler called for a halt close to sundown.

Nathan picketed Ben's horse with the other animals and made his way through the busy caravan toward the Harrisons' wagon. Several men nodded to him and one shouted a *well done* with a wave.

Well done? What?

Ah. He must be referring to the river rescue earlier. Nathan flushed, unused to the approval. But something inside made him meet their gazes and return their nods.

As he was passing by, three men worked on a wagon. It looked as though they were replacing one of the wheels that had two broken spokes. Two of the men supported the front corner of the wagon while the third was removing a wheel from the axle. Another wheel, a good one, rested nearby, no doubt waiting to be placed on the axle.

As Nathan watched, one of the men lost their footing and the wagon tipped.

Reacting quickly, not really thinking, he stepped up

behind the man—a stranger to him—and put his shoulder into the wagon's sideboard. It steadied.

Both men, with sweat beading on their foreheads, nodded their thanks.

The broken wheel fell away and one of the men grunted, "About time, Rollins."

The man replacing the wheel kept working, tossing the broken wheel on the ground and picking up the new one.

"C'mon," the first man urged. "This is heavy."

"I'm goin' as fast as I can manage," the smith replied.

Finally the wheel was in place and the bolts replaced. Nathan stood straight, relieved of the heavy burden. He squared his shoulders, working on the kinks from a long day in the saddle and the unexpected lifting.

The man closest to him stuck out his hand. "You're the one who jumped in after little Ariella Harrison. Brave thing you did."

Nathan shook his hand, words sticking behind his teeth. He should tell the man how it wasn't brave if a body didn't really think about it, how he'd only reacted and didn't really deserve recognition.

But he swallowed it all back.

"Thanks for your help," the second man said, also with a shake of his hand.

Nathan continued on his way to find the Harrisons' wagon, a little flummoxed by the whole transaction.

He'd only seen a need and filled it, but the men had been thankful. And they'd praised him for saving Eight—Ariella.

Why were things so different in this caravan than in the Hewitts'? Had Stillwell poisoned the other travelers against him?

Nathan's lip curled at the thought of Stillwell and

his wrongful accusations. There was something, some motive deeper behind Stillwell's presence in the wagon train, Nathan knew it. It didn't make what the man had done to Nathan right, but that couldn't be changed now.

Or was the travelers' reactions to Nathan his own fault? Had his standoffish behavior made him seem more suspicious to them?

That thought put a rock in his belly. Could it be true? If it was, that meant *he* was the reason people looked down on him.

He found the Harrisons' wagon and caught sight of Emma's honey-brown hair as she bent over one of the children, listening intently to what they were saying. Paying attention.

His entire being quickened just at the sight of her.

He was in too deep, and he didn't know what to do about it.

Emma was relieved that the wagon master had called a halt a little before sundown. Sarah's pains were getting closer together, she'd had to stop walking frequently as the discomfort turned to pain more and more.

But now she'd disappeared into the family tent with Harrison helping to settle her.

Nathan appeared with a nod and an inscrutable look, before moving to help Chris with the oxen.

Emma helped Sam disembark from the wagon. Some of the residual pain had eased from the boy's expression, to Emma's relief.

She settled him on a blanket not too near the fire pit, and kept the other children busy with small tasks, getting the fire built up, hauling buckets of water, finding clean linens and locating the baby gown and diapers that Sarah had packed in a special satchel for just this night.

The Harrisons shared their fire with a family of three, the Gearys. The forty-year-old couple and their nineteen-year-old daughter, Millie, greeted her pleasantly. The mother disappeared to help Sarah, which left Emma and Millie to watch over the children and prepare the evening meal.

The children started to stir in their anticipation, wondering whether the new baby would be a boy or a girl and suggesting names that were getting louder and more absurd the longer it went on. Chris joined them, but Nathan remained out of sight, though she had a feeling he was nearby.

When Anna's animated antics almost resulted in a fall into the fire, Emma went looking for Nathan.

He stood in the shadows behind the wagon. Alone, just as he'd been since he'd come into their caravan to drive for the Binghams. He watched her approach without speaking.

But there was something in the expression on his face. A wish...

Maybe the same wish that was in her heart.

Stunned that he'd allowed her to see it, he who was usually so closed off, she swallowed hard.

He'd revealed the truth after his swim in the river, and he couldn't take it back. Things weren't settled between them.

But she wouldn't acknowledge it, not now.

"I need you, Nathan," she said softly, reaching out a hand for him.

He jolted, as if her words had physically touched him.

"The children are restless. Come and tell a story. Please. At least until supper."

And he came.

He settled near the fire, but far enough away to be

out of her way. His surprise was evident in the vulnerable cast of his expression when Sam crawled into his lap and rested his back against Nathan's chest.

As she worked with Millie to cook the stew and some pan biscuits, he told of tracking a cougar on a weeklong hunt. Of the winter that another trapper had stolen furs out of Nathan's traps until he'd figured out what was happening. Of losing a favorite horse and having to pack out a season's worth of furs on foot.

"Your beau is so brave, going on so many adventures," Millie said softly at one point, as they began ladling the stew into bowls for the children. "And not bad to look at, either."

Emma looked up to find Nathan's eyes on her. Had he heard Millie's *beau*? He went on telling the story and she couldn't tell from his demeanor whether he had or not.

She didn't think quite the same about Nathan's stories of life in the wilderness. Each adventure sounded… *lonely.* He hadn't had a brother to help him track the cougar, his stories reflected that he was alone most of the time.

The isolation would have driven her crazy, she was sure. Not having someone to talk to, to listen to her joys and sorrows…

She regretted the resentment she'd held for her siblings over the trip West. She'd been at fault for not expressing her fears and desire to stay back home. She was thankful she'd come, or she never would have faced her fears.

But more than that, she wanted to give that to Nathan. Family.

Would he let her? Would he let her in?

Chapter Sixteen

Sarah hadn't had the baby until well into the night. Emma had settled the kids in the family's second tent, well after they should've been abed. Her limited nursing skills didn't extend to childbirth and she'd been more than happy to know that several experienced mothers in the caravan were standing by to help Sarah.

She'd lain awake a long time, listening for the small cry and muted voices that signaled a baby's arrival. Safe and healthy, judging by the squalling.

Sarah had birthed a baby on the trail. She hadn't been afraid, even though the dangers of the trail had affected her family, with Sam's injury and Ariella's near-drowning.

Their family was strong.

But Emma had let her own fears weigh her down along the trail—including her fear of speaking in front of people. She'd let Nathan down with how she hadn't defended him to Stillwell.

Had she ever really apologized to him for allowing it to happen that night? Perhaps he thought *she* was ashamed of their friendship. Could that be why he pushed her away?

She was lost in the tangle of her thoughts when she noticed Sam start to twist and turn in his sleep. She sat up, the other children a mass of bodies, elbows and knees. She'd isolated Sam on her opposite side so his leg wouldn't be jostled in the night.

She reached out and touched his forehead and quickly discovered that he was burning up with fever.

Carefully, she scrambled out of the tent. Movement in the shadows nearby startled her and she whirled with a hand at her chest, letting the tent flap fall closed behind her.

Near the wagon, Nathan sat up, his legs encased in a bedroll, hatless with his dark hair rumpled.

"Whatsa matter?" His voice slurred and in the almost complete darkness she couldn't see, but imagined, his dear face lax and open from sleep.

"Sam has a fever—I'm worried about the infection."

Without questioning her further, he struggled to get out of the bedroll and came to her.

"It's very dark," she whispered when he'd met her near the tent. Even the stars didn't seem as brilliant tonight.

"It's very late," he countered, "and the moon is new." He was close enough that his exhalation stirred the fine wisps of hair at her temple. He touched her elbow as if to say *I'm near, there's nothing to be frightened of,* and she wasn't afraid.

Something had changed between them today, unacknowledged, but it was there.

She leaned into his touch slightly. The night was cool around them, the temperatures dropping overnight, and she missed the warmth of her own bedroll in the tent. But Sam's fever was a worry.

"You want me to get the boy or stoke up the fire?"

he asked. Ever present, at her side, ready to help without her asking.

"The fire," she decided quickly. "And can you fetch some water?"

He was gone before she'd bent to pull Sam out of the tent, careful not to wake the other children.

The fact that Sam didn't rouse as she lifted him carefully in her arms was a worry. She knew some children slept more soundly than others—her brothers were a fine example of that—but she was afraid the fever had rendered him unconscious, which would be a very bad thing.

She stumbled out of the tent toward the fire.

When she made her way carefully near the fire pit, praying all the while, she found Nathan squatting beside it, tending to the slowly growing flames. A bucket of water waited nearby with a washrag folded over the handle, and Nathan's own bedroll was laid out close enough to take advantage of the light but not too close that the fire would overheat the feverish boy.

Emotion clogged her throat for the thoughtful care Nathan had given even as she'd roused him from his much-needed rest. "Thank you," she whispered as she laid Sam out on the bedroll.

Nathan slid one more small willow log on the fire and shifted toward her, his boots rotating on the flattened grasses.

"I didn't wake his parents," he said. "I didn't know if…"

She nodded, reaching for the cloth and dipping it into the bracingly cold water. "Sarah must be exhausted, and Harrison will have care of all the children tomorrow. If he gets worse, we can wake them."

Nathan settled back onto his haunches as she squeezed

excess moisture out of the rag and then applied it to Sam's forehead like a compress.

Nathan watched her movements.

"Wasn't so long ago I was bathing your forehead," she said softly. "I'm grateful you've recovered."

He nodded. "Your nursing pulled me through and that's the truth. Being around you has…done me a lot of good."

The hesitant admission sent a thrill through her. For someone as taciturn and silent as Nathan, his words meant a lot.

"You've been a blessing to me, as well, Nathan," she said shyly, keeping her eyes on Sam's small face.

Nathan made a noise of disagreement and she looked up to see him staring off in the distant darkness, his jaw tight and expression drawn.

"You have," she insisted, her eyes remaining on him this time. "You allowed me to share my fears about the journey, and you didn't treat them as trivial. You've lived out in the wilds enough to probably dismiss my fears, yet you never made me feel silly."

She swallowed and looked down at the boy lying prone. "Your…friendship has become very important to me." She wanted it to be so much more. But she was afraid to put herself out there, afraid of what he would think of her if she pursued him, especially after what had happened.

"Nothing about you is silly, Emma." She couldn't help but notice that he hadn't responded to her comment about their friendship.

She left the rag across Sam's forehead and moved to lift the boy's nightshirt, just enough to get at the bandaged shin.

When she touched his ankle, Sam moaned and his head rolled to one side.

Nathan moved to sit beside the boy, careful not to block her light. He put one hand on the boy's opposite leg. "Don't need you getting kicked again," he said gruffly. Taking care of her.

Beneath the bandage, the wound had become inflamed and pus-filled again.

"That's bad, right?" Nathan asked at the soft catch of her breath.

"I believe his tissues are trying to rid themselves of the infection," she murmured. "The fever is the body's attempt to help, as well, but it is dangerous."

She washed his wound with soap again, and again left it open to the night air.

Her worry intensified when Sam didn't rouse even through her ministrations. Earlier in the day, he'd thrashed through the pain, but now he barely moved.

She bathed his forehead and chest with the damp cloth, her fears rising in the dark quiet of night.

What if her efforts weren't enough? What if he died because there wasn't a doctor to be found out here in the wilds?

She hadn't realized her movements had turned jerky and uncontrolled until Nathan's large hand covered hers, stilling her and enclosing her hand with warmth.

"Why don't you go lie down? Get some rest. I'll stay up with him."

Nathan wasn't surprised when Emma dismissed his suggestion she return to bed.

Sitting beside her in the night, with the crackling fire near, he was lost. Not physically. He trusted himself to be able to locate water, game for food if they needed it.

Even finding the wagon train come tomorrow wouldn't be an impossible challenge.

But traversing the terrain of Emma's emotions was fraught with dangers. He cared about her. There was no denying it after what had happened earlier in the day.

He could tote water and tend fires, even nurse a sick child, but sharing himself with Emma frightened him worse than anything.

He'd heard what the young neighbor had called him earlier. Emma's *beau*.

The words—and that Emma hadn't refuted them— had knocked the wind out of him as if he'd been socked in the gut.

Did she really consider him her beau? She had to have simply let the comment pass, not wanting to embarrass him. Knowing they would likely never see these folks again after they parted ways.

But the words had stuck in *his* mind all night.

Igniting his hope.

He wished there was some world in which she would have meant it.

Now, faced with her fear and upset over the boy, Nathan was frozen. Impotent.

Maybe they never should have come. Then she never would have been here, to be upset.

What would she feel if the boy didn't survive?

But if they had never come to this caravan, what would've happened to Ariella when she'd fallen in the river? Would someone else have rescued her? Or would she have drowned?

Mired in uncertainty and self-blame for bringing Emma out here, Nathan did nothing.

But he didn't have to.

Emma leaned toward him, first a brush of her shoulder against his arm, then more fully, her weight against his chest.

Sam had calmed, and was resting quietly now. It was so very late that there was no other noise from their fellow travelers. Everyone except the watch was sleeping.

His arm went around her shoulders of its own accord and her head rested in a hollow between his jaw and shoulder. It fit there naturally, as if he'd been made to hold her.

That was a dangerous line of thinking.

And then she whispered, "I feel safe with you."

And that was an even more dangerous thought, one that filled him with both joy and terror.

She shouldn't. He'd failed Beth. What if he did the same with Emma?

"Tell me a story," she whispered.

Because his throat closed tight with memories, he whispered, too. "Once upon a time, I was twenty years old and even though I didn't come from much or have many worldly goods or an education, I thought I had a future."

She remained quiet, breathing steadily in the quiet night.

He cleared his throat because it was hard to talk about this, but maybe if he did, she would finally see why they could never be a match.

"Growing up, my pa was…difficult. Always drunk. Often mean. My sister, Beth, got married 'bout as soon as she could find someone. Only the man she married was even meaner than our pa."

Old anger stirred, that someone would hurt a woman like Beth.

"Beth was… She was something special. Always so

cheerful. Always with a kind word. Telling me I was better than our upbringing."

In the fire, a log split and sent sparks spiraling into the night sky.

He took a deep breath so he could go on.

"She came to me and asked for help. Needed to get away from her husband. It was the first time she told me how he'd been treating her."

He still remembered the violent anger that had coursed through him, but also the helplessness.

"I had no money to speak of. She had things all planned out, if I could get her a sum of cash, she could buy a train ticket and escape him.

"I did every job I could think of. Went town to town, begging for work. But it wasn't fast enough. I went to the cabin and found her dead on the floor, beaten by his hand."

He swallowed, the memories pressing in on him even after all these years.

"Later, a doctor told us she'd been pregnant when she died. I couldn't save her or her baby."

He waited for her recrimination, but when she said, "Oh, Nathan," it was only to put both arms around his neck in an embrace.

He sat there dumbly, one arm slung around her slender waist, mind mired in the past while part of him soaked up the comfort she offered so freely.

For once, he couldn't deny himself.

Emma didn't have words to comfort Nathan. Knowing what he'd gone through, the guilt he carried…she didn't know how he'd borne it.

He was strong, so much stronger than he'd given himself credit for.

It was no wonder he had trouble trusting people, no wonder he kept things about himself so private.

"I'm sorry you went through that," she whispered.

He was shaking.

Maybe that's what he needed, to share his past, to realize he could be forgiven of his guilt.

Sam stirred beside them, breaking the intimate moment when she had to pull away. His skin was mercifully cooler to the touch.

"Miss Emma?" he rasped. "Where's my ma?"

She smoothed back his hair from his still-damp forehead, aware of Nathan still close at her side. "She's with the new baby, remember?"

He nodded sleepily. "C'n I have some water?"

She fetched him a dipper, relieved beyond measure at his animation. When she asked about his leg, he said the pain had lessened. And then he wanted back in the tent with his brothers and sisters.

Nathan helped her stand with a hand beneath her elbow, his presence steady at her side.

He carried Sam to the tent and helped her settle him just inside before backing out of the canvas.

She caught him by the hand, as he was still halfway bent over with only his head still inside the canvas flap.

"Thank you for telling me—for trusting me," she whispered.

It was too dark to see his face, but he squeezed her hand, hard, letting her know he'd heard.

Chapter Seventeen

By midmorning the next day, Nathan and Emma had traversed the last of the familiar landscape that they had seen two days ago when they'd been with the Hewitts' company, passing through a course of thickets and narrow ravines.

Once past the landmarks he recognized, Nathan followed the signs of recent travels. A scrape in the dirt at the bottom of the ravine, where a wagon tongue must've dug into the earth. Hoofprints. A bush that someone had raided for its blackberries.

As far as he was concerned, the faster they caught up to the company, the better. He didn't like traveling on their own.

He felt exposed, as if eyes watched them constantly.

Maybe it was superstition, or maybe it was because he was responsible for another person.

He was still reeling from the revelations he'd made to Emma last night, and the fact that instead of turning away from him, she'd turned toward him.

He had been unable to crush the wild hope that had taken root inside him and refused to be quashed.

He wanted Emma in his life. He wanted it badly.

And if he *could* be forgiven, why couldn't he have it?

He guided the horse out of the ravine and over a stone ridge. There was still no sign of the caravan when he caught sight of movement on a high bluff to their north.

He took a longer look and what he saw sent chills down his spine.

"Indians," he murmured to Emma.

A whole line of them, maybe a dozen, sitting on paint ponies. From this distance, he couldn't tell if the men wore war paint on their bodies.

Emma's hands clutched his waist. "What should we do?"

He didn't know. Indecision held him immobile as thoughts of what could happen ran through his mind.

If they tried to run, and the horse went lame, they would be dead.

If the men were friendly, the best thing to do was face them and see what they wanted.

But Emma's presence complicated things. She was the most beautiful woman Nathan had ever met, with a crown of beautiful, long hair.

What if the Indians tried to take her? Nathan was just one man.

Worst-case scenarios played through his head in quick succession.

"Nathan." Emma's frantic whisper galvanized him into action.

"We'll keep going as we were," he answered, affecting a calm manner when he felt anything but. His heart pounded frantically in his rib cage. "You keep watch on them. Tell me if they move off the ridge."

He guided the horse along the same path they'd been following, parallel to the wagon train marks in the grass, but nearer the woods concealing the creek.

If the Indians gave chase, they would attempt to out-run them, and catch up to the wagon train. Ben Hewitt's horse was larger, faster than the Indians' paint ponies, but also carrying two passengers.

If forced, they could attempt to hide in the woods, but Nathan knew the Indians were excellent trackers.

Did they have a chance of survival?

His mind spun with self-recrimination. If he'd argued harder, maybe Ben wouldn't have allowed her to go and she wouldn't be in this danger.

Or if he'd insisted on leaving yesterday afternoon, as he'd wanted, they would already be back in the caravan with her family.

Nathan laid the blame right where it belonged.

He could've insisted on leaving yesterday and she would've had no choice but to go with him. He could've manhandled her onto the horse with him. He was larger than her; he could've done it easily.

But he'd allowed weakness in himself, he'd *wanted* to give her what she wanted, *wanted* to be a part of the camaraderie with the Harrison family.

And his weakness had put Emma in danger. If something happened to her, he would have failed her, just like he'd failed Beth.

Imagining Emma's body lying broken, all the life gone out of her, sent fear worse than he'd ever felt chilling through Nathan. The hairs rose all over his arms and down the back of his neck. His breath came in painful gasps.

He couldn't lose Emma.

Sitting close behind him on the horse, with her arms about his waist, Emma felt Nathan's tension vibrating through his entire body as he hurried the horse through a copse of scrubby pine.

She couldn't tear her eyes away from the men and horses silhouetted on the far-off plateau. Were they armed? Dangerous? Would they attack?

But beneath the fear was the reassurance that Nathan wouldn't let anything happen to her. He would take care of her.

She felt as if she stood on the edge of a precipice. One breath, one movement and she could fall in love with him. Watching him with the children last night, being beside him while she'd cared for Sam…hearing about what he'd gone through with his sister. All of it made her care about him more.

He was a man of honor, whether he could see it or not.

He kept the horse to a fast, steady walk, as the road flattened out into a plain now that they'd navigated the ravines.

When he turned his head, she could see the tightness of his jaw, the bright intensity in his eye.

Relief fluttered through her when she realized the Indians hadn't moved.

"They aren't following us," she told him.

But the tension in him didn't ease.

"There could be another group somewhere up ahead," he said quietly, and his voice held no warmth in it. His tone was flat, emotionless. Dead.

Something was wrong.

"Surely we can't be far behind the wagon train."

She meant the words to be comforting, maybe to them both, but he still didn't ease.

"We'll make it," she said softly. Surely.

He kept his face resolutely ahead.

Where had the tender man from last night gone? Had

he frightened himself, allowing himself to open up, sharing some of his hurt with her?

Or was he really that worried that they would be attacked?

If it was the latter, he needed his concentration, so she let him be and prayed she wasn't allowing him to stew over their relationship.

The sun had long passed its zenith when they came across signs that the wagon train had stopped for the noon meal.

Some of the fires hadn't fully been covered over and a forgotten tin plate and fork littered the ground near their feet.

And there had been no further sign of Indians.

Nathan brought the horse beneath the cover of trees and to the nearby creek, but he didn't dismount, only let the animal have enough reins to reach the water.

Emma's back and legs were stiff from being in the saddle all day. Surely the horse could use a rest, too.

"Can we stop for a bit?" she asked.

Getting down and stretching sounded delightful.

"It is too much of a risk," Nathan said shortly.

He was still upset. From earlier today or from last night?

"Risk of what? We aren't being followed." She made her voice as cajoling as possible.

"We don't know that," he returned.

"Nathan, we haven't seen hide nor hair of another soul all day."

"It's too dangerous."

Wasn't he overreacting? She didn't see any danger.

And she needed a break.

Before he could protest, she swung one leg over the horse's back and slid free.

She landed with a jolt, her left ankle taking the brunt of her weight and buckling at the sharp slice of pain. She stayed upright by sheer force of will, her legs wobbled terribly.

"Emma! Give me your hand. Get back up here."

The horse must've taken offense at his abrupt, demanding tone because it neighed and sidestepped away.

"It seems we both need a break," she said.

"Emma!" he barked, but she'd already turned and hobbled in the opposite direction.

She kept her face averted even when she heard his boots hit the soft ground with a muted thud.

She kept walking, even as he called out, "Emma. Get back on the horse."

There on the bank, she found a spot bare of brush, and she sat and then flopped back, lying flat on her back. She could see patches of blue sky interspersed among the tree branches that provided the shade.

Until Nathan's angry face interrupted her view.

His eyes flashed fire, and his lip was curled slightly. He was *angry*.

Well, so was she. Looking at him, she started to get good and riled. She could take a five-minute break if she needed it!

"Get up," he said, and his voice was more dangerous than she'd ever heard it. A shiver went down her spine even though she knew he would never hurt her.

"No," she responded calmly, though her insides were rioting. "I need a few moments off the back of that beast."

He leaned over her and gripped her upper arms, pulling her to a sitting position. She could feel that he was shaking, through his hands.

"Nathan, how far could the caravan outdistance us in

a few minutes? Surely it won't hurt to allow the horse to rest, and us, as well."

"It isn't about rest," he said.

He didn't reach for her again, but he looked as if he might at any moment. His eyes positively *burned*.

She looked around, gesturing with one hand. "We are completely alone. What danger are you afraid of?"

"Everything," he burst out, and this time he did reach for her.

He wasn't rough with her, lifting her by her upper arms. She stood up, because he gave her no choice.

He was shaking badly, but she didn't think he was angry.

"The Indians could come after us. A wild animal could attack. You hurt yourself getting off the horse, didn't you?" He didn't wait for her to reply, but rushed on. "What if you get thrown? There are so many ways I could fail you…"

"None of those things are up to you," she cried, looking up to him, trying to express what she knew in her heart.

"Nathan, you can't take the blame for everything. Sometimes it *isn't your fault*."

"And sometimes it is," he replied fiercely.

She knew exactly what he was referring to, exactly where his thoughts had gone. "Beth's death was not your fault."

"You can't know that."

"I know that you tried to help her, Nathan, that your heart was in the right place. If anyone carries the blame, it was her husband."

His face crumpled, as if her words of absolution hurt. Maybe they did, because his guilt had controlled him for all these years.

"Beth's death wasn't your fault," she repeated.

And because of the terrible, wild hurt on his face she reached up and placed her hands on his cheeks. The bristles of his unshaven jaw scraped her palms.

"If something happened to me, it would not be your fault, either."

The terrible truth was, he *could* cause her harm. By breaking her heart. Because for all her good intentions, she was falling in love with Nathan.

Nathan wanted to deny Emma's words. Looking down on her earnest expression, her blue eyes wide with hope and *belief* in him, the only response he could make was nonverbal.

He crushed her to him, his mouth seeking hers. She met his kiss sweetly, as if pouring her heart into his.

And he had no more defenses against her. She'd destroyed all his walls, refused him his isolation, made him fall for her.

He kissed her, trying to express everything he couldn't verbalize. How much he admired her, how she'd changed him, made him better.

How much he cared about her.

When he broke away, breathless, and she held him tightly around the waist with her face pressed to his chest, all he could do was bury his own face in her fragrant hair and hold her.

He was past the point of denying himself. He wanted a life with Emma. Whether she was too good for him or not, whether he deserved her or not, no longer mattered.

He couldn't deny himself any longer.

He was starting to fall in love with her.

But he held the words back by gritting his teeth together, locking his jaws together painfully.

He had no right to her. He had no job when they got to Oregon, no future except what he hoped for with her. If he were a better man, he would make his declaration to her brother, swallow his pride and ask Hewitt if he would help Nathan get a start.

How could he, when he had nothing to offer her except himself? He'd never amounted to much and still didn't.

He held her for longer than he intended. He would have kept on holding her for as long as she would allow but for the knowledge they were still alone out here without the protection afforded by the caravan.

"We should go," he finally said, his voice rusty with all the emotion crashing through him.

She nodded. "I think I can bear getting back on the horse now."

They let each other go, him smiling in spite of their continued precarious situation.

He didn't let her go far; he kept her hand as they moved back the few paces to where he had tied off the horse to a tree branch.

He wasn't kidding himself. Things would change when they got back to the wagon train.

They wouldn't have time alone, not like this.

Folks there still didn't trust him, although now he wondered how much of that had been his fault, carrying a chip on his shoulder like he had when he'd come into the caravan.

But if he could be the man Emma would be proud to stand next to… If he could ignore Stillwell's suspicious nature and things other folks might say behind his back…

Was there a chance he could prove himself worthy of Emma?

Chapter Eighteen

The sun was setting, illuminating the valleys and pine-covered mountain range, with the Powder River snaking its way through the landscape in the distance, when Nathan and Emma rode up to the company.

The tentative hope that had grown in his chest—hope for a future with Emma—was quashed nearly before it had begun to take root, almost as soon as they rode into the camp.

They'd caught sight of the snaking trail of white-capped wagons from the top of a rise just before sunset and Nathan had let out a whoop, a rare show of emotion that he almost immediately regretted until Emma had squeezed his waist with a joyful laugh.

The caravan had apparently just circled up for the night, and there was a lot of movement near the horses. But from outside the circle, Nathan hadn't been able to tell what was going on.

If there was trouble, he might be needed. And he planned to make himself useful to the caravan. He swallowed. *Make friends.*

He saw Ben's light brown head and shoulders above the other men near the horses and saw the moment when

Ben looked up and recognized him. Ben called out to the other men, though Nathan couldn't hear what he said, and started toward them, followed by another man that Nathan didn't recognize.

"Emma! I'm so thankful you're all right."

Ben met them at the horse's shoulder and reached up for his sister. "What happened? We expected you back much earlier."

He brought Emma to the ground and embraced her while a handsome fellow followed close behind, as if he had a right to be there. Nearly as tall as Nathan with reddish-brown hair and green eyes, the man was well-built and handsome. And watching Emma with a proprietary gaze.

"It's a long story," Emma said, glancing over her shoulder at Nathan, her eyes shining. She didn't realize something was happening, didn't even see the man standing near her brother.

Her serene joy didn't stop the awful feeling in his gut.

"The little boy was worse off than we thought—and then his mother went into labor…"

Ben chuckled. "And of course you had to stay on and make sure everyone was all right."

He still had her tucked against him and turned her in one smooth move to face the man at his side.

Nathan dismounted, boots hitting the ground at the same time Ben's words pummeled him.

"This is Tristan McCullough."

Nathan heard her faint reply. "Tristan?"

The ruddy man grinned widely at her, and as Nathan couldn't tear his eyes from the tableau, saw how handsome the smile made the other man.

Nathan swallowed, the pain in his chest growing stronger, radiating out in waves.

"This part of the Blue Mountains can be treacherous in the best of times. I've come out to assist the wagon train—and to meet you."

"Umm, well, I—"

Nathan couldn't see her face over Hewitt's shoulders, but their feet carried them away from him.

And she went, with Ben's hand at her back.

His breath hitched, and everything stilled inside him.

They left him standing with the horse.

Hurt, along with despair, ratcheted through him, erasing the hope and warmth that had filled him just hours ago when he'd held Emma in his arms.

Things were still the same for him. He was alone.

And Emma had just walked away, too.

He wanted to hit something. Emotions roiled through him.

But he still had the horse to take care of.

Shaking with the force of his hurt and disappointment, he took the horse by its halter and led it over to where the rest of the animals were gathered and began unsaddling it.

The familiar motions calmed him somewhat, although they didn't erase the sting of disappointment still reverberating through him.

Hadn't he promised himself he would be a man that Emma could be proud to be with?

Did his promise hinge on Emma's desire to be with him, or *was he that man*?

He could still make the effort, attempt to make friends with those in the wagon train. Prove Stillwell wrong.

Only the success would be empty without Emma at his side.

He didn't know if he could do it without her.

Just one glimpse was enough to know what kind of

man McCullough was. He was handsome and his fine clothes spoke of a job, a life already made in Oregon. What could Nathan offer her? A life of work and drudgery, just trying to survive.

How could he have even thought of asking that of her?

He didn't know where to go—he didn't want to return to the Hewitts' campfire and watch McCullough court Emma.

But he had nowhere else to go.

He checked on Clara, who had already turned out the Morrisons' oxen and grumbled a welcome.

"I guess you saw who showed up," she said in a grudging show of solidarity.

Nathan worked to keep any expression off his face. Had he gone so soft by being with Emma that even Clara could see his upset?

"You know anybody who needs help?" He surprised them both with the words. He chewed on them—they left a bad taste in his mouth. Her eyebrows had disappeared under her hat and he was hot all over.

"Hauling water from the creek? Injured animal needs doctoring?" The words tasted like ash in his mouth but he soldiered on.

Realization passed over her face. He looked away, not wanting to see pity, not if she knew McCullough would win Emma.

"The Davies family," she said softly. "I don't really know 'em, but I overheard the father got a lucky shot and took out a deer late this afternoon—the family needs the meat—but I doubt he knows a thing about skinning it."

He nodded.

It wasn't where he wanted to be—with Emma—but he couldn't face being alone and wouldn't mope.

If any time was for action, it was now.

* * *

Emma was bundled along back to the family campsite, sandwiched between her brother and Tristan McCullough.

Tristan McCullough. Who had come to meet the wagon train so they could *get to know each other*.

Her heart beat in her ears and throat, blocking out other sounds and making her catch only snatches of her brother's conversation with Tristan.

Ben approved. His prideful gaze flicked in her direction, but she couldn't follow the conversation the men were having over her head. Something about the route they would travel tomorrow. She could barely register their words with the thoughts circling through her mind in a panicked whirl.

Her pulse raced through her veins. She threw a glance over her shoulder.

Where had Nathan gone? Had he simply walked off and left her with…her brother. Why would he have inserted himself into the conversation, demanded he be allowed to walk Emma back to the family wagon?

She was the one who should have said *stop* and *I'd like to wait for Nathan to accompany us*.

Again, her shyness, her inability to speak up for herself, had left the man she cared about behind.

Did Nathan think she'd been happy to see Tristan? After what he'd shared with her over the past twenty-four hours, they'd become close. Was he angry, hurt?

She didn't want to meet Tristan, didn't want to get to know him.

She didn't have a choice, as Ben stopped several paces off from their camp. When she would've kept walking, he tugged gently at her elbow to make her stop, as well.

"Rachel and Abby are taking care of supper. You can take a few minutes to say hello…"

And he abandoned her to Tristan McCullough's company.

"What…?" She could only splutter, uncomfortably aware of the man beside her.

"He wanted to give us a few moments of privacy." Tristan's voice was pleasant, with just a hint of a brogue.

She swallowed hard.

If Tristan was right, her brother couldn't have been more obvious in his approval of the courtship.

The courtship she didn't want.

The man at her side—an inch or so shorter than Nathan—looked down at her and smiled, a wide spread of his lips that revealed white teeth in straight rows.

Her own teeth chattered as she glanced down, not even attempting to return the friendly expression.

Nathan hadn't smiled at her when they'd first made acquaintance. It had taken him days to warm up to her.

And even in the beginning when he'd tried his hardest to push her away, she'd never felt this uncomfortable with him.

And it was uncomfortable, knowing Tristan had expectations of her. Courtship! She wasn't ready.

"You're surprised to see me," he said in a gentle voice, no doubt in an attempt to put her at ease.

It had the opposite effect. Nathan had been gruff.

Her upbringing made it impossible for her to be rude, so she flicked a glance upward and saw his eyes on her. Her face flamed and she cast her eyes back down.

"I— That is, *we* just returned to camp." The excuse felt as feeble as it sounded, but it was the best she could come up with. "It has been a harrowing two days." In some ways. In others, the best of her life.

"Did that man—was it Reed? Did he act inappropriately?"

His tone had changed from warm and friendly to something dangerous and cold, and her startled glance flew to his face.

"No!" she cried. "Nathan was a perfect gentleman."

His eyes narrowed slightly and she realized she had used Nathan's given name. She worked to lower her voice, not wanting to give him any reason to be suspicious of Nathan, as many in the wagon train were.

"Sam—the little boy was worse off than expected. And we saw Indians as we traveled this morning."

Her rushed words had the effect she had hoped in distracting him.

"How many?"

"About a dozen. They didn't follow us, but it was frightening."

"I'm sure it was. I'm exceedingly glad that *Nathan* returned you safely to us."

She averted her eyes. She had the feeling that he saw too much. His obvious interest made her uncomfortable, but she also didn't want him to be suspicious of Nathan. Stillwell's agenda against Nathan was enough.

They stood in silence for moments that stretched far too long for Emma's taste. She could see Rachel and Abby just beyond them, in the circle of firelight just past where she stood with Tristan, heads bent together as they worked over the fire.

She desperately wanted to be over there with them.

He sighed. "You're as beautiful as your brother said."

Heat flamed in her face and she couldn't look up at him. He didn't sound terribly happy about the statement.

"I suppose it is forward of me to say so, but my whole

purpose in coming to meet you was to determine if we'd be a match."

She gasped softly, really more of an inhale. She'd known that Tristan waited in the Oregon Territory, but since Nathan had come into her life, she'd pushed her brothers' plans to the back of her mind.

She didn't want to marry Tristan. She couldn't look at him.

"My daughters need a mama."

She heard the hard edge beneath the simple statement. "I love my little girls. I'm not looking for a love match for myself. My wife…"

He swallowed audibly, holding back more that must've been painful for him. The moment of vulnerability softened the outright rejection that she wanted to give.

She and Rachel had both wanted for a mama, after their mother had died. She knew how those little girls must miss their mama, how much love they needed.

Her hesitation must have encouraged him, because he cleared his throat and went on. "Grayson and Ben both told me you'd be shy. I'd like to spend as much time together as we can, before we reach Oregon City, but I think it'll just confirm what I'm already discovering. You'll be a fine mother for the girls."

Anything she might've said to refute his words was lost as he ushered her forward into the circle of firelight where Rachel and Abby exclaimed over her.

She could barely find words to tell them about Sam, about Nathan's daring rescue of Ariella, of the Indians and danger.

She was numb. Completely numb.

It sounded as if Tristan had already decided to marry her, and expected her to go along with it.

And if Ben and Grayson already agreed, as well, they would encourage—push—her at the handsome sheriff.

When she wanted something else entirely.

Emma had never stood up to her brothers, never asked for what she wanted. They didn't even know she hadn't wanted to come West.

If she didn't stand up for herself now, would she end up married to Tristan when they reached their new home?

Nathan stood just outside the circle of firelight, heart heavy.

He carried a packet of venison from the Davies family, who had been uncertain of his help at first but readily accepted it as he helped them skin and butcher the animal.

Had he really thought that bringing this to Emma like a gift would earn her affections?

She sat next to McCullough on a fallen log someone had dragged into the campsite. McCullough spoke earnestly to her, and although Emma's face was turned down, Nathan could see she was listening.

Was he too late already? Was Emma already lost to him?

McCullough laughed, his face transformed with a freely given smile. He was handsome. Emma would notice—she noticed everything.

And what Nathan had shown her many times before was his rough attitude, the chip on his shoulder, the fact that he had a difficult time trusting people.

If she put him side by side with McCullough there was no contest. Nathan would lose.

"Mr. Nathan! I heard you was back. Can we please finish the book? I figure we got two more nights, maybe three at the most…"

Nathan looked down to see Georgie's earnest face. For weeks, Nathan had purposely stayed away from the campsite in hopes of distancing himself from Emma, but during that time the boy had become a fixture, sticking close to Emma and her family.

If Nathan had hoped to sneak away and lick his wounds over Emma, that hope was crushed by the kid's exclamations. But he found he was happy to see the boy. He'd been worrying—a bit—about Georgie in his uncle's care and now he could check up on him.

All heads turned toward Nathan as heat enveloped his face and neck. He stepped into the circle when he really wanted to sneak off in the darkness.

He handed the parcel to the closest woman, Ben's fiancée, with a muttered, "Some venison steaks."

He rubbed the back of his neck and stood awkwardly, unsure whether he should sit or leave.

"Where'd you get it?"

Ben's question was conversational, but Nathan knew he could be casually fishing for information. Seeing if Nathan was causing trouble. While Tristan was welcomed into the family.

It stung.

But he forced his voice to a normal, if not upbeat, tone. "Helped butcher the stag and they gave it to me as thanks."

He felt Emma's eyes on him and looked at her. She smiled tentatively at him, and his heart punched.

Was it possible things weren't over between them?

His eyes flicked to the man at her side. McCullough watched him with an inscrutable gaze. Nathan nodded at the other man.

"Mr. Nathan's gonna read to us," Georgie announced.

And then seemed to realize the almost palpable tension among the adults. "If…if that's all right," he faltered.

Nathan put a hand on the kid's shoulder. He hadn't actually agreed to read, but he didn't want the kid upset, either. Georgie had been a friend to Nathan when no one else had wanted to.

"Of course it's all right," Emma said, standing and sweeping her hands down her skirt. "I'll get the book."

Was it Nathan's imagination, or were her words tinged with relief?

Georgie gave a *whoop* and then a piercing whistle and several more kids ducked into the circle of firelight, some wearing sheepish grins.

"We been waiting for ya to get back, Mr. Nathan."

He couldn't help but laugh as three or four of the children came right up to him, one pulling on his sleeve in excitement.

Maybe the making friends part wouldn't be as difficult as he'd thought.

He sat cross-legged on the ground with the kids crowded around him, Georgie close at his side.

"Here we are." Emma carried the book tucked between one elbow and her side. In one hand she carried a candle, while the other hand was cupped around the sputtering flame.

Nathan expected her to deliver both to him and return to McCullough's side, but was pleasantly surprised when she sat close beside him and smoothed her skirts. Georgie was too big to sit in her lap, but he sat at her knee with the other children gathered around.

He opened the book under the watchful gazes of Emma's siblings and her suitor and started reading.

Her elbow brushed his knee as she held the candle where he would have light enough to read and he lost his place, had to clear his throat before he could start reading again.

This. This was what he wanted. Emma at his side. A passel of children, whether they were helping orphans like Emma's dream or it was their own children, that part didn't matter.

But how could he prove his worth when everything he did would be held up against the golden boy McCullough?

Nathan would never measure up, no matter how desperately he was falling in love with Emma.

Chapter Nineteen

"Good job." Nathan cleared his throat after saying the rusty, unfamiliar words.

The young man at his side looked up, lowering the rifle still smoking from the muzzle where he'd just shot it.

"I hit the pheasant?" the teenager asked incredulously.

"Yep. Let's go get it."

Four days after they'd returned to the company, four days after Tristan McCullough's arrival, and he'd barely seen Emma. But instead of sulking and keeping to Clara's company, Nathan had branched out, reaching out to some of the other travelers.

Nathan and the boy traipsed through the dry grasses to the pheasant he'd felled. The Blue Mountains were almost close enough to touch. They would begin the ascent tomorrow, and the wagon master had given them the afternoon to rest for this arduous portion of their journey.

"Your ma will be happy to have some fresh meat tonight."

The boy looked at him sideways. He carried the gun the way Nathan had shown him earlier, barrel pointed to the ground.

"Will you show me how to skin it for her?"

Nathan nodded.

The idea of helping the boy—and getting out of camp—brought welcome relief.

Nathan had overheard McCullough asking Emma to go walking with him and Nathan had needed an escape.

For the past four days, it seemed every time he turned around, McCullough was beside her. Emma was too kind to tell him to leave off, but Nathan remembered the woman who had fiercely told him she would never give up.

If Emma would have been motivated enough, she would have gotten rid of McCullough.

Which must mean she wanted him around.

This morning, when one of the children he recognized from their readings had found him, dragging along her older brother, Nathan had been relieved for the distraction.

Word had gotten out among a few families that he'd helped butcher that deer and this boy hadn't had meat for his family in weeks. But instead of offering to go out and get some, Nathan had heard himself volunteering to teach the boy how.

No doubt that was more of Emma's influence.

But he also felt proud that he'd helped a family in need, that this young man would be able to continue helping his family eat.

It was a small sense of accomplishment, but it was something for a man who'd spent so many years pushing folks away.

He might become a man Emma would be proud to be with, but he didn't kid himself.

Many of the folks still harbored suspicions about him. Stillwell could be overheard muttering about Nathan, though Nathan worked to let the suspicions roll off his back.

Maybe he would never win over everyone. He would settle for Emma, but the longer McCullough stuck around the less likely that seemed.

"Thanks again, Mr. Reed," the young man said as they neared the circled wagons.

"Sure, kid."

He hesitated. He didn't want to go back to the Hewitts' campsite and see Emma with McCullough. But clouds massed on the horizon, possibly indicating a gathering storm. He didn't want to wander away from camp if the weather was going to worsen.

He didn't have to. He heard a female voice calling his name and ducked through two wagons to find chaos— more than normal—inside the circle of wagons.

A frantic Emma was arm in arm with Rachel and looking for him, apparent by the calling of his name.

"What's the matter?" He waved them over and Emma's relief was the only thing he could see.

Hooves thundered up outside the wagons. He couldn't make out the rider.

"There's a little girl gone missing," Emma said, letting go of Rachel to grip his hand.

He was aware of Rachel's curious gaze, but couldn't bear to let go of Emma, not when *she'd* reached for *him*.

"The men are mounting a search party. Her mama thinks she wandered off."

"Do you think you can track her?" The strident male voice from behind made Nathan turn, and Emma dropped his hand at the same moment.

McCullough.

"How old is she?" Nathan directed the question at both the man and Emma.

"Three years." Emma's voice held a trace of tears and Nathan wanted to clasp her to him, but didn't dare with her suitor and her sister looking on.

"Have the men already left?" Nathan asked.

"Yes," McCullough said. "Emma insisted on looking for you, said you're an expert tracker."

Hg shrugged off her praise, thought it heated him from the inside out.

"It's likely they've trampled any sign of her."

McCullough frowned. "I thought the same. What if we ride out and then circle back, maybe you could catch some sign of her that way."

It was worth a shot, but... "I don't have a horse," Nathan admitted, hating showing weakness to the man who was challenging him for Emma's heart.

If McCullough was surprised, he didn't show it.

Thunder rumbled and he felt Emma go still beside him.

McCullough didn't seem to notice her distress. "We can ride double. It isn't ideal, but it'll serve the purpose."

"Can we talk to the girl's ma?" Nathan asked.

Emma trailed behind the two men as they strode around the edge of the camp to the mother who had lost her little girl. All the while the gathering storm grew closer and more threatening.

Every roll of thunder in the distance made Emma jump.

"She was playing hide-and-seek with her older brother and some friends from a nearby wagon. They didn't tell me she was missing because they were afraid I would be angry—"

The mother broke into sobs. Rachel moved to comfort her and the two men exchanged glancces.

"We can't waste any more time," Tristan said.

He didn't seem to register Emma's unease at all, while Nathan hesitated at her elbow.

"I know it is dangerous for her to be out in the storm," she said, raising her chin.

"It'll erase any tracks she might've left," came his quiet, steady response.

She knew that. But it didn't erase her worry for the man.

She wanted to reach for him, but was aware of Tristan's close proximity. She still hadn't found the courage to tell him she didn't want to marry him.

When they were alone, on the walks he often asked her to take after the wagons had settled for the evening, he told her about his girls. It was obvious from his manner that he loved them very much. And if she hadn't met Nathan, she might've accepted a marriage where three little girls came first.

Was it selfish to want to be loved for herself?

She followed the two men, leaving Rachel with the distraught mother.

"Please be careful." Her words could've been for both of them, but it was Nathan's dark gaze she held for a moment too long.

The men mounted up and rode out, beneath the sky that grew heavy with clouds.

Emma watched them, a prayer on her lips.

She sensed when Rachel joined her, standing just behind her elbow. "You're in love with him."

The softly spoken words startled Emma out of her trancelike stare after the departing horse.

She attempted to keep her face expressionless, but the fear and emotion overwhelming her made her lips tremble.

"With Nathan Reed," Rachel continued.

And Emma was tired of pretending. Tired of being the quiet sister, the one who never made waves. Tired of not standing up for the man she loved.

"Yes, I am," she said calmly. She wasn't ashamed of it.

"Does he feel the same?"

Rachel's question wasn't idle curiosity, Emma knew. Her sister was her closest friend.

"I…don't know. I thought so, but since we returned to camp he's been distant."

"Since Tristan's arrival," Rachel murmured. She looped her arm through Emma's and they began walking toward their wagon. "Does Tristan know?"

Emma shook her head. "He wants a mother for his girls."

Rachel fell silent, unlike her usual self.

"What a mess," Rachel finally said with a sigh. "Does Ben know?"

Emma shook her head.

"If you told him how you feel, perhaps he could ease over things with Tristan."

"Ben and Grayson are in favor of the match."

Rachel pulled a face. "Are you really willing to let those two determine who you marry? Like you let Ben convince you to come West?"

Everything in Emma went still. "You knew?"

Rachel's arm slipped about her shoulders. "You're my sister. Of course I knew you didn't want to come—that you'd put aside your happiness for ours."

A sudden case of sniffles overtook Emma and she half laughed and wiped at her eyes.

Her heart beat high in her throat just thinking of what must happen. "I need to tell Tristan how I feel. Even if… even if nothing happens with Nathan—"

Rachel snorted.

"—I can't marry Tristan when I'm in love with some-one else."

Nathan wanted to dislike McCullough. But the man grew more focused as the storm brewed right over their heads. He understood how deadly the situation could be for the little girl.

And then when Tristan muttered, "I've a daughter that's four. I can't get it out of my mind—what if it was her, lost out here…"

And Nathan didn't want the flare of compassion for the man, but felt it nonetheless.

They had traveled a far piece from the wagon train, in the direction the children believed the little girl had gone. Tristan began guiding his horse in a perpendicu-lar pattern, in hopes that they would see some sign of the girl as they rapidly lost the late-afternoon sunlight to the storm clouds. Men fanned out from the wagon train in the distance, moving slowly toward where they rode.

Lightning flashed, momentarily blinding Nathan. Thunder boomed in quick succession. The storm wasn't far off. Every moment that passed without finding her was a moment lost.

They were running out of time.

And then the first fat drops hit his shoulders.

"Let's split up," he called out above the sudden rush-ing wind.

McCullough seemed to understand how desperate the situation had gotten, because he didn't argue.

He pulled up the horse and Nathan slid from the ani-mal's back, his boots crunching in the dried late-summer grasses.

"I'll head west," Tristan said, the horse wheeling in its nervousness.

"I'll take east. There's a ravine about a half mile." Nathan and his hunting partner had come across it earlier in the day.

They parted and Nathan scanned the ground as he walked as quickly as he could.

Rain began pattering the ground around him. He called out the girl's name. Would she be frightened of him if she did see him, hear him? Would she stay silent so he would miss her?

Had Beth felt the same terror he felt right now? The entire caravan was counting on him to find this little girl.

Beth had been trying to protect her unborn baby.

And he'd been trying to protect Beth, but he'd failed.

If he failed at this, would Emma see him differently? He wanted to think *no*, but there were no guarantees in life.

The rain began to pour harder and his hopes plummeted. The rain would obscure any chance of spotting a footprint and made it hard to see anything out of the ordinary—a hair ribbon. Anything.

God? He reached out with the prayer, as rusty as his words of praise for his young hunting partner had been. *Emma said You would forgive me if I asked. I can't bear this burden any longer. Please. Forgive me.*

The prayer made him feel lighter, freer in a way he hadn't expected. He noticed some blades of crushed grass and followed the trail. It could be a small animal. Or a small girl.

Please. Help me find the girl.

And he heard a mewling cry, just before another loud crash of thunder.

He had reached the ravine and called out for the girl. Above the rain, he heard her soft sobs.

He edged to the cliff side and glanced down. A dozen feet down. And there she was.

Coincidence? He didn't believe so.

God had answered his prayer.

She was clinging to the cliff face, with another drop of twenty feet—deep enough to be deadly—just beyond.

He turned and whistled, waving his arms for McCullough, but the man was out of sight.

He let out another shrill whistle, just in case, then turned back to the girl.

Thunder boomed again and she cried out.

"Hello, little one," Nathan called down. He tried to gentle his voice, but it was impossible with the rain and thunder booming around them.

"Are you all right?"

She just sobbed louder.

She was so small—there was no way she would be able to climb back up from where she'd fallen. And she might be injured.

He glanced over his shoulder again, but there was no sign of McCullough. No sign of help.

But McCullough had known which way Nathan had gone, toward the ravine. He would get here, eventually. If Nathan couldn't get them out, they would wait. A little rain wouldn't hurt them—as long as it didn't flood and wash away the ledge where they would be standing.

"I'm coming down to you, all right?"

He made sure he was off to one side, so if he knocked off any dirt or rocks, they wouldn't hit her, and began scrambling down to her.

The ledge was narrow, barely enough room for them

both, and he didn't want either of them to take that twenty-foot drop.

He bent as much as he was able while keeping his balance. He didn't want to frighten her and have her dart off that ledge.

"Honey, I'm here to help. My name is Mr. Nathan."

She looked up at him and he worked to gentle his expression.

And she lifted one arm to him, as if she recognized that he was there for her and wanted him to pick her up. That was when he noticed her other arm was tucked up next to her body, and a little crooked. Had she broken it, falling down onto this ledge?

He gathered her up, wincing at the tiny whimper when her arm was jostled.

"We'll be all right, honey. They're gonna find us."

The ravine was too steep for him to climb out with only one arm, especially since she was hurt.

And it started pouring even harder. He tucked his coat around her as best he could, sheltering her between himself and the rock wall.

It seemed an eternity—hours of her tiny sobs shaking her body, cold rain dripping down the back of his coat—before he heard McCullough's shouts.

He hollered back and McCullough found them. It didn't take long for the other man to get a rope tied to his saddle and pull Nathan and the girl out.

"She's injured," he said as he handed her over to the other man.

He saw the gentleness McCullough treated her with and knew he could be trusted to get her back to camp. McCullough's horse sidestepped nervously, as if threatened by the thunder.

"Take her back to Emma. Emma can set her arm. I'll find my way back."

McCullough met his gaze just as lightning lit up the landscape. Something passed between them, some knowing.

And McCullough nodded.

He mounted up, taking care with the girl, and rode off, leaving Nathan alone.

Except this time, Nathan wasn't alone. He couldn't forget the prayer that God had answered.

But…he also knew that McCullough was a man who could be trusted. A man who was good for Emma.

Where did that leave Nathan?

Alone in the cold rain.

Chapter Twenty

Rain poured down on the family tent. Emma and Rachel huddled inside waiting and praying while Ben had gone out searching with the other men.

Emma's thoughts and prayers ricocheted between Nathan, Tristan and the missing girl.

If anyone could find the missing girl, it was Nathan. But he had said the rains could wash away signs of her. Emma couldn't imagine the mother's grief if they didn't find the little girl.

And then there were shouts and hoofbeats above the sound of the rain and the storm.

Rachel opened the tent flap, but all that did was bring in rain blowing sideways.

"There's definitely something going on out there," Rachel said over her shoulder.

And then a voice was shouting Emma's name.

Her heart thrummed high in her chest. Nathan?

But it was Tristan who appeared out of the swirling rain, holding a small, prone body in his arms.

"Broken arm," he said after a loud crash of thunder. "Can you set it, Emma?"

Rachel vacated the tent with a quick response. "I'll get your supplies."

And then Tristan filled the tent with his overwhelming presence.

He knelt close and laid the girl out on one of the bedrolls.

"Where's Nathan?" She couldn't help the words, but she kept her focus on the little girl, stretching out the arm as best she could with the little girl clutching it to her chest.

"He saw how bad off she was and sent me ahead."

How very like Nathan.

Emma's gentle fingers probed the break at the girl's forearm and the little one cried out.

"I'm sorry, sweetie," Emma crooned. "It hurts now, but we're going to make it better."

She couldn't think with Tristan so near and her worry for Nathan overpowering her other thoughts. Was he in danger from the lightning strikes out on the prairie? Was he cold, alone?

She loved him for putting the little girl's needs first, above his own safety. Hadn't he been doing that for Emma?

"Will you splint it?" Tristan asked. At her elbow, he was steady and strong, handsome and well-spoken.

And she didn't want him.

"What do you need?" he asked.

And she didn't hesitate as she said, "Nathan. I need Nathan."

Lightning chose that moment to split the sky, illuminating his features and his intent gaze.

Her stomach dipped. Maybe he realized what she really meant, maybe he didn't.

And this wasn't the time for a candid conversation. Even though she needed to initiate one.

He ducked out into the storm without a word.

She bent to try to comfort the young girl, but who would comfort her? Was Nathan hurt out there?

The fear she'd kept carefully hidden from her family—until now—threatened to overtake her.

And then Rachel put her head through the tent flap. "Here's your bag. I put some pieces of wood inside, if you need a splint."

Her sister pushed the satchel inside the tent and turned away.

"A candle, Rachel—"

But it wasn't Rachel who ducked inside the tent.

"Nathan," she gasped.

He dropped to his knees beside her.

The girl's cries quieted. She seemed to recognize Nathan.

"Are you all right?" she managed.

His jaw tightened as he nodded. "Just a little wet." It was an understatement. He was sopping wet, dripping water everywhere.

"Sorry," he apologized.

Despite the tight quarters, he shrugged out of his coat and stuffed it on the floor near the tent flap, leaving himself in shirtsleeves. His dark hair hung dripping about his shoulders.

And he was so dear to her.

But he barely glanced at her. "What do you need me to do?"

They worked together to set and then stabilize the girl's arm with the splint, wrapping it with lengths of cloth.

Nathan's calm presence soothed Emma, in contrast

to Tristan whose hovering had only gotten her more and more worked up.

But something was off with Nathan. He didn't look at her once in the flickering candlelight.

His voice was low and soothing, but he spoke only to the little girl.

It didn't take long, and the little girl's cries had calmed to sniffles.

"I want Mama," the little one said.

"She's right outside," Nathan answered.

He was nearer the door and handed out the girl into her mother's waiting arms.

And Emma realized the storm had passed. Thunder rolled in the distance. Rain pattered softly on the tent roof, at much longer intervals than it had earlier.

Nathan rubbed the back of his neck. "I should go."

She wanted to reach out to him, to somehow close the distance that had grown between them these past few days. But she didn't know how.

And she had to speak to Tristan first, and maybe Ben, and settle this once and for all.

But if Nathan's feelings had changed, was it all for naught?

She followed him out of the tent into a crowd.

"Who's to say he didn't hide that little girl away to distract us all while his partner stole our belongings." James Stillwell was holding an accusatory finger pointed at…Clara.

The woman in disguise was clearly in distress.

Emma looked around for Ben, but he was nowhere around. Tristan had also disappeared.

The little girl's mother held her toddler in her arms, her gratefulness evident in her expression but quickly fading.

"Clara—"

"Ence is no thief," Nathan finished for Emma when she would have fumbled over the name and possibly revealed Clara's secret. She sent him a grateful look but he had his arms crossed and chin raised as he stared down Stillwell.

"And neither is Nathan," she said, her volume finally obeying her.

She felt her heart beating in her throat as all eyes turned and landed on her.

Her voice trembled but she forced herself to go on.

"He…he risked his own life to save an eight-year-old girl, Ariella Harrison, from drowning."

Stillwell shrugged off her words. "So what? He could've done it to draw attention from himself, make everyone think he was some hero when he's been the thief all along."

At her side, Nathan bristled, fists clenching on a deep inhale.

She prayed he wouldn't do something in retaliation— like slug Stillwell the way she wanted to for the awful accusations he was making against Nathan.

A young voice piped up from the gathered crowd. "Mr. Nathan wouldn't do nothin' like that. He's a hero, like from the book he's been readin' us."

Georgie had puffed out his chest and raised his chin, practically daring Stillwell to say something else bad about the man he'd come to think of as a good guy.

And she was afraid Stillwell would do it.

"He spent all morning teaching me how to hunt," came another voice. This from a young man she didn't recognize. "So my family could have meat—we ain't eaten meat in three weeks. How'd he sneak away with that little girl if he was with me all that time?"

Nathan was barely breathing at her side. Whether he felt it or not, her insides swelled with pride for him. He'd been doing a good deed.

And it was paying him back because the young man had offered him an alibi.

"He helped us mend the wagon bonnet," another voice said, a grown man this time. Quietly, as if he almost didn't want to admit to it.

The tide was turning against Stillwell.

"Whatever crime has been committed, Nathan wasn't a part of it." For once, Emma's voice rang out clear and true.

And the crowd heard her. And listened.

"Clarence wasn't a part of it, either," Nathan stated unequivocally.

Stillwell looked as though he would start up again, but Tristan and Ben chose that moment to walk up to the fray.

"What's going on?" Ben demanded.

It was enough to get the attention off Emma and Nathan.

He ducked around the wagon, escaping the commotion inside the caravan.

And she followed.

She had to know if his feelings had changed. He'd kissed her twice. The first time he'd declared it a mistake but the second… The second time she'd begun imagining a future for them together.

If he didn't care for her anymore, she had to know.

And if he did, well, after standing up for him—the way she should've from the beginning—she was ready to speak to Tristan.

Nathan was aware of Emma following him. He couldn't face her, not with all the emotions crashing through him in waves.

He was certain McCullough was the better man. He'd proved it out searching for that little girl.

And trouble continued to follow Nathan around. Now Stillwell had attempted to drag Clara into his unfounded suspicions. Whether he really believed the disguised woman was involved, or just brought her into it because Nathan had been helping her, Nathan didn't know.

How could he ask Emma to be a part of his life if the stigma of being an outsider, someone to be suspicious of, followed him around?

How could he ask her to stand by him when he was just getting his life back together?

It wasn't fair to her, not when she had someone like Tristan waiting to give her the perfect life.

His triumph at saving the little girl had been short-lived. Now all he felt was the heavy weight of his decision to let Emma go.

He wanted privacy, but somehow he knew Emma wasn't going to let go, not without talking to him.

So he steeled himself and whirled to face her. She drew up, shoulders heaving. She'd been almost running to keep up with his strides. The bottom of her skirt was soaked, probably dragging her down with its weight as it had picked up mud and water from the wet grasses.

"Are you all right?" she asked quickly.

"I'm fine," he said shortly, and saw her draw back slightly at the harsh tone in his voice.

Being hard and cold was the only way to get through to her.

"It's just—" she pushed. "I thought I saw you'd scraped your knuckles—"

He glanced down at the back of his hands and saw she was right. His knuckles were raw, even bleeding in places. "Must've happened when I was scrambling down to get the girl."

"Scrambling…down…?"

He waved off her tentative question. Let McCullough tell where he'd found Nathan if he cared to. "I'll wash up in a bit. I'm fine."

He waited a beat, not sure how to continue. Not wanting to continue, even though he knew it was for the best.

Her blue eyes were wide, shadowed. Was she trying to do the same? Find a way to let him down easy?

His jaw tightened at the thought, he was unable to stop his back teeth from grinding.

"You shouldn't be out here with me." The words gritted like dust in his mouth. He almost choked on them, but he forced himself to be stoic, to reveal no emotion.

Her chin went up, but he saw the slight tremble in her lower lip. "I'm a woman grown. I'll go where I want."

"McCullough won't like it."

She flinched and he felt a pang of guilt for hurting her. But he couldn't keep on like this, live in this limbo.

He would do what he had to do.

"There's no understanding between Tristan and me," she said. She held his gaze for a moment, then looked away, her chin shifted to the side as her eyes went past him.

What wasn't she telling him? There was something underneath her words.

Then she looked back at him and her eyes seemed to be communicating something, but he knew not what.

Everything inside him protested. Everything inside him wanted to reach out for her, pull her into his arms and kiss her again.

But he didn't.

He couldn't.

He knew Emma, knew her pure heart. If he kissed her when she was meant for someone else, all he would do was hurt them both.

And he refused to do that to her.

"McCullough is a good man," he told her, his voice low to hide the huskiness in his tone.

"So are you," she said quickly, adamantly.

He shook his head. He was a work in progress. He might get there one day, be a man Emma could be proud to stand beside, but he wasn't there yet.

She opened her mouth with her expression scrunched and petulant, as if she might argue with him.

He needed to get away before he succumbed to her sweet nature, before he started believing again.

"He'll make you a fine husband," he said with a firmness he tried to feel.

He was telling her that he, Nathan, wouldn't ask. If there was a moment to argue that they should be together, this was it. And he wasn't arguing for them.

He was giving her to McCullough.

She realized it, too. Her beautiful eyes filled with tears and pain sliced through his midsection. Maybe his heart was breaking. Or maybe his whole self was breaking, because they weren't meant to be together.

Then she averted her gaze, hiding her eyes from him, hiding her emotions. Shutting him out.

And that hurt even worse.

It took everything in him to remain still, not to reach out for her as she turned and walked back toward the circled wagons.

He'd done it. He'd let her go.

But despair choked him.

It was the best thing for her, but he was bereft. Bereft of her company, her smile, her gentle presence.

He knew there would be no more evening readings. No more companionable conversations in camp.

He was well and truly alone, and it was no one's fault but his own.

Chapter Twenty-One

Early the next morning, Emma worked feverishly at scrubbing the skillet where eggs had congealed in one side.

Nathan sat on a crate across the campsite, finishing his breakfast. Alone. Neither of them spoke.

Emma had lost her appetite.

She felt his occasional glances as acutely as if he had touched her. But he never met her eyes.

He wanted her to marry Tristan. Or so he said.

Tristan, who had spent ten minutes chatting with her quietly as they'd both eaten breakfast, asking about the little girl with the broken arm and Emma's medical training at her father's side, then telling her about his daughters.

He hadn't understood from her request for Nathan last night that she'd chosen Nathan. Nor he had sensed that something had happened between them.

Nathan, who wanted her to marry Tristan.

Nathan, who wouldn't even look at her.

The Blue Mountains standing silent sentinel, so close now, were supposed to have been a sign that they were close to finishing the journey. They'd almost made it.

But she was not happy. Not one bit.

Hence the near-violent scrubbing.

"Um…I think it's clean."

Rachel's voice broke Emma out of her chaotic thoughts.

She looked up to see that Nathan had vacated his spot and only she and Rachel were left in the camp.

Her heart dropped, even though she hadn't expected Nathan to speak to her. She'd hoped.

Rachel began gathering the few items that had been left out.

"Are you all right?"

"Of course," Emma answered. There was nothing physically wrong with her.

But she felt Rachel's gaze on her as she lugged the heavy skillet toward the wagon.

Her sister was far too perceptive. Emma didn't particularly want to discuss the events of last night. They were too fresh, stung too much.

"Ben said to make sure everything was as secure as we can make it. Apparently there will be some rough terrain today."

She nodded. She could imagine so, with the granite mountains hovering above them, both beautiful and treacherous.

Just like her love for Nathan had turned out to be.

With her emotions too close to the surface, she brushed past Rachel at the tailgate of the wagon.

"Do you want to talk about it?" Rachel asked softly.

Emma inhaled reply through her nose. "Not really."

"All right."

Shocked at her sister's easy acquiescence, Emma snorted an indelicate half laugh, shaking her head. Rachel was always a surprise.

"He told me that Tristan would make a good husband."

"Who, Nathan?"

Emma nodded, her eyes filling with tears as she thought about the entire conversation again.

"Why would he say that?" Rachel's tone revealed how perplexed she was.

Emma shrugged, unable to speak over the lump that filled her throat.

"Did something happen between you? Did you argue?"

Emma laughed, though the sound emerged suspiciously like a sob. "No. We've barely spoken since we returned to camp, since Tristan's arrival."

"You didn't talk to him about your feelings?"

"I—I tried to bring it up, but he was already turning me away."

Rachel was silent for only a moment as they tied down the crates in the rear of the wagon. "Do you suppose he thought that's what you wanted? To marry Tristan?"

Emma's thoughts whirled.

"I can barely speak to Tristan when we're together. Surely he would see that…"

"Nathan certainly has sharp eyes, but perhaps viewed through a lens of jealousy…"

Had Nathan been jealous? Because she'd taken too long to decide to speak to Tristan?

She remembered his hot temper, his jealous kiss when the soldiers had escorted the sisters back to the wagon train at the fort.

Why would his reaction be different this time?

Unless…

Nathan had a negative view of himself. What if, in his mind…

"He decided Tristan was the better man?"

It seemed a bit ridiculous when Emma said it aloud.

"Without talking to you," Rachel agreed.

Emma's ire built. How could Nathan just give up on them because Tristan had appeared?

Of course, they hadn't exchanged any promises. And things weren't always easy for him—as evidenced by Stillwell's continued accusations and suspicions.

But for him to give up... She knew he carried a burden of guilt over his sister's death. Did he think that somehow he was protecting her by pushing her at Tristan?

He couldn't be more wrong.

"I thought you were done allowing the men in your life to make all your decisions for you," Rachel said, a mischievous smirk on her lips.

"I am," Emma felt a sense of determination as she said the words.

Perhaps there was no future for her with Nathan, but she wasn't going to let him decide on his own.

Nathan buckled the last of the harness straps on the Morrisons' oxen, his movements jerky and uneven. He hadn't tasted a bit of his breakfast. It had all tasted like sawdust, watching Tristan lean close to Emma in conversation.

He'd given her his blessing, but oh, it hurt seeing the two of them together. Imagining her in McCullough's home, his girls gathered around her in the family Nathan knew she wanted.

Imagining the child she would bear for McCullough.

He gritted his teeth so hard he thought he heard them grinding.

"I'd appreciate you not frightening the Morrisons' animals with your temper."

He took a step back from the oxen. He'd thought Clara was behind the wagon, securing the tailgate and any loose belongings for the arduous journey they were in store for today.

"Sorry," he mumbled.

The oxen stood placidly in their traces. They hadn't seemed to notice Nathan's inattention or his ire.

Clara crossed her arms, which only brought to attention the bulge of her belly. He couldn't help his eyes going there, and the sharp knife of pain imagining Emma in the same condition—with McCullough's baby—made him scowl.

She looked down and realized that her posture revealed the secret she'd been trying so hard to protect and let her arms fall to her sides.

"I didn't take you for stupid," Clara said.

Nathan bristled. He had taught himself how to read. He wasn't stupid.

"You're letting Tristan McCullough step in and court Emma."

Yes, he was doing that. And he didn't want to talk about it. "It ain't your business."

She shook her head. "Maybe not, but I still say you're making a big mistake, not fighting for her."

She had never wanted his help, now she wanted to give him advice?

He saw red just thinking about it. "What good would it do, delaying the inevitable? Her brother wants her to marry McCullough."

Saying the words was like hot knives tearing through his gut.

"What does she want?" Clara asked softly.

That was what hurt the most. He could see Emma accepting him, temporarily. But when she tired of him, of the trouble that followed him around, she would end up with someone like McCullough.

And the hurt would incinerate him.

"Have you even asked her what she wants? Told her you're in love with her?"

He had barely admitted it to himself and ignored Clara's pointed words.

Clara shook her head again, disgust evident in the set of her mouth.

"She deserves better than me," he muttered.

"It ain't really fair of you to decide that for her."

Maybe Clara was right, but his way was safer. For them both.

"This way, she won't get hurt." He didn't know why it was important for her to understand. Clara was a friend, of sorts. Something he hadn't allowed himself to have in so very long…in years.

"How do you figure?" Clara asked, a bit perplexed.

"I… A long time ago, I failed someone I loved. She… died and I could've stopped it." All of Emma's assurances on the matter rolled through his head. Maybe he hadn't been completely at fault, maybe he was forgiven, but he still felt he could have prevented it if things had been different.

"If something bad happened to Emma because of me, I couldn't bear it…"

And Stillwell and his accusations proved that it could. If the altercation with him had gotten out of hand, she could've been in danger.

Clara nodded, as if it was all making sense to her now.

"So instead of hurting her later, you're hurting her now. Protecting yourself."

His head came up and he immediately protested, "No—"

He shook his head, denying it even as his heart pounded loud in his ears. Was she right?

He raised both hands and gripped the hair at his temples, pressing the heels of his hands into his head. "I can't fail Emma." It would kill him.

He could feel Clara's eyes on him but he stared at the ground. Admitting it made him vulnerable, but… it was the truth.

"What if you are failing her, right now?" Clara asked quietly.

He jerked his head up and found her looking at him with compassion that made his gut tighten painfully.

"She's in love with you, Reed. If you walk away from her, you'll be failing her."

The bugle rang out, clear in the morning air. It was time to start moving, and Nathan had been so distracted by the conversation that he hadn't gotten Mr. Bingham's oxen in their traces.

When he rushed to the wagon, he found that the same young man he'd helped with hunting had put the oxen in their harness. Unfamiliar gratefulness expanded his chest and he nodded his thanks to the kid.

He needed his full concentration to maneuver the wagon over the rough terrain today, but he couldn't ignore Clara's words as they bounced through his head over and over in a continuous loop.

She's in love with you.

He couldn't forget how she'd confronted him in the woods after they'd seen the Indians. She hadn't let him hide behind his fears. Would she have been so passionate to make him face his demons if she didn't care about him?

If you walk away, you'll be failing her.

The last thing he wanted was Emma hurt. If she

was in love with him and he was pushing her at Mc-
Cullough…could Clara be right? *Was* he hurting her
with his actions?

The hope that he'd thought disintegrated last night
when he'd pushed Emma away had been brought back
to glorious life by Clara's words. Was it possible that
Emma wanted to be with him?

There would still be obstacles in front of them. He
would only have the little money he'd earned driving Mr.
Bingham's oxen on this journey West, and no job waiting for him. But with Emma by his side, those obstacles
suddenly seemed smaller…

But what would her brother think? Would he approve
of Nathan's courtship with those obstacles in place? Or
would he refuse Nathan's suit?

And there was also McCullough. He had traveled out
of Oregon City just to meet Emma. He'd spent days talking with her, taking walks, sitting next to her at breakfast.

If Nathan was serious about pursuing Emma, he
would have to talk to Ben. He owed it to Emma to do
things right, to act in an honorable manner.

But it also made him nervous, thinking about speaking to Emma's brother. Ben might not think he was the
wagon train thief any longer, but Ben's allegiance was
to McCullough.

What would he say to Nathan?

And…he'd hurt Emma. Her silence this morning was
proof of that. Would she forgive him…would she still
care about him?

Nervous anticipation filled Nathan. He was through
hiding.

It was time to change his future.

Chapter Twenty-Two

Nathan had chewed over his words all morning, in between traversing the difficult, rocky trail.

They reached a part of the pass where each wagon had to be hefted up a cliff face, using ropes and pulleys. The oxen turned uneasy. The whole day had already been grueling.

And McCullough mentioned there was another cliff just like this one to be found in the afternoon.

And Nathan still had to talk to Ben.

The wagon master called for a break after they'd managed to get all the wagons up with only a few minor mishaps. By that time, the sun was high and bright in the sky.

And Nathan had no excuse.

He found Ben and McCullough together, near a pretty little stream flowing over some rocks. Thankfully, they were alone, speaking in low tones.

His palms were sweaty and when the both glanced at him, his mouth went dry and all of the words he'd planned to say dissipated in the fine afternoon breeze.

"Something wrong?" Ben asked.

"No."

Nathan's face flamed. He hadn't expected to face both of them together and this was the most uncomfortable situation.

But it was for Emma. He had to remember that.

He jerked his chin in Ben's direction. "First, I wanted to say thank you for taking me in when I was sick. And for being at my side when Stillwell wanted to make more trouble for me."

Nathan cleared his throat. "The truth is, I've come to…deeply admire your sister. Emma," he amended, so there was no confusion. Admiration didn't properly express the depth of his feelings for Emma, but he had no intention of admitting he loved Emma to her brother first.

Ben crossed his arms over his chest, his brows drawn low over his eyes. He glanced at McCullough and back at Nathan. McCullough's expression remained stern, unsmiling.

Nathan blew out a breath heavy with tension. "Emma is…amazing. You know." He directed the words at Ben, but he was sure Tristan had sensed it, as well.

"And she deserves to be with someone she loves," he finished.

"Does she love you?" Ben asked bluntly.

That was the question, wasn't it? Nathan shrugged helplessly. "I don't know. But I intend to find out. And I'd like your blessing to marry her, if she'll have me."

"But…" Ben shot another glanced at Tristan, who finally moved.

He took a step toward Nathan and Nathan's hackles rose, but he remained where he was, hands relaxed at his side.

"I didn't come out here looking for a love match," the sheriff said. To Ben, he said, "If she loves Reed, I'll bow out." Then he turned his intense gaze on Nathan again. "But if she doesn't have feelings for you, my goal to get to know her on the rest of the journey remains."

Nathan looked to Ben, who still stood with a slightly perplexed look on his face, as if he had never even considered that Nathan might notice Emma.

"I had a lot of guilt from my past that Emma and God have helped me resolve. But I can promise you that I'll do everything in my power to be the man who will make Emma happy."

And very slowly, Ben nodded.

Emma shook, literally trembling all over as she stood half-hidden behind the wagon.

She watched Tristan where he stood amid a group of other travelers, in conversation. She'd heard the wagon master pass by moments ago, saying they were getting ready to pull out after the break.

She'd intended to talk to Tristan in private while they were stopped, but a mother had brought her little boy who'd had a huge, jagged splinter embedded in one palm. Once she'd got the splinter out, Emma had had a hard time stopping the bleeding.

Rachel had been impatiently murmuring about something and then disappeared, but Emma had paid her little mind.

And then Emma had had to bandage the wound and now there was no privacy to be found with Tristan.

Her heart thundered in her ears. She could always go—interrupt—and fetch him.

She didn't want to wait until they stopped for the evening to speak to Tristan. Because tonight she intended tell Nathan how she felt about him.

And if they were getting ready to pull out, her time to speak to Tristan was dwindling.

What was the worst that could happen? She would suffer embarrassment while everyone watched her ask to speak to Tristan.

Was Nathan worth a bit of embarrassment on her part? Absolutely.

She took one step on a leg shaking so badly it felt like jelly. Then another.

He was in profile to her and didn't see her approach. The two men at his side looked up at her, curiosity showing in their expressions. Heat flamed in her chest and rose into her neck and face.

"Excuse me. Tristan?"

The tentative whisper that emerged wouldn't do. He hadn't heard her at all, though another head turned her direction and her palms began to sweat.

She forced strength into her voice, though she felt anything but strong. "Tristan."

Now his head turned toward her, his eyes familiar and friendly, but she felt nothing for him. "May I speak to you? In private?"

He excused himself and followed her away from the group. She thought she heard him murmur, "Not you, too." What did that mean?

She marched away from the group of people, past the wagon to the edge of the rocky incline that led back down the mountain.

When she turned back to him, he'd taken off his hat and held it against one leg. And if she wasn't mistaken, there was a very slight pink tinge to his cheeks. Did he somehow suspect what she was going to say to him?

"I—I wanted to say how very flattered I am that you came all this way to meet me." Her voice trembled and she took a breath to steady herself. Unfortunately, it gave him time to speak.

"And to help with the wagon train," he said gently.

She fumbled for words. Took another deep breath. It didn't help.

"I've enjoyed getting to know you, and hearing stories about your daughters." She swallowed hard. His eyes glinted, but he didn't look away from her and his patience, his intensity, made it that much harder to say the rest. "And I admire that you want to find a mother for your children."

He seemed to brace himself, just slightly, as she finished, "But I am not that woman."

"I see." His jaw had tightened a minuscule amount. If she hadn't been watching so closely, she might not have noticed.

"I count you as a friend," she went on, but she doubted it made it any better. "It's just…I have feelings for…I feel very strongly about…"

"You're in love with someone else," he said with a bluntness that sent heat up her spine.

She'd admitted it to Rachel. She suspected Clara knew, but Tristan was a spurned suitor, she supposed.

She simply nodded because she wasn't ashamed of it.

He looked at her for a long moment, taking her measure and she had the sense that he was accepting her words.

Tristan mashed his hat on his head, muttering something about Rachel.

"What? What did you say?"

Now she was sure he was blushing. "Nothing."

"It wasn't nothing. Something about Rachel." She crossed her arms, wondering what her impatient, impudent sister had done. If his embarrassment was any indication, maybe Emma should be the one embarrassed.

"She confronted me earlier and mentioned the same. That you were in love with your Mr. Reed."

Beneath his breath, he muttered, but this time she didn't call him on it.

Had Rachel thought Emma would lose her nerve? Was that why she'd confronted Tristan? Waves of emotion flowed through Emma. She didn't know whether to be thankful for her little sister or embarrassed.

She could only hope Rachel hadn't confronted Nathan!

"You'll have to forgive her for sticking her nose where it doesn't belong. My sister can be…"

"Brash?" He offered the word with a raise of his eyebrows, as if daring her to contradict him. "Impertinent?"

"Protective," Emma put in. "She has the best of intentions."

"She wants to see you happy." He smiled a little at that, though there was a subtle strain beneath it. "I cannot fault her for that. And I would never stand in the way of love. I had it with my wife, and…"

His voice trailed off and she saw his Adam's apple bob as if he had swallowed hard. His eyes cut away, looking off in the distance.

Compassion stirred in her breast for what he'd lost. She couldn't think about how she would feel if she lost Nathan, and Tristan had years with his wife to build their love.

"I'm truly sorry that I can't marry you."

"Don't be." He visibly pulled himself out of his thoughts with an intake of breath. "I wish you the best. And I'm certain we'll still have the chance to be friends. Ben has become a good friend to me, as well."

She noted he did not mention Rachel.

The wagons began moving and he motioned her back toward the caravan. "Come along. We don't want to be left behind."

And that was that.

Her knees were still shaking as they walked back to the now-moving caravan and she rejoined Rachel. Her sister shot her a questioning glance and with Tristan still in earshot, all Emma could do was glare at her. She would save the set down for her sister later. Nosing into Emma's private business like that!

Nathan pushed the Binghams' oxen past, sitting tall on the back of one of the animals. Their gazes met and held. Had he seen her speaking with Tristan?

But he didn't look angry, he looked… He smiled at her and her thoughts fled. It wasn't a huge grin, a baring of his teeth. It was a small smile by all accounts, but for Nathan, it was something she'd rarely seen.

And a stark contrast to how he'd avoided her entirely this morning.

Had something happened?

Now that they were on the trail again, any discussion between them would have to wait.

But her impatience knew no bounds. She wanted things settled between them.

Chapter Twenty-Three

Emma shuddered as she considered the imposing cliff face only hours after they had conquered the first. At least thirty feet, nearly straight up.

The family wagon had already been lifted—without mishap— but Nathan remained at the bottom of the cliff as the Binghams' wagon was tied off with strong ropes in preparation to be lifted.

She could admit, if only to herself, that she was glad the journey was nearing its end. After the caravan crossed the Blue Mountains, they had only a short time left until they would reach Oregon City.

She had faced many of her fears out here on the prairie. Lived through storms with only a thin sheet of canvas as protection from the elements. Mostly overcame her fear of speaking up in a public setting.

Her family had made it this far without injury. It was much to be thankful for. And she couldn't wait to see Grayson.

And start a new life, with Nathan at her side.

She desperately wanted to speak to him, to tell him how she felt. But she also didn't want him distracted on this particular leg of the journey.

The men at the top of the cliff began hefting the Bing-hams' wagon. It rose a foot off the ground, then another.

Nathan called out—she couldn't hear his words—and one corner of the wagon slipped. A rope snapped.

The men on the top of the cliff didn't hear him.

He shouted again and Emma couldn't breathe as he rushed to steady the wagon that now wobbled.

A second rope broke with a sound like a whip and a scream rose in her throat.

Nathan disappeared behind the wagon. She lost sight of all but his dark hair, and then another rope snapped and the wagon fell with a loud crash.

"Nathan!" The cry was ripped from her lips and her feet carried her forward before she had even considered moving.

Had Nathan been crushed by the falling wagon? If he'd suffered internal injuries, there was no doctor here to help—

Her thoughts rioted as several men swarmed over the fallen wagon. Ben scrambled down the embankment feet away, sending a small spill of rocks falling loose.

Why hadn't she told him she loved him before?

Her breaths came in short gasps. She couldn't speak, couldn't tell all the men to move so she could see the man she loved.

And then she did get a glimpse of Nathan, pinned be-tween the broken wagon and the sheer rock wall.

His face was creased with pain, but he was alive!

She pressed her fingers against her trembling lips. He was alive.

Almost as if he sensed her nearby, he looked up, his dark gaze boring straight into her.

"I'm fine," he mouthed to her.

Her heart pattered hard against her breastbone. Of

course he would say that. He was trying to comfort her and couldn't know the extent of his injuries when he was still pinned in place.

She wiped a hand across her face and discovered tears tracking down her cheeks.

It seemed so silly now, that she hadn't had the gumption to tell him that she loved him last night when he'd tried to push her at Tristan. What, she'd been afraid to be the first one to speak? Even knowing how Nathan's past had shaped him, had made him afraid of getting too involved.

Well, she was afraid now. Afraid she would never get the chance.

I love you, she mouthed to him, tears still running down her face.

She was ready to shout it, uncaring who might hear.

He must've taken her meaning because his expression shifted. His face almost crumpled, and then the men were moving the wagon and someone stepped between them, blocking her view.

The conveyance shifted and then Ben pulled Nathan free, lugging the taller, broader man with Nathan's arm slung over her brother's shoulder.

Nathan's color was good.

She met the two men a good piece away from the fallen wagon—men were already working at getting it out of the way so it could be repaired, and more wagons waited to be toted up the cliff.

"All right?" Ben asked as he lowered Nathan to the ground.

"I think so," Nathan replied as she knelt next to him. "I saw the rope unraveling but—"

"They didn't hear your shouts at the top until it was

too late," Ben said. He sighed. "I told Abby's pa he needed to lighten his wagon…"

His voice trailed off but her brother didn't have to finish. They all knew Abby's mother had packed the wagon, and after her death on the trail, Bingham had refused to part with the items that held her memory—all of them.

Emma stopped listening to the men speak of inane things. She had to make sure Nathan was all right.

She touched his nearest arm first, running both hands down the length of it. Then reached across his torso for his other arm, pressing with her fingertips from shoulder to his fingers.

She ran her hands down his legs, demanded he bend his knees and rotate his ankles.

He did so, looking down on her with what she would call on anyone else a bemused smile. It wasn't something she was used to seeing on him.

He had a scrape across one cheek and just looking at it made her eyes fill with tears as Ben faded away into the background.

"Does your chest hurt?" she asked, still worried about an injury she couldn't see. "Does your stomach pain you?"

"Here," he said, taking her hand and placing her palm over his heart.

Her breath caught. She could feel the muscle pounding beneath her fingertips.

"But I don't think this pain will ever go away."

Nathan's pulse tripped, sending vestiges of adrenaline from the wagon crashing atop him through his veins.

Or maybe it was just being near Emma.

He could still feel pain radiating throughout his body from his rib cage—likely he'd bruised a rib or maybe even cracked one—but it barely registered, with her here, with her hand beneath his, pressed again his heart.

He was flying above the ground because of the words she had given him.

I love you.

Could he have really seen what he thought she'd said to him, albeit silently? She loved him?

He felt as though he was on Hewitt's horse again, getting ready to plunge into the river rapids. He didn't know what to expect, chaos and danger to pull him under.

But he did it. He dove off.

He cleared his throat. "It's never going to go away because I'm never going to stop loving you."

The tears standing in her blue eyes overflowed and he dared to reach up and cradle her face in his hand. "Emma—"

She leaned forward and kissed him, a tender brush of her lips that wasn't enough, before she sat back on her heels.

"I love you, too, Nathan."

She had said it. Aloud. He didn't have to guess. And the knowledge filled him with a quiet joy that he knew would never leave.

He reached for her, but a sharp pain from his ribs made him inhale and abort the motion.

She frowned at him. "You *are* injured."

He exhaled a long breath that eased the pain some. "It's nothing. Maybe a bruised rib."

She began poking his ribs with her fingers, muttering, "Bruised rib or you're bleeding internally and might die…"

She hit a tender spot on his left side and he gasped, grabbing her hand in his to stop her.

When her eyes flicked up to his face, he saw the apology in their depths. "Sorry," she whispered.

"I'm not going to die," he murmured, squeezing her hand. "I'm too stubborn for that, or I would've already passed from the measles, or drowned, or been shot by an Indian."

She sniffled slightly, and he used her hand to tug her into the curve of his arm, ignoring the sharp flare of fire in his ribs. Some things were just worth the pain.

He rubbed his chin against the softness of her hair. "You really love me?"

She nodded, her cheek against his shoulder. "I couldn't help it. You saw me. You listened to me."

"We saw each other," he murmured.

There was a part of him that couldn't believe this was happening. That couldn't believe his good fortune, that God would bless him with a woman like Emma, who loved him back.

"I'll need some time to get settled once we get to Oregon City. Find a steady job so I could support a…family, before we get married."

He could hardly believe he'd said the words.

"Are you asking me to marry you?"

"Not very well." He breathed in deeply, ignoring the pain in his rib. He pushed her away slightly, so he could look down into her face. "Emma, I love everything about you. I know you could find a much better man than me—" like McCullough "—but I'll do my best to be worthy of you. Will you marry me?"

A small smile played around her lips. "Yes. And I won't hear this nonsense about you not being worthy. You've proven your character many times since we've met. I'll be proud to be your wife."

He leaned down and kissed her, and she met him sweetly. Behind his closed eyes, tears welled.

He'd come on this journey looking for a way out of his old life, a new start. But he'd never dreamed he would meet Emma, someone who challenged him, someone who made him better, someone who loved him.

And along the journey, he'd found forgiveness for himself, found a way to let go of his guilt over what had happened with Beth.

He didn't deserve either, the freedom or Emma, but he had his hands outstretched to take both.

God had blessed him beyond what he could have asked or imagined, all because of this journey West.

* * * * *

Dear Reader,

Since I started writing for Love Inspired Historical four years—and eight books!—ago, I have written settings in the same fictional Wyoming town/area, so this journey West with my characters was a new adventure for me. Although I did the best I could using the research resources available to me, I also used a bit of literary license to make the story flow.

My favorite research tool while writing this book was *Journal of Travels over the Rocky Mountains* by Joel Palmer. I also did quite a bit of research about doctors on the trail and found that it wasn't uncommon for a doctor to be summoned to another wagon train—that's where I got the idea to have Emma called out to help a very sick little boy.

I would love to know what you thought of this book. You can reach me at lacyjwilliams@gmail.com or by sending a note to Lacy Williams, 340 S Lemon Ave #1639, Walnut, CA 91789. If you'd like to find out about all my latest releases in an occasional email blast, sign up at http://bit.ly/15lA19O.

Thanks for reading!

Lacy Williams

WAGON TRAIN PROPOSAL
Journey West
by Renee Ryan

When Tristan McCullough's intended wagon train bride chooses someone else, Rachel Hewitt accepts a position as his children's caretaker—not as his wife. She'll only marry for love...yet perhaps the McCulloughs are the family she's always wanted.

HER CONVENIENT COWBOY
Wyoming Legacy
by Lacy Williams

When cowboy Davy White discovers a widowed soon-to-be-mother in his cabin, he immediately offers her shelter from the blizzard. As their friendship grows, so does Rose Evans's belief that Davy is her wish come true for a family by Christmas.

THE TEXAN'S TWIN BLESSINGS
by Rhonda Gibson

Emily Jane Rodgers dreams of opening her own bakery, not falling in love. Then she meets William Barns and his adorable twin nieces, and soon the ready-made family is chipping away at Emily Jane's guarded heart and changing her mind about marriage and happily-ever-afters!

FAMILY OF HER DREAMS
by Keli Gwyn

As a railroad stationmaster and recent widower, Spencer Abbott needs help raising his young children. He's surprised when Tess Grimsby fits so well with his family—maybe she's meant to be more than a nanny to his children...

LIHCNM0515

REQUEST YOUR FREE BOOKS!

2 FREE INSPIRATIONAL NOVELS
PLUS 2 FREE MYSTERY GIFTS

Love Inspired® H I S T O R I C A L

"Are you my new mommy?"

Rachel blinked in stunned silence at the child staring back at her. She saw a lot of herself in the precocious six-year-old. In the determined angle of her tiny shoulders. In the bold tilt of her head. In the desperate hope simmering in her big, sorrowful blue eyes.

For a dangerous moment, Rachel had a powerful urge to tug the little girl into her arms and give her the answer she so clearly wanted.

Careful, she warned herself. *Think before you speak.*

"Well?" Hands still perched on her hips, Daisy's small mouth turned down at the corners. "Are you my new mommy or not?"

"I'm sorry, Daisy, no. I'm not your new mommy. However, I am your new neighbor, and I'll certainly see you often, perhaps even daily."

Tristan cut in then, touching his daughter's shoulder to gain her attention. "Daisy, my darling girl, we've talked about this before. You cannot go around asking every woman you meet if she's your mommy."

"But, Da—" the little girl's lower lip jutted out "—you said you were bringing us back a new mommy when you got home."

"No, baby." He pulled his hand away from her shoulder then shoved it into his pocket. "I said I *might* bring you home a new mommy."

When tears formed in the little girl's eyes, Rachel found herself interceding. "I may not be your new mommy," she began, taming a stray wisp of the child's hair behind her ear, "but I can be your very good friend."

The little girl's eyes lit up and she plopped into Rachel's lap. No longer able to resist, Rachel wrapped her arms around the child and hugged her close. Lily attempted to join her sister on Rachel's lap. When Daisy refused to budge, the little girl settled for pulling on Rachel's sleeve. "You don't want to be our new mommy?"

The poor child sounded so despondent Rachel's heart twisted. "Oh, Lily, it's not a matter of want. You see, I'm already committed to—"

She cut off her own words, realizing she had no other commitments now that her brother was married. He didn't need her to run his household. *No one* needed her. Except, maybe, this tiny family.

Don't miss
WAGON TRAIN PROPOSAL
by Renee Ryan,
available June 2015 wherever
Love Inspired® Historical books and ebooks are sold.

SPECIAL EXCERPT FROM

Love Inspired®

*Can a widow and widower ever leave their grief in the
past and forge a new future—and a family—together?*

*Read on for a sneak preview of
THE AMISH WIDOW'S SECRET.*

"Wait, before you go. I have an important question to ask
you."

Sarah nodded her head and sat back down.

"I stayed up until late last night, thinking about your
situation and mine. I prayed, and *Gott* kept pushing this
thought at me." He took a deep breath. "I wonder, would
you consider becoming my *frau*?"

Sarah held up her hand, as if to stop his words. "I…"

"Before you speak, let me explain." Mose took another
deep breath. "I know you still love Joseph, just as I still
love my Greta. But I have *kinder* who need a mother to
guide and love them. Now that Joseph's gone and the
farm's being sold, you need a place to call home, people
who care about you, a family. We can join forces and help
each other." He saw a panicked expression forming in her
eyes. "It would only be a marriage of convenience. The
girls need a loving mother and you've already proven you
can be that. What do you say, Sarah Nolt? Will you be
my wife?"

Sarah sat silent, her face turned away. She looked into
Mose's eyes. "You'd do this for me? But…you don't
know me."

"I'd do this for us," Mose corrected, and smiled.

The tips of Sarah's fingers nervously pleated and unpleated a scrap of her skirt. "But we hardly know each other. What would people think? They will say I took advantage of your good nature."

Mose smiled. "So, let them talk. They'd be wrong and we'd know it. I want this marriage for both of us, for the *kinder*. We can't let others decide what is best for our lives. I believe this marriage is *Gott*'s plan for us."

Sarah's face cleared and she seemed to come to a decision. She smoothed out the fabric of her skirt and tidied her hair, then finally took Mose's outstretched hand with a smile. "You're right. This is our life. I accept your proposal, Mose Fisher. I will be your *frau* and your *kinder*'s mother."

Don't miss
THE AMISH WIDOW'S SECRET
by Cheryl Williford,
available June 2015 wherever
Love Inspired® books and ebooks are sold.

Nicholas Cole hurried toward the White House special in-house security chief's office in the West Wing, gripping the leash for his K-9 partner, Max. General Margaret Meyer stood behind her oak desk, a fierce expression on her face.

The general moved from behind her desk. "This office has been searched."

He came to attention in front of his boss, having a hard time shaking his military training as a navy SEAL. "Anything missing?"

"No, but someone had searched through the Jeffries file, and it would be easy to take pictures of the papers and evidence the team has uncovered so far."

"What do you want me to do, ma'am?" Nicholas knew the murder of Michael Jeffries, son of the prominent congressman Harland Jeffries, was important to the general as well as his unit captain, Gavin McCord.

"I want to know who was in my office. It could be the break we've needed on this case. With the Easter Egg Roll today, the White House has been crawling with visitors since early this morning, so it won't be easy." She shook her head. "Especially with the Oval Office and the Situation Room here in the West Wing being used for the festivities. If you discover anything, find me right away."

"Yes, ma'am." Nicholas exited the West Wing by the West Colonnade and cut across the Rose Garden toward where the Easter Egg Roll was taking place.

He scanned the people gathered. His survey came to rest upon Selena Barrow, the White House tour director, who was responsible for planning this event. Even from a distance, Selena commanded a person's attention. She was tall and slender with long, wavy brown hair and the bluest eyes, but what drew him to Selena was her air of integrity and compassion.

Selena would have an updated list of the people who were invited to the party. It might save him a trip to the front gate if he asked her for it. And it would give him a reason to talk to her.

Don't miss
SECURITY BREACH by Margaret Daley,
available June 2015 wherever
Love Inspired® Suspense books and ebooks are sold.